The Killing Tree
&
Other
Afflictions

The Killing Tree
&
Other
Afflictions

Shannon Lawrence

Warrior Muse Press

Warrior Muse Press
TheWarriorMuse.com

Cover Design © 2025 Jeff Lawrence
Author Photo © 2015 Jared Hagan
Cover Image Dead tree isolated on white background, 3d rendering © 2017 geerati@gmail.com | Depositphotos.com
Cover Font - Author – DCC Ash © 2013 dccanim | Dafont.com
Cover Font – Title – Archivo (Adobe Open Source)

Disclaimer:
This is a work of fiction. Names, characters, businesses, events, and incidents are the products of the author's imagination even when sharing a name with a real entity. Any resemblance to actual persons, living or dead, or actual events is purely coincidental. If any of these events have happened to you, this is a terrifying coincidence, and you lead a scary life. We should have coffee.

AI Note:
No AI has been used in the writing of this book or these stories. Nor has it knowingly been used for the cover art. We have vetted the art to the best of our ability.

ISBN: 979-8-9898381-3-4

Table of Contents

Dust Bunnies

Carol put on a white glove and ran two fingers along the mantle. They came away clean, just as she expected. Still, she couldn't help a sigh of relief. This new cleaning lady would do. For now.

It took about half an hour to finish her inspection. The previous cleaning person had grown lazy, no longer moving the curios or sweeping behind the doors. Carol hated dust. Her mother had taught her that. It was so deeply instilled that she checked for dust in any room she passed through, judging whoever might be responsible. Public spaces were unbelievable. They paid people to keep them clean, yet there was always dust. Always.

Her house wouldn't hold any dust. She couldn't stand it. Clumps of human skin, dirt, and living creatures that fed off the waste of unclean human bodies. She exfoliated twice each day, scrubbing at her body, plucking at loose hairs to ensure they wouldn't fall and settle into the nooks and crannies of her home. It took very little for dust to gain a foothold. One had to take control or risk losing it completely.

Carol checked that the replacement filters for each air purifier were in stock. They were meant to last several months, but she had them changed out once per week to keep them in top functioning shape. She also checked her inventory of dust cloths, furniture polish, and all associated cleaning items.

Satisfied with her rounds, Carol headed back to work in her sterile office. She'd long ago had to quit working in regular offices. Dust everywhere. She'd been fired, encouraged to quit, under-scheduled, and experienced many other means of being pushed out, all because she demanded a clean work environment. One would think that would be important to everyone in that space. Did they know what they were breathing in? No. Humans had a way of looking the other way about things. It was no different in the workplace.

The online commute simplified things in many ways. She had her own space, wasn't exposed to other people's germs and filth, ate in her own kitchen at lunch time, and saved on gas. As far as Carol was concerned, there were no benefits to working in an office. She'd always been a private person and working in an office meant that people were always in her space and in her business. No thank you.

The cleanliness of her space made her happy. She straightened her back, turned on her computer, and got to work with a smile on her face, the air purifier behind her zipping and zapping away at the isolated dust motes that floated through the air.

~~

The next morning, Madison, the housekeeper, swept through for her daily cleaning. Carol kept a close eye on her, watching to be sure she got all the hidden caches of dust. Tomorrow she'd have the woman dust out the attic. It hadn't been dusted in a week. The thought of the piles of dust lurking up there gave Carol a chill of disgust. Her stomach turned, and she held back a gag working its way up her throat.

Madison walked past a potted plant without cleaning it.

"Absolutely not!" Carol called.

Startled, Madison jumped and looked over to Carol, her eyes wide, mouth partially open.

"The plants need to be cleaned each day, as well. Otherwise, the dust gathers then settles into the soil. Then I'll be forced to change it out."

"Sorry, Ms. Tulliver. I'll be sure to do it from now on."

Carol arched an eyebrow. "See that you do."

With Madison thoroughly chagrined, Carol went to her already cleaned office to get to work. Really, as incompetent as these so-called cleaning people were, she might as well do it herself and save the money. That would mean making contact with the dust, though, and she hated that. She'd give Madison one more chance tomorrow.

She tried to settle into work, but she was too frustrated. It was hard not to follow the woman around to make sure she did a good job, but they usually quit if she did that too often. Perhaps she should just tell them in the interviews that it was part of the job. If they didn't like it, she wouldn't hire them. Things would be simpler that way. It took too long to train them properly, only to lose them. A complete waste of her time.

Carol huffed and shut down her computer. No work would get done today. Not until Madison left.

Well, if she had to deal with dust at home, she might as well venture out to the store, where there'd certainly be plenty of it. If her mother were still alive, she'd go to her house. It had always been, if nothing else, even cleaner than Carol's home. She could only strive to reach the same level of cleanliness as her mother. Of course, now her mother lie in a coffin, surrounded by dirt. The alternative would have been to be cremated, which turned you into dust. It may have worked in the bible, but neither Carol nor her mother had come from dust, so it would be irrational to return to it. The coffin was as airtight as Carol could find, and Carol had paid the funeral home additional money to ensure they cleaned it out before sealing it. No sense tormenting her mother in the afterlife. Though Lord knows her mother had tormented her enough in life.

Carol snatched up her purse and keys, and left without telling Madison. She didn't want to look at her right now, let alone speak to her. She got into her car, wiping the dashboard down with a pre-wetted wipe. Sun shone in the windshield, illuminating the clean surfaces of the car. Today would be a good day to get the car detailed, as well. Perhaps she'd catch a meal in town. She knew of a mom-and-pop restaurant that was kept spotless.

The drive didn't take long. It was only about fifteen minutes to get into town. She dropped her car off at her favorite carwash and asked for Paco, who she knew would treat her car with the utmost respect. She paid him well enough to make sure he kept doing so.

Happily, the restaurant she wanted to visit, Mona's, was located a mere five-minute walk away. Carol had intentionally put on comfortable shoes, knowing she'd be walking. Light clouds had moved over the sun, making it a pleasant walk. The quaint, white stucco building came into sight before she knew it, a tidy garden decorating either side of the front walkway. The freshly painted blue door beckoned her.

As usual, Mona greeted Carol as she came through the door. "Carol, so good to see you! Your table just freed up a few minutes ago."

Mona led her to the corner table, a lush fern sitting on a shelf over it. The tidy proprietor set a menu on the table and went to get Carol her water and diet soda.

Carol studied her surroundings. No dust on the table or chairs, the fern was bright and clean, the shelf tidy. Even the baseboards were spotless. Content, Carol sat back to study the menu. She almost always got the same thing, but Mona's had put her in the mood to try something new, live a little. When the owner bustled back with her drinks, Carol asked, "Do you have any specials today, Mona? I'm in the mood to try something new."

"Of course! I've got a California chicken sandwich, with avocado and ranch, on a croissant. Our soup is tomato bisque. And I've got a lovely pasta, with spinach and bell peppers, and a light cream sauce. It comes with soup or salad. Any of those sound good?"

"I'll get the pasta, with soup. Thank you, Mona."

Carol felt downright perky. She might even have dessert after her lunch. She rarely imbibed, but today was the day for it. Amazing how a clean space could elevate her entire day. Thank goodness for Mona, a bright light on a dusty day.

About fifteen minutes later, Mona brought out her soup and refilled her drinks. Carol relished the soup, which had a lovely touch of cream in it, then moved on her to entrée as soon as Mona dropped it by. The woman had her timing down. She swooped in to remove the bowl and plop down the steaming bowl of pasta within seconds of Carol having finished up. A lovely, toasted bread sat in the pasta, golden with glistening butter. It melted in her mouth with the first bite, the rich butter lilting across her tongue.

The pasta tasted so good that, despite being full, Carol ordered a brownie a la mode. It also proved to be a pleasure. She paid and started her walk back to the car wash, humming and studying the cute houses and well-tended gardens she passed. The previously five minute walk took a solid twenty minutes due to her dalliance. Her car sat, brightly polished, in front of the car wash. She paid and picked up her keys, starting for home.

The closer she got to her house, the more her mood dipped. Usually it went the other way. She realized that the hesitation she felt to go home was actually fear. Fear that Madison had left dust mines around the house. It had happened before. The house would look so tidy and clean, no dust in sight, then Carol would reach onto a shelf or brush her hand across a surface, unprepared for the grimy coat of dust that would come away on her skin.

Her breath caught in her chest. She didn't want to go inside now. This day had been too perfect.

"It will be fine," she said aloud. "Madison cleaned the house thoroughly. There's no dust waiting for me."

She took deep, healing breaths. Nothing but a panic attack. She had them sometimes. It was so easy to get lost in them, to not realize the irrationality of her thoughts while they streamed through her head. Today of all days, she felt she should have been exempt from them. All she wanted was one perfect day.

How long she sat in the car, she wasn't sure. The snuffing of the sun beyond the neighboring houses drew her out of her thoughts. It had become cooler, and goosebumps dappled her arms. In fact, she'd been out here long enough that hunger once again gnawed at her belly. A light dinner must be in order.

One more big breath, and she marched toward her front door, chin up. Her anxiety would not get the best of her. She did everything in one fluid set of motions so she'd have no means to procrastinate. Keys came out of the purse as she climbed the stairs, which were then inserted in the lock. A push, and she was in the door. Shoes got tucked into their cabinet, coat in the closet, purse set on the foyer table, keys in the bowl. She padded around the house to check the cleaning job. So far, so good. No hidden traps of dust. Everything in its place. Just the way she liked it.

She relaxed enough to make her dinner, and even ate it on the sofa while watching a romantic comedy, rather than sitting at the table as she usually did. The evening flew by, and the finish of the movie told her it was time to go to bed. After putting her pajamas on, she grabbed her toothbrush and plopped a dollop of toothpaste on the bristles, perfectly proportioned, as always. She ran a drizzle of water over it to soften the bristles then put it into her mouth.

It tasted funny.

It felt weird, too.

The mint tasted dull, and it felt almost gritty, like there were bits of grime in it. When she pulled the brush out of her mouth and examined it, it looked perfectly fine. She rinsed off the brush and put more toothpaste on. This time, she put less than usual, just in case.

Sure enough, when it went back in her mouth, it still tasted and felt wrong. Maybe it was her toothbrush.

Carol kept a supply of toiletries in a cabinet. From this, she took a new toothbrush, still sealed in a bag, as well as a fresh tube of toothpaste, still in the box. She opened the packages, prepared her toothbrush once more, and tentatively stuck the brush in her mouth.

Darn it all. Still off.

Could it be the water? She grabbed a fresh glass and filled it with water from the bathroom faucet, putting it up at eye level to examine the contents. It looked fine. Clear. Nothing floating in it.

She must just be having an off day. Maybe something about dinner had stuck around and made things taste and feel different. She grimaced and finished the job of brushing her teeth, trying to ignore the disgusting taste and sensation. Her tongue curled away from the foam in her mouth, almost of its own volition. She shut her eyes and muscled through, grateful when the time came to spit out the final mouthful and rinse the toothbrush. She threw both toothbrushes and tubes of paste in the garbage, brushed her hair, and climbed into bed, settling down with her e-reader to unwind. Books were so musty. The invention of e-readers and e-books had to be one of the best, right behind dust mops, and the pre-wetted dust wipes. She really loved those.

When she opened the decorative cover of the e-reader, she saw that dust covered the screen.

"No!"

She jumped out of bed to grab one of those dust wipes, and thoroughly cleaned the e-reader and its cover before nestling the e-reader back into it. It took a moment for her heart to slow and her breaths to return to normal. The moment over, she decided she wasn't in the mood to read anymore. She put the e-reader into her nightstand drawer and turned out the light. Today had been a wash. Tomorrow would be better.

~~

A frantic scuffing sound awakened Carol. She opened her eyes and looked around the dark room, straining to see the corners. Greedy shadows hid parts of the room from her.

The scuffing came again.

Carol tried to figure out what direction it was coming from. She closed her eyes to listen more intently.

Only, it came from everywhere.

Every part of the room.

In addition to the scuffing, she heard scratching and crunching. Then whispers. Not whispers like someone talking. Just whiffs of air bouncing around the room. When she put her head under the covers in fear, the sounds grew louder.

With a shriek, she tossed the covers away from her, leapt out of the bed, and fled to her bathroom, shutting the door against the noises.

Only, they were in the bathroom, too.

In the bathroom, the sounds echoed off the tiles and hard surfaces. They crashed into her eardrums. She threw her hands over her ears to try to muffle the sounds. When that didn't work, she grabbed a clean towel and covered her ears with it.

The sounds grew louder.

Whatever was making these sounds, it was everywhere, in everything. She threw the bathroom door open and raced through the house to the front door. Unbolting it, she ran outside, only to freeze. The sounds were out here, too. The ground, the air, everywhere.

She ran back inside, bolted the door, and pressed her back to it. Looking around, frantic, she tried again to find the source of the sounds. Her chest heaved with panted breaths. Her mouth dried out and filled with something grainy and dusty at the same time. It coated the inside of her cheeks, her tongue, the roof of her mouth, her throat.

Carol choked, and dust exploded from her mouth in a living cloud.

She slapped a hand over her mouth. Her fingers smelled musty. When she looked down at them, she saw they were covered in dust. Not only that, the dust *moved* across her skin, crawling in different directions like nearly microscopic ants. The skin on her hand dried out as the mass of dust moved over it.

Her eyes darted around the foyer. From beneath the walls came mounds of dust, a tiny army approaching. The rustling grew louder.

Carol scrambled to her feet, still choking, her nose drying out now. She grasped at the lock, struggling once more to open the door. Her legs tickled as the dust armies reached them and climbed. She stomped her feet and tried to scream, but only a garbled yelp came out.

The lock turned, and she pulled at the door. The dust had reached her waist. It felt like her legs were mummifying, the intense dryness itchy and unpleasant. The door opened to show that dust had gathered everywhere on the porch. She slammed the door again, looking around desperately.

Where wouldn't there be dust? Was anywhere safe?

She ran to the bathroom again. This time she threw the towels out, along with everything from the shelves, sink, and medicine cabinet. She shut the door and started to clean the surfaces with industrial strength bleach. A thousand tiny screams filled the air. With glee, she cleaned faster. Harder.

That finished, and with the dust mass up to her neck, she stepped into the shower with her clothes on and turned on the water.

Only, no water came out.

Instead, more dust gushed out of the shower head. The dust mites within joined the others swarming over her body. Everything had dried out. Her eyes felt full of grit. Her mouth and nose were entirely coated. The mites writhed over her tongue, through her nostrils, and on the surface of her eyes.

Carol gagged and tried to spit out the dust in her mouth, but saliva turned it into a paste she couldn't expel.

With a sigh of resignation, she held the bleach bottle over her head and poured. The screams came once again, the mass of dust and mites falling back from her body and sloughing into the tub. The bleach burned its way into her sinuses then her lungs. She gasped against the fire within her. Then her skin began to itch. Squinting her eyes open, she tried to get out of the tub, but tripped on the rim and fell headfirst onto the tiles.

The blow briefly stunned her. She lie in a small, dust-muddied puddle of bleach. It was the itching of her skin that brought her the rest of the way back. The bleach had started to eat at her flesh. Itching became fiery agony, and blisters broke out on her arms. Her eyes stung and watered.

When she was able to lever herself up from the floor, she saw that the dust horde stayed a few feet away from the bleach. There was more in the kitchen—if she could get there.

The room spun as she got to her feet. She nearly slipped in her puddle, but she caught herself and kept going. The dust no longer coated her throat and mouth, but she could feel blisters there instead. The burning in her lungs caused labored breathing. Suffering, wavering, she wrenched the bathroom door open and went into her room.

The air was full of dust particles. Carol waved a hand in front of her face to clear them, but others instantly took their place. She couldn't see an inch in front of her. Her legs hit something soft, but solid, and she flopped forward onto it. Her bed. All she wanted right now was to lie down and go to sleep, to shut it all out.

Instead, she pulled the comforter off her bed and wrapped it around herself as thoroughly as possible to block out the dust. She stumbled forward, eyes now red and swollen. The bleach seemed to be eating through her eyeballs. Everything had become blurry.

With ragged breaths, she made it to her bedroom door and opened it. The dust cloud was equally thick out here, and she almost gave up. No. If she could get to the bleach, she'd be okay.

What she'd forgotten was how much dust was in the typical quilt or duvet. Inside her cocoon, the dust mites moved on her. The bleach was evaporating from her skin, leaving her susceptible to their attack once more. If only it would evaporate from her lungs.

She felt the cold of the kitchen tiles under her feet and knew she'd made it across the living room. Dropping the comforter, which only served to smother her now, she fell to her knees, ambivalent toward that minor pain, and crawled toward the sink. If she could just reach the bleach.

Her movements slowed, while those of the dust mites quickened. They swarmed over her and inside her throat, attacking her already lacerated lungs. Her hand closed on the cabinet, and she opened it, feeling inside for the telltale curve of the bleach bottle. She could no longer open her eyes against the searing burn, but she knew the feel of that bottle by heart. She pulled it out, twisted the cap off, and once more poured the bleach over herself and down her throat.

She would kill these bastards if it were the last thing she did.

She sunk to the floor, knowing they must be screaming, even though she couldn't hear it any longer. They must be feeling thousands of times worse than she did. They wouldn't be able to get past the bleach. Nothing defeated bleach.

Not even people.

A Few of His Favorites

Glen pulled the blanket from the trunk and walked over to their spot, spreading the chenille throw gently where shade covered the soft, thick grass. The trees shivered in a gentle breeze, wildflowers bopping heads in a colorful dance. The rustling of the moving air soothed him and cooled his walk back to the trunk for the picnic basket.

The basket was heavy, stuffed as it was with all the food and drink Glen had gathered for the special day. He closed the trunk, leaned in the driver's side window to turn up the music, and hefted the basket over beside the blanket. Strains of Nirvana, Evan's favorite band, filtered through the open window of the car.

Lovingly, Glen took each item out of the basket, arranging it on the blanket. The fresh fruit he'd sliced that morning went toward the corner. Fried chicken on a platter was placed beside the fruit, along with a bowl of mashed potatoes and a plate of corn on the cob. Two mason jars of real sweet tea went to the far end of the blanket. He uncovered each plate and bowl and put the wrappings back into the basket.

Then dessert. The final touch. Glen had stayed up all night making various chocolate items, including chocolate dipped strawberries, chocolate caramels, and chocolate chip cookies. As he laid these out, he thought back to how they'd met. It had been a building party at work. Glen's accounting firm had been responsible for the desserts; Glen, himself, had brought his various chocolate specialties, those which he now laid out.

Evan had come in, an employee at the law firm downstairs, and headed straight for the chocolate. He'd talked about the cases he'd dealt with that day, how people were always crankier near the holidays, and especially the weekend. Two bites into a chocolate caramel, and he'd sagged in relief, moaning about the quality of the dessert. When he found out Glen was the baker, he held a cookie aloft and the two of them toasted to the end of the week, biting their cookies to seal the toast.

They'd chatted for the rest of the party, finding out they had plenty in common outside the building. They both enjoyed genuine sweet tea, long strategy board games, and romantic comedies, especially if they happened to star the one and only Hugh Jackman. Though Glen was typically shy about asking anyone out, on that night the stars had aligned in just the right way, and he'd asked Evan out, holding his breath for the mockery that would surely follow. Glen had gotten it wrong before, and he'd paid the price.

Instead, Evan accepted, throwing out the idea of watching "Australia" at his place. "But only if you bring dessert!" he'd said.

"Deal," Glen had said, and they'd set the date.

Leading up to that date, Glen had been so nervous. Evan was the type of attractive that came with such ease and confidence. Glen couldn't compete with that.

The beauty of their burgeoning relationship turned out to be that there was no competition at all. Evan treated him like a prince. Though Glen brought the dessert, Evan had home fried chicken, chopped up fruit, and made mashed potatoes with cream and real butter, all served with fresh corn on the cob, buttered and seasoned to perfection. To cap it all off, he'd made a pitcher of sweet tea so sweet that Glen's first sip had drawn a moan.

While the chicken Glen had brought today was fried, he hadn't done it himself, but had gotten it from a local soul food restaurant to be sure it was the best. The mashed potatoes came from the same place, but he'd made the corn on the cob, hoping it was just right, and he'd brewed the sweet tea from a recipe he found online. He felt certain Evan would love it all, even if it wasn't as perfect as that meal he'd made on their first date.

From then on, they'd had a whirlwind romance, spending their free time together. Glen's work had started suffering for it, as he'd set aside work he'd brought home if it meant spending that much more time with Evan. He skipped sleep sometimes, just to catch up when he got behind. Nothing could steal away his time with the man he intended to marry.

They went to movies, played board games, and went dancing. They dined out at the best restaurants, listened to music, and had intense, intelligent conversations. In short, Evan was the perfect man for Glen, and they were well on their way to eternal happiness, enjoying everything they did in the meantime.

Or so it had seemed to Glen at the time.

Evan had started pulling away a little bit, not always making himself available when Glen suggested a date or some time spent together. He'd been withdrawn. Sometimes Glen's calls had gone straight to voicemail, where before Evan had answered every call. Every one.

When he'd asked Evan if he'd done something wrong or if there was some other problem, Evan had acted surprised and said everything was fine.

"I'm just really busy at work right now," he'd said. "We're good, you and I. I just don't have as much time as I did before. They're looking at me for partner."

Glen had believed him. At first.

In fact, things had improved for a time. Evan had been better about answering his calls. They'd gone out more. Intimacy had returned. The sex had been amazing. It had felt like Evan was back and fully invested in their relationship.

That is, until he ghosted.

He no showed a date. He didn't answer the calls or texts. Glen left messages and never heard back. Not a word. No goodbye. No explanation. Evan didn't exist anymore, as far as Glen could tell.

Desperate, Glen showed up at Evan's apartment. After he pounded on the door for ten minutes, the door opened, and there was Evan, shirtless, with another man's hands on him. As soon as Evan realized who was at the door, his face fell. "What are you doing here?"

"You couldn't be a man and tell me it was over?"

"It was implied by my ignoring you."

The other guy had backed away. "I'm going to, ah..." He disappeared into the apartment.

On the dining room table, Glen could see the remains of a meal. Fried chicken, mashed potatoes, corn on the cob, freshly sliced fruit, sweet tea, and a half-eaten box of chocolates.

The pain had been instantaneous. Glen had seen red. He'd never seen red before, never been so angry that the blood pulsated in his eyeballs and shot through his head, making him see pure red overlaying everything.

When the red had faded, his senses returning, he had been horrified at what he'd done.

Now here he sat, in their special spot. The place he'd buried Evan's body. The place they would always be together. No more anguish. No more betrayal.

"I brought your favorites." Glen removed a spade from the basket and started to dig.

Sweet Nothings

Melanie lie in bed, tears coursing down her cheeks, puddling in her ears. They left a cold trail across her skin, but she wouldn't wipe them off. Instead, she pressed her arms to her sides, her body rigid. Tremors ripped through her.

It felt like she would shake apart, shredded into pieces. Her jaw clenched.

Then the rattling began. Movement in the walls. Grinding, rasping, sliding.

They spoke to her the only way they knew how.

The tears stopped. The tremors, too. Her body relaxed into the softness of the bed. Soon she fell into a restful oblivion, one hand pressed to the wall where she could feel their movements.

~~

Upon waking the next morning, Melanie felt refreshed and much more able to face her day. She ran her hands along the papered walls on either side of her in the hall to the bathroom. The slight bubbles under the age-worn paper read like braille greetings when paired with the rattling behind the walls. They always moved when she was near, attuned to her rhythms.

Her sweet nothings.

Soothed by their murmurings, she showered and dressed, completing her morning toiletries. She put her hair up and did her makeup in a professional, neutral fashion. Sliding her feet into dressy flats, she went through the motions of eating then commencing with her morning commute. The sun beat down on the car. The barren heat of an August morning radiated around her. But it couldn't touch her. Not today. This would be a good day.

Her office, located downtown, squatted between taller, historic buildings. It was stucco and stone, a dreary brown.

Despite the outside, the inside looked welcoming and homey. Overstuffed sofas rested around a glass coffee table. A bookshelf sat against one wall, full of colorful books, graphic novels, and comics. A flat screen TV arched out from one corner, and a small shelf beneath it held a remote. A small fountain gurgled in one corner.

Melanie turned on the peaceful pipe music and tilted her head to listen before turning it up slightly. She checked to make sure the clipboard was loaded with a sign-in sheet, and added new patient pages to a second clipboard sitting beside the first. Then she went through the adjoining door to her desk to check her messages. The familiar motions of her day, every day, flowed from her as they always did. She wasn't even conscious of doing them at this point.

As she finished jotting down notes from the final message, the front door opened. Footsteps padded across the carpeting, and the sound of weight being lowered onto a sofa drifted in, followed quickly by a muffled sigh. Her first patient of the day had arrived ten minutes early.

Melanie pulled her stack of files across her desk. Just like every other day, she'd set them out the night before. Her first appointment was on top of the stack, and she flipped the folder open. Boredom coursed through her when she scanned her past notes. This sad sap and his first world problems was a pain in the ass. Every week he came in and complained about the random jerk who stole his parking spot at the grocery store or the fast food worker that had been rude to him. Nothing major had happened in his life to cause him issues, but he insisted on a weekly appointment to talk about the little things that impacted him. He paid good money for it, so who was she to tell him no? She'd tried. Lord knew she'd tried. He wouldn't hear of it. "Therapy isn't just for people with serious issues," he'd told her. It took everything in her not to tell him that was kind of the definition of therapy.

She should discharge him as a patient, but for all she knew that would be the trigger that finally set him free to do something horrible. Maybe the therapy really was the only thing keeping him sane. Certainly, he had self-esteem issues, and he didn't understand why he was still single, even though he was a nice guy. A nice, dismal, boring guy. Besides, there was an edge to him when he spoke of being single. There was a part of him that blamed women for his singleness, made him resent them. Why he'd come to a female therapist with that being the case was still a mystery between them.

With a sigh, she carried the folder and her notepad to her chair, set them down, and went to get him from the waiting room. He looked up expectantly from his phone when she stopped in the doorway, and she smiled. "How are you today, Simon?" Simple Simon.

His mouth turned down then up into a half-assed, pitiful smile. "I'm okay, doc. How are you?"

"I'm good. Why don't you come on back?" She moved to her chair, lifting the pad and folder into her lap and getting settled in, legs crossed before her. She felt the slight drag of stubble, and noted a shave was in order tomorrow morning. That, or pants instead of a skirt.

Simon settled onto the couch across from her, draping himself across it. He always insisted on lying down for their sessions. "It feels more real that way," he said. Her response, as always, was, "Whatever makes you feel the most comfortable." Once in his usual prone position, he knitted his fingers together on his stomach and gazed up at the ceiling

"How have you been since our last appointment?" she asked.

"It was a kinda' crummy week. I got a flat tire and had to put the spare on. They told me they couldn't sell me just the one tire, because the others were too worn down, and it would mess things up. Shouldn't that be my choice? It's my car, after all."

The drone of his familiar voice filled her head, and she nodded, doodling as he spoke. He liked it when she took notes. She'd long taken notice of his hungry eyes on the movement of her pen, the peace it seemed to bring him that she took him seriously enough to take notes. Keeping her pen busy kept him happy. Without real issues, that meant filling the space with something else.

Near the end of the hour, when she'd reached her limit and he'd launched into a discourse on the indignity of having to pay for the privilege of parking downtown, she cut in. "Tell me something you're looking forward to, Simon."

This caught him by surprise, and he stopped and stared at her, mouth agape. After a moment, he asked, "What do you mean?"

"I think it would be helpful for you to think of something to look forward to in order to not dwell on the negative."

"I..."

"Do you have anything good planned for the weekend? Any shows you enjoy watching? A meal you're looking forward to?"

"Well, I like a show that's on Friday nights."

A rush of hope filled her. "Do you do anything special for yourself when you watch it?"

"Like what?"

"Pop some popcorn or have some ice cream?"

"No, but..."

"Go ahead," she pressed, pen held to paper.

Simon's eyes strayed to the pen. His tongue jutted out between his lips. "I turn out the lights to make it more like a movie theater and I have a soda."

"There you go!" She surprised herself with her own outburst, and the way he jerked back showed she'd startled him, as well. "Try adding a snack you like. Make it a routine. That sort of positive experience can go a long way toward helping you relax and removing the negative feelings."

Simon nodded. His eyes darted to the clock, and he sat up. "I guess it's time for me to go. Thanks, doc."

"I'd love to hear how Friday goes when I see you next. Maybe try writing down how you feel and what you change."

They both stood and shook hands. After he'd left through her secondary door, which kept her patients from having to see each other, she settled behind her desk to write down some notes. The notes were sparse, as usual, but at least this time she had the assignment to add to his folder. Her next patient wasn't for another hour since she'd had a cancellation, which left extra time, but not enough to do anything of consequence.

The silence of the room pressed down on her. The walls were so quiet here. She itched to hear even a faint rustle. Instead, the sounds of traffic, deeply muffled, drifted through the glass of the closed window. Her clock ticked on the wall. A mild electric buzz filled the room, though she didn't know if she was actually hearing it or if it was a physical sensation.

Raising her hand, she fluttered her fingernails against her teeth, enjoying both the sensation and the sound. It soothed her enough to get through her notes for Simon and to review the next patient's previous session notes. Today was shaping up to be an exhausting day.

She wanted to go home, to hear her sweet nothings. Only three more appointments for the day. It was a short one. Her skin crawled from the silence, and she finally grabbed her phone and started her playlist on random to fill the void space in the building. It struck her that the time had come to make this office officially hers. After all, she'd been in this location for several months now, with no intention of switching any time soon. Eyeballing Simon's folder, she took it back out and combed through his information, absorbing his personal details.

A plan formed. Peace settled over her.

~~

Friday night, Melanie spoke directly to the wall beside her bed. "They won't take your place, but I have to have backup at work. I'll go crazy having to face that silence if it continues."

No sound greeted her words. No answering scrapes or mutters. Her sense of isolation grew, and she curled inward, hugging herself tightly. Tight pain filled her chest.

"I need to know you're okay with this."

Nothing.

A tear drifted down her cheek. "Please?"

When she still didn't receive a response, she pressed her damp cheek to the wall and slid down it until her head rested on the bed. She pressed as much of her body against the wall as possible, reveling in the stiffness of the paper, the almost rough surface, but also the solid strength of it. Their approval meant the world to her. Absolutely everything. She couldn't face the stark loneliness of the outside world if she didn't have them to come back to. They filled the emptiness, both within the house and within her.

Just when she'd given up on her idea, a soft muttering began. It wasn't the full bore rasping she'd hoped for, but consent had been given, albeit grudgingly. Joy filled her, cascading into the empty spaces within, and she kissed the wall, both hands pressed lovingly to its surface. Their vibrations tickled her palms in a delicious dance of acceptance.

"I hear you. Thank you!"

With one final kiss, she grabbed her shoes and her coat, taking a moment to double check she'd packed everything she'd need. Her kit still sat on the bookshelf where she'd left it. A final glance in the mirror to check her hair and makeup, and she was ready to go.

The drive to Simon's wasn't long. He lived in a simple house in an older neighborhood. One of the ones old enough to not have HOAs to force neutral colors and uniform houses. His house had a big white wraparound porch, the square footage probably equaling the entirety of the interior floor plan. He'd decorated it in an eccentric fashion, with metal and wood sculptures all over the lawn. She counted at least five bird feeders hanging from a giant old oak in the center of his lawn, plus three more hanging from sculptures. Dusk had already fallen, so no birds graced the feeders with their presence, lending his yard a rather pathetic appearance. The dim gaudiness of it all expressed his constant need for attention, despite his mundanity.

The TV's flickering light shone through the front window. He'd left the blinds open, his living room exposed blindly to the dark outside. She could see in, but he couldn't see out. Even his home situation showcased his prey nature, a rabbit within a glass cage, waiting for the wolf to find it.

With the brisk fall temperatures, everyone in the neighborhood had tucked themselves into their houses, most with their shades drawn. The beauty of cooler weather was everyone's withdrawal from the outside. No nosy housewives to peer at her from their porches, or late-night lawn mowing suburbanites to notice her. Neighbors and friends sat inside instead of on their porches. She continued past his house and drifted down a parallel street until she found a good parking spot in front of a darkened house.

In her dressy pantsuit, she looked like a professional getting home from work. No one would look twice at a nicely dressed woman in her thirties walking down the sidewalk. Her briefcase reinforced this innocent appearance.

She walked back around to his house, watching for faces in windows, of which she saw zero. Everyone had settled in for their evening programming, just like Simon. She had the night to herself. The brisk air felt amazing on her flushed skin, and the clack of her high heels on the pavement created a pleasant rhythm. She found herself adjusting her steps just enough to change the patterns.

Outside his house, she took a moment to plump her hair and rub her teeth with a finger to be sure no lipstick stained them. Her knock rang out sharp and loud in the quiet evening. The chatter of the television shut off, and there was a quiet pause. She could imagine Simon inside, staring at the door, wondering who might be knocking at this hour. Or at all. He'd never mentioned getting visitors, had in fact never mentioned friends or even going out with co-workers. His parents had died years ago, and he had no siblings to speak of. Simon was alone.

A creak sounded and the light disappeared from the peephole. She directed a smile toward the curious eye she knew watched her right now. After about twenty seconds, the light returned. The deadbolt scraped and the door opened.

He squinted at her. "Ms. Zahn? Hi. Uh, what are you doing here?"

"I wanted to check in on you. Thought I'd pay a visit."

"Oh." He studied her for a moment then blushed. "Sorry, I'm being rude. Please, come in."

She stepped past him into a clean, pleasant living room. Southwestern paintings decorated the walls, and a flat screen hung over the fireplace. "Thank you."

He took her coat and hung it on a hook by the door then gestured to the sofa. She kept her briefcase and sat in the spot next to where a can of soda and a bowl of yellow and white popcorn sat. The soda, freshly opened, still fizzed. The rich smell of butter filled the room. Melanie took a deep breath and eased against the back of the sofa. She recognized the show paused on the screen, though she couldn't remember the name. A cooking show, of which there were at least dozens on TV at any given time.

"You can start the show back up. I just wanted to keep you company for a little while. Maybe shake up your routine a bit. I feel it will be a healthy change."

He stood at the end of the sofa, thumbs rubbing over his index fingers. He shuffled on his feet. "You want a drink? I have soda, water, and some orange juice. Or I could make coffee."

"I'm good, but thank you."

He sat down, pressing himself against the arm as far away from her as he could get. His darted glance at the other sofa told her he wondered why she hadn't sat there. Her mouth twitched up into a half smile before she could stop it, and she turned it into a full wattage smile for his benefit. She didn't want to hurt his feelings.

With a mildly shaking hand, he used the remote to start the show. Instantly, voices filled the room, shouting back and forth in desperate agitation. Reality shows were a great way to study people. They took the competitions so seriously when, in the scheme of things, they weren't important. Not really. They certainly weren't life and death situations. Competitiveness was a strong compulsion that couldn't be fought and often made people do stupid, even aggressive things. Without more important resources to compete over, such as food and water, people instead invented reasons to battle each other. Mostly in terms of money.

As she sat there breaking the contestants down into personality types from their actions on the show, it struck her how pleasant this felt. Like Simon, she spent most of her time alone. She never brought people home with her. If she wanted a distraction, she went out, had a drink, flirted, danced. In the end, if she decided she wanted more it was at their place or even a hotel, though never a seedy rent-by-the-hour motel. She only left with the ones who could afford to treat her appropriately. Her house wasn't to be sullied.

But she'd never done this—sat peacefully next to a man, watching TV. It felt nice. Maybe she should have had a drink with him. She reached over and took a handful of popcorn, relishing the buttery saltiness of it when it hit her tongue, the crunch as she chewed it. Warmth caressed her. She felt drowsy, and decided to let herself go with this pleasant situation.

After about an hour, when they'd both been lulled into a comfortable peace, she reached into her briefcase for the syringe she'd brought. When he was in his natural surroundings he looked so much more relaxed, so natural. He even looked more masculine when he wasn't whining. Amazing how that worked. She hadn't noticed before now how strong his chin was or the soft fullness of his lips. His eyelashes stretched out from his lids for miles, and his clean hair curled softly against his neck. He might even be considered handsome. If he wouldn't look at life through his tainted personality, he'd be a catch.

He paid no attention to her movements, more at ease with her now. With care, she brought the syringe up to his neck, quickly injecting him before he could jerk away from her. She slipped the syringe back into her briefcase and placed both hands in her lap.

Simon stood up, stumbling over the end of the sofa. He fell back against the wall, facing her, eyes wide, one hand slapped to his neck.

She frowned. "Are you okay, Simon?"

His brows furrowed. He pulled his hand away from his neck, looking between her and the palm of his hand as if he could conjure answers from thin air. His eyes rolled up, and he slid down the wall into a slouch, head bent onto his shoulder.

She moved to his side, crouching beside him, and took his hand. "Don't worry. I'll be gentle."

~~

Three hours later, sated, she strolled down the sidewalk to her car. It had grown colder, the air harsh on her face, but she welcomed the wind's assault. It felt good to feel so thoroughly when so much of her life existed in a cloud of numbness, surrounded by other people's emotions. Her mind and body screamed for more stimulation. In fact, she often ached for it to the point of frustrated tears, as she had last night.

She left the car windows open on the drive to her office, her hair flying free, drifting around her face. The burning chap of the cold air on her cheeks kept her drowsiness at bay. She was exhausted from the last three hours, but sleep would come soon enough. For now, she had to finish what she'd started.

With hammer in hand, she entered the office and went

directly to the clock ticking on the wall. Pulling it down, she made a small circular hole in the wall about three inches below the nail that held it in place. After gently clearing the bits of drywall from the opening, she reached into her coat pocket and pulled out a handful of bloodied teeth. One by one, she fed them through the hole, listening to the clatter of them falling through the aged, thinned insulation and bouncing off each other.

Once she'd put all the teeth into the wall, she re-hung the clock, slid down the wall, and placed a cheek to its surface.

"Whisper to me, my sweet nothings."

And they did.

Shelter From the Storm

Malin squatted by the front door, feet sinking into the deep, red sand. It was hard to hear through the hood she wore, but she strained her ears, listening for any sound that might indicate someone inside. A dry wind rustled past, sending sand skittering across the wood of the door.

With no other intact buildings nearby in what appeared to have been a small settlement, long burned and buried, the risk of ambush was heightened.

Her thighs quaked in response to the awkward position. She stood, back scraping along the rough-hewn wood wall, probably making more noise than she would have liked. Lucky for her, everyone had to wear something over their heads to keep out the toxic air, so she wouldn't be the only one at a disadvantage.

She'd already circled the building, checking for risk factors inside. What she'd seen was a single large room and two doors leading to other rooms. The windows on that side had been boarded over, ensuring she couldn't get a thorough check before going in.

She grasped the knob and turned. It scraped, sticking, rasping loudly. The door opened, stopping abruptly after about two inches.

Was someone on the other side?

She stepped back, away from the partially submerged stoop, heart pounding. The steady, rapid thrum of her pulse filled her ears, blocking out the growing howl of the wind. She had placed a hand on the knife at her thigh without thinking about it, even unsnapped the sheath. The rough handle rested against her gloved palm. She swiped at the goggle lenses to clear the sand dust from them, eyes back on that door. She looked down for shadows that might indicate someone on the other side.

What she saw instead was accumulated sand.

Breathing heavily, her breath sour in the mask, Malin stepped forward and pushed, leaning her shoulder against it. Sand had piled up behind the door, slithering in through the crack in the bottom and creating a blockage. The more she pushed, the more it tumbled around the door. It took several minutes to force the door enough to squeeze inside.

The room before her was about thirty-by-fifteen feet, empty of furniture and appliances. The lack of a kitchen or even roughed-in plumbing meant this house had been built post-comet. The few post-comet houses she'd run into had been utilitarian and simple, lacking bathrooms and kitchens. After all, without electricity and plumbing, those additions became redundant. Sand had gathered into piles in a fan beyond the open window. One of the interior doors sported its own pile of sand, which had obviously sifted under it. Odd, considering the window to that room had been intact from the outside. She decided to check the other one first.

The floor felt strong under her feet, except for a couple boards that had loosened over the years. These sunk underneath her, and she wondered if they'd creaked. Being inside the building had dampened the storm's sound, but the wind had reached a new level of high-pitched screech, and it covered up everything but the sound of her own breathing, which roared in her ears.

The worn door sported deep grooves in the lower half. There were also dents, as if it had been kicked or rammed with something. It opened the moment she touched it, the latch broken.

Inside were the first signs of life she'd seen, so far. Two filthy blankets and a sleeping bag lay on the floor. There were also two backpacks, similar to her own. Maybe there would be something useful in them.

Only one room awaited examination, and then she could get settled. She hadn't eaten or peed in hours, and her full bladder and empty stomach nagged her now that she'd found shelter. Her level of dehydration had reached misery status, as well. Her mouth felt like it was lined with sandpaper, and her dry sinuses ached. Every blink was minor torture, eyelids dragging across dry eyes.

She hesitated at the door to the second room, hands flat against its splintered surface. There were odd, unfamiliar markings in the sand at her feet, feathery striations overlapping each other and facing different directions.

A hole gaped at chest level, and she bent down to look inside. The boarded window let in a small amount of light between the slats. Like the big room, it sat empty. Something dark and irregular stained the visible flooring. The floor had been broken from below. Large chunks of wood stood like ragged buildings, jutting up from a large central hole. What looked like strips of fabric stuck to one of them, caught in the splintered wood. Since there was no sign of anything living inside, she turned the knob and pushed the door open.

She approached the hole, careful to look around and check every corner first. The room was as empty as it had appeared through the door. Careful to avoid the splintered boards, Malin peered down into the hole. It was deep. Not just foundation deep, but vast enough that she couldn't see a bottom. The edges of the hole were ragged and uneven, desiccated roots dangling from the sides. The edges didn't match up with the hole in the floor, instead stretching away on the sides, underneath the flooring. Whereas the broken wood would allow something the size of, say, a black bear through it, the actual hole was large enough to fit a small car, if they hadn't all rusted into oblivion.

Malin took off a glove and held her hand over the hole. Cool air caressed her skin for a second before the toxicity began to burn it. She put the glove back on. She bet it would feel magical to take off her filter mask, goggles, and hood, and let the air run over her sweaty face. But she knew better. It would only feel good for a second.

Backing out of the room, she shut the door. The hole creeped her out. Something had to have tunneled up and broken through the floor, and she couldn't think of one creature that could do something like that. Not that size. Most mammals and all birds had died off when the comet hit, blocking out the sun's rays for several years. After all, people could make masks and protective clothing, but animals couldn't. The only ones that had survived up to this point were insects and creatures that thrived in the sand and soil. All of these were small, though. Certainly not as big as a car or a bear. Then again, she'd heard mention of creatures that had come with the comet, animals that thrived in the new atmosphere. She'd long figured that for the tall tales of people living in constant fear and discomfort. This hole made her wonder. She shuddered and backtracked from the room, pulling on the door to make sure it latched securely.

The house officially confirmed as empty, she blocked the front door closed with the sand that had made it so hard for her to get inside. Then she turned her attention to an open window that allowed the wind to bring in swaths of sand that swirled around the building, creating airborne sandpaper. All attempts to close the window failed; it wouldn't budge. Frustrated, and sweating harder than before, she used a roll of thick, black tape to seal her insulated sleeping bag over the opening.

Once that was settled, she pulled three cans out of her bag: beans, corn, peaches. Since she hadn't eaten all day, she got a triple course, with protein, veggie, and fruit. She also extricated a small machine with what looked like an old-fashioned milk bottle, a series of clear tubes, a capsule with a filter inside, and a second milk bottle. With great relief, she urinated into the first bottle on the contraption by opening a small flap in her pants that would only expose the small area necessary. Once finished, she covered herself up, flipped a switch on the machine, and waited. The battery was low, and for a moment panic edged at her mind, fear that it wouldn't work. Happily, the green light popped on, and a suction noise began, followed by trickling fluid. The dark yellow urine disappeared from the first bottle, shooting through the tubes into the capsule. It came out the other side crystal clear.

She opened the cans, grabbed a grubby fork from her bag, and settled onto the floor with her meal, eager to fill her veins and her belly at the same time. The gas mask came off, leaving a small circle around her mouth uncovered. Her lips dried instantly, skin flaking onto her gloves. A quick application of a thick lip balm from a squeeze tube helped, and she made quick work of her meal.

Once she'd packed everything back up, she went through the backpacks in the first room, finding a couple cans of food, another water extractor, and a sizable flat-head screwdriver. She put these in her bag and set it against the wall.

That finished, she took her ankle-length coat off to form a makeshift pillow, leaving the rest of her clothing on to protect against the air. Curling into the fetal position, she fell asleep quickly, despite the muffled howling and the shifting of the building as it faced off against the wind's heavy currents.

~~

Malin awakened to pure darkness. It took her a moment to process the stillness. The wind had ceased. She rolled to her other side, groaning at the soreness already infiltrating her joints from sleeping on a hard floor. She was just nestling into the coat pillow when she heard it: the slamming of a door.

She froze, instantly alert.

Her heart pounded in her chest, veins pulsing with panicked blood cells. It hadn't been the door to this room, which left two other options, both terrifying. Somehow, either the blocked front door had opened or the door standing between her and the giant hole had. Either way, she wasn't alone.

She heard no further sounds, but that might be a lie. They might be too quiet for her to hear them through the walls. If the door hadn't slammed, she'd be asleep. After some debate, she loosened the laces on the back of her hood and pulled one side forward, exposing her ear, neck, and the back of her head. She didn't move, holding her breath and listening intently. She ignored the discomfort as the moisture sucked out of her skin, the beginnings of a chemical burn spreading across it.

There. A scuff.

Another one.

Someone was out there.

For now, she left the ear uncovered. Someone else would have their own safety gear on, which meant they wouldn't hear her coming. Her only advantage was that she knew they were out there, but they probably had no idea she was in here. She'd just have to deal with the burn.

She got up, slipped her coat on, and crept to the door,

standing in the corner, bare ear pressed to the wood. In her backpack, she had a flare gun and a real gun with a single bullet. On her person, she had a hunting knife. She was better with a knife than a gun.

The way she saw it, her choices were to hide in the room and hope whatever it was didn't come in or to make a surprise attack on whoever lurked out there. Cringing behind this door and waiting for someone to come in after her sounded like torture. On the other hand, she couldn't be sure of where they were. She could make a mad rush for them, only to expose herself to attack.

The sleeping bag. If she could make a run for the window and rip the sleeping bag off, she might stand a chance.

Her ear and neck were in excruciating pain, and she figured she'd burned off a couple layers of skin. She replaced the hood, afraid the eardrum would burn.

She breathed rapidly, rank air pulsing in and out of her nose. The condensation made it hard to inhale, and she purposefully slowed her breathing. Sweat trickled along her spine, down her forehead, and between her breasts, quickly soaked up by the thick safety gear she wore.

Malin placed one hand on the doorknob, knife in the other.

Did a stranger stand on the other side of the door listening to her, breathing mere inches away?

Her spine crawled at the thought.

She could change her mind, stay behind the door, wait it out. If it was someone simply seeking shelter, they might leave before she got up. They might have no reason to search the rooms. Or perhaps they'd go inside the other room and stumble into the hole. She'd never been that lucky, though, and she knew she had to do something. Staying in the room wasn't an effective option, and she had nothing with which to prop the door closed.

A deep breath, and she pulled the door back a small amount, bracing herself against it, waiting for an attack.

Nothing came.

She pulled the door slowly toward her.

Still nothing.

The door now stood open as far as it would go with her

standing behind it, huddled and underweight as she was. There should be plenty of room for an individual to come through the door, but no one came.

It was too soon to be relieved. They could be out there waiting for her to come out, biding their time. She bet her life each time she made another decision. One misstep and she'd be dead. Or someone else would. Her whole body quaked at the thought of having to kill again. Most people didn't want to fight or steal. They just wanted to survive. Like her.

She stepped out from behind the door, moving to the wall on the other side of the frame, and knelt down by her backpack. Clutching the bag to her chest, she slid the knife back into its sheath and took out both guns, shoving each into a pocket. Her head pounded from all the blood rushing to it, the beginnings of a headache snaking their way around her brain.

The clouds outside must have shifted, because a small amount of light filtered through the doorway. She took advantage of the light and stuck her head out, not giving herself time to think about what could happen.

No figure stood in the room, as far as she could see. She jerked her head back inside, leaning it against the wall behind her.

Bracing herself, she stepped out of the room completely, sweeping with her goggled eyes, which meant turning her head fully in each direction she needed to check. There was still nothing to see. Swiftly, she walked across the room to the sleeping bag covered window and ripped one side off the wall, exposing most of the window. More light filled the room, a faint and eerie green in color.

If there was someone in this room with her, they had to be hiding under the blankets she'd heaped in the corner. She swallowed, an uncomfortable move with so little saliva, and moved toward the pile. Was it bigger than before? She hadn't paid too much attention to the size of the pile earlier, but it was possible it was slightly bigger than it had been.

She leveled a fierce kick at the center of the pile then stomped down on it.

Her foot met wall then floor. She snagged the top blanket with her boot and pulled it away from the other one, spreading them both out. No one hid there, and she could see that the front door remained closed, the sand undisturbed.

Her skin crawled, goosebumps breaking out across her body. She'd left her back exposed to the rest of the building. The room with the hole was behind her.

She spun around, panting, flare gun held out before her. Someone could have snuck up behind her. Or something. Now that it was down to that room being the one occupied, she couldn't bet on there being a human behind the door. Something had entered this building from that massive hole. It waited behind the door. Not only that, but it could open the door, had done so once already.

This could be a trap. It might have woken her up, hoping to lure her into the room, drag her into that never ending hole in the ground.

It wasn't safe to go outside at night, even without a storm raging. The ground shifted in the winds, the sand moving at will. She could fall in a hole, be trapped or killed. She'd once found a corpse in a hole hidden by a hill. Had almost joined said corpse when she popped over a hill at a rapid pace, only to stop on the edge of the drop. He couldn't have been dead long, considering the sand covered several inches while she stood there. If he'd been dead more than a few hours, he would have been covered entirely, invisible to everyone who traipsed across his grave.

There was also quicksand. The only place water existed was beneath the ground, but there were pockets of it close enough to the surface to create quicksand.

These were at least known threats. What she faced in here was unknown.

With a suddenness that caused her to jump, a gust of wind slammed into the building. She not only heard it, but felt it. Then the howling began. The storm had returned. She'd woken up during the lull. All thoughts of possibly leaving the building were squelched just like that. The storms were not only dangerous, they guaranteed death.

She took a moment to gather her wits. With such limited resources, she needed to be mentally prepared to respond to whatever threat awaited her.

Crossing the room was one of the hardest things she'd ever done. Even when she'd been trapped in that room figuring out what to do, she'd at least been fairly confident she'd be facing a human. There was something comforting about that, because chances are they wouldn't have intended to invade an already inhabited space. Now she had no idea what she was dealing with or what its intent might be. Her legs shook so hard they barely held her up. Her arms and hands felt weak. She wasn't positive she'd be able to pull a trigger if it came to that.

That was stupid. She'd have to. Therefore she would.

Guns secure in her hands, she moved to the door. Two deep breaths, and she kicked the door right at the handle. It flew open on the first kick, fragments of wood raining down on her feet and legs in a soft pitter patter felt through her protective clothing.

She charged inside, deflecting the door swinging back at her with an elbow.

She ran directly to the corner behind the door, holding the guns out in a "V" in an attempt to cover both sides of the room.

Frantically, she turned her head from side to side, seeking whatever had opened and closed the door.

Everything looked just as she'd left it.

That left only the hole.

She aimed the flare gun and fired. Red light shot out from the muzzle, the flare arcing down into the hole. She ran forward and peered down.

A horde of glowing, white forms looked up at her, briefly pink in the flare's light. They looked humanoid, but insect-like at the same time. Their heads were oversized, bodies shrunken, limbs bent at weird angles, with long hairs coming off them. The tumbling flare illuminated an endless mass of them, clinging to the dirt walls and looking directly up at her.

Malin screamed, throwing the now empty flare gun at the closest form before fleeing toward the doorway. She grabbed the door to close it, realizing too late that she'd obliterated the one thing that stood between her and these creatures. She let go of the door, staring into the room as it opened the rest of the way.

The creatures poured out of the hole, accompanied by a

high insectoid clicking that penetrated the material of her hood.

She ran toward the front door. The other door didn't latch, so trapping herself inside the room wouldn't help her unless she could hold out against them until morning, her strength against their combined mass.

Throwing herself to her knees, she scooped at the sand, aware that at any moment they would be upon her. Then she remembered the window.

Giving up on the pile of sand, she stood, pressing her back to the door. The creatures had stopped not far outside the door. They were the same distance from the window as she was, and she had no idea who could move faster.

She saw now why their limbs had looked weird. They were jointed in the opposite direction as humans, and they had six limbs each, all equal lengths, though they stood upright on only one set. The more that poured out of the room, the louder the clicking became, joined by a rough rasp. Their throats moved with the noises, rather than their mouths, which sported giant mandibles. Their large eyes stood out, pitch black against the light glow of their skin, bottomless like the hole.

She pondered the window, the creatures, and the sand at her feet. She could keep scraping the sand away until it became possible to squeeze out through the crack once more, or she could dive through that window. One option required turning her back on the creatures and hoping she could squeeze through fast enough to beat them out; the other option required racing them to the window and hoping her aim was true, which was always tricky with the lack of peripheral vision around the goggles.

That still left the storm to deal with. She'd also be leaving her bag behind with all her supplies. Hopelessness coursed through her. There was no good solution. Every option meant death for her, just in different timeframes. But escaping to the outside gave her the option of finding shelter, leaving the possibility of retrieving her things once they crept back to their hole.

Assuming they didn't follow her out.

Reaching behind her, she turned the knob and pulled as far as the door would go in order to test it. It only opened wide enough for her to stick a hand out.

She shuffled at the sand on the floor with her feet, staring at the creatures. Her motion alerted them, and they moved forward several steps. When she froze, they froze.

No discreet way to get the sand away from the door then. She had to try the window. It wasn't large, so she'd have to leap headfirst through the center. If she could pull the sleeping bag with her, it might provide additional shelter from the storm.

Gathering her last shred of courage, she tensed her muscles in preparation to run.

The creatures tensed, mirroring her actions. Their mandibles flexed, and the sounds silenced. Or at least got quiet enough she could no longer hear them.

They knew she was going to try something.

One of the creatures moved forward like lightning, a bright blur, zigzagging at great speed. She held the gun up in front of her and fired. The bullet found its mark, demolishing its head. The others shrieked and reared back.

Malin tucked the gun into her pack and unsheathed her knife. She stared at the creatures, willing them to do something other than merely stare back. She was afraid to move, but had to do something.

The creatures calmed, no longer frantic. Another stepped forward, once more mirroring her actions.

Malin took a wider stance, making sure she had good balance. She held the knife before her, ready for the attack.

Sure enough, it raced at her the same as its predecessor. Only this time it stopped short of where the other one had landed after being shot. It bent down and examined the other creature, nudging it with a leg. Then it looked up at her, hunched low, and came for her.

When it leaped, she brought the knife up, straight into the soft underbelly, bracing for the impact. She wrapped her other arm around it, thrusting upward with the knife the best she was able. Its weight crashed fully into her, legs closing around her, squeezing. One claw punctured the material of her shirt, tearing at the flesh, which then began to burn. She screamed, tearing with the knife while keeping her face turned away from the snapping mandibles.

Finally, it stopped moving, head sinking to her chest. She shoved the body off her and stood, covered in dark gore, knife ready. Her blood drenched glove felt damp against her skin.

The creatures eyed her, but now they retreated a slight distance toward the door they'd come out of. Underneath their wide open mandibles were human mouths, teeth bared in grimaces behind thin, black lips.

Malin shuddered. She sheathed the knife, tucked her head, bent her arms, and ran like she had never run before. She couldn't hear the creatures, nor could she move her visual focus from the window. She had no idea if they were retreating or crashing toward her. No idea if they would be upon her before she reached the window.

Though only a matter of feet, it seemed to take forever. Every second was another second one of those foul things could be on her. The back of her neck buzzed with a feeling of vulnerability, spreading down her back. Her muscles tensed.

Any second now.

A foot away from the window, she threw herself into a headlong dive, arms over her head, aimed at the center of the opening. Her feet left the ground, and she became fully airborne.

As her head cleared the windowsill, she reached out to grasp the sleeping bag, gripping the slick material as firmly as she could.

Now her torso was through. Now her waist.

Something grabbed her ankle, and she jerked to a stop, slamming down on the windowsill. Her pelvis hit, the bones slamming into the frame. Pain rocketed through her abdomen. She dangled above the ground, releasing the sleeping bag, which hadn't had a chance to loosen. The pressure on her ankle was intense, and she scrabbled at the ground with her gloved fingers, tearing the fabric over a couple of them. The air burned her fingertips, but she couldn't care about that. She clawed for all she was worth, pulling at the sand, but it only slid around, not giving her any purchase.

She kicked back with the other foot, striking the creature. Her blows were useless, and it dragged her back over the sill by her leg. She screamed into her mask, breath heating her face.

Groping for her knife, she continued to thrash against the creature's hold, kicking out, twisting her body, but nothing seemed to make a difference.

Her hand landed on the sheath, and she gripped the handle before unsnapping the covering. She held the knife close to her chest, waiting for a clear shot, and curled inward as much as she could, hoping to keep her head from striking the ground.

It worked, though the hit her shoulder took jolted through her entire body. It took her a second to recover, but she twisted onto her back, legs crossing, and arced out with the knife, hearing a crisp sound as the knife bit into the creature's torso. She slashed out again. The blade bit into one of its appendages, which fell to the ground with a thump. It screamed, mandibles opening wide, the eerie human mouth once more visible, pearly white teeth reflecting the moon's light.

She stabbed out with the knife, aiming for the head. It caught her wrist in a strong grip, twisting. She heard and felt the snap, the sound preceding the pain. The knife fell from her now limp hand, smacking the wood with a solid thud.

Two more of the creatures reached her, grabbing her even as she struck out at them. Together, they dragged her backward, chittering. Her coat drifted above her head, tugging at her arms. Her wrist burned and throbbed simultaneously.

She twisted herself around and scrabbled for purchase along the floorboards. Nails broke off with quick, sharp pains. Her fingers found a knothole, and she gripped it as hard as she could. One of the creatures lost its grip. She took the opportunity to kick out at the other one. Her blows landed on its head repeatedly, with no result. Switching directions, she kicked at the appendages holding her. One snapped, and it released her entirely.

Leaping to her feet with her last bit of energy, Malin ran for the door once more, blinded with panic. This time she made it through. She didn't look back until hidden behind the blackened boards of one of the burned buildings.

Moonlight reflected from multiple sets of eyes, staring her way through the window she'd used to escape, but they made no move to leave. Malin sank to the ground, exhausted, the air burning every bit of exposed flesh. With no supplies, her only chance at survival would be to venture back into the building in daylight and hope the creatures were nocturnal. She rolled into a ball and pulled her coat more tightly around her, blocking out the poisonous air in an attempt to make it to daylight.

Following the Rules

When the dark comes, I have to lock my bedroom door. That's when my night parents come out. I have to follow the rules.

I've never met my night parents, but I've heard them. My day parents tell me to turn my music up, and to sleep with headphones on. Sometimes they're louder than the music. It's not my fault.

There was one night where I heard screaming. There was a lot of booming outside my door, and I heard it even when I kept turning my music up. I heard a lady crying. She said, "No, no. Please, no. No." It sounded like she was right outside my door, and I wanted to open it to see if she was okay. Maybe she was hurt. When I got a bee sting, I said "No." I cried, too.

But then there were growls. My door went *clang-clang*, *clang-clang*, *clang-clang*. I heard choking sounds and more growls.

I got in bed and put my pillow over my head. I did a little hum, too, and it felt tickly on my mouth.

My day parents say I'm never to look outside or open my door or windows. There are bars on my windows, so I don't understand why I can't open them. I don't understand why I can't open my door, either.

My door is very thick. When I knock on it, it goes *clang-clang*. It smells like pennies, but it's dark grey, not penny-colored. I guess that means it's metal, but not the same kind as my pennies. The lock is thick and slides all the way across the door and into the wall. I know it's locked when it goes *DONG* and vibrates in my hands for just a second.

Sometimes things hit the wall. One time, something *tap-tap-tapped* behind my bookshelf. It scared me so bad I peed my panties. It was warm when it went down my legs, but then my feet and legs were cold and wet. It smelled icky, too. I took off my nightgown and wiped myself off with it. Then I put it on the floor where the wet spot was so it could clean it up. When my day mom came in the next morning, she didn't get mad. I thought she might, but she didn't. She just made a clicking sound with her tongue and helped me get cleaned up. We made my bed with "My Little Pony" sheets. Those are my favorite.

The rules are written in my bedroom and by the front door, so I don't forget:

Always be home by 5:00 PM for dinner.
Always be in your room by 7:00 PM. Lock the door.
Never get up before 8:00 AM.
Keep the music on from 7:00 PM to 8:00 AM.
Don't look outside.
Don't stick your fingers through any cracks.
Don't look under the door.
Never go in the basement.

I remember a lady a long time ago who used to stay in my room all night with me. These memories are fuzzy and blurry and weird sounding, like I'm listening through a seashell. Maybe I remember her voice, but maybe it's Mary Poppins' voice. They sound the same.

The lady was nice. She looked like grandmas look in books. Her hair was white, and she had dark, round glasses that made her eyes look double-big. She always had on a skirt and a sweater. The only difference between her and book grandmas was that her hair was long and flowy, like Rapunzel, and she never put it back in a round thing on her hair. I liked to touch it. Even though the looks and sounds are blurry, the softness of her hair isn't. Sometimes I close my eyes and touch my hair and pretend she's there with me. Especially when I'm the scaredest.

One day, the not grandma lady opened the door. I told her that was on the list, but she said she needed to check, that she thought someone might be hurt. She told me to close the door and turn the music loud. I was listening to Disney songs. I closed the door and made the lock go *DONG*, and then I turned up the music. I kept turning "Supercalifragilisticexpialidocious" up more and more and more, because there were screams. Loud screams. Not like just bee sting screams.

Something hit my door. *Clang-clang*.

I put my blanket over my head and sang "Circle of Life" real loud with the music. I screamed it. I sang all the songs like that until my throat felt scratchy and my voice got whispery. Then I went to sleep.

The not grandma lady wasn't there when I woke up. Or when I went to bed again.

Or when I woke up again.

No more pretty white hair or big glasses eyes.

My day mom said I was old enough to follow the rules on my own, so no more nanny.

I read to myself until I go to bed. There are lots of books in my room, and my day parents get new ones all the time. Sometimes I have a bedtime hot chocolate party with my dolls and stuffies. My day mom makes me special hot chocolate with a bowl of marshmallows, and she puts them on the table in the corner of my room. Then she kisses me on my head and tells me, "Remember the list."

It's right there on my wall. I would have to be stupid to forget it. Or a baby, and I'm not a baby. I'm a big girl. Six years old. I don't understand why she says that to me all the time. When she says it, her mouth is crinkly with a smile, but her eyes look scary and they don't crinkle.

My day dad says goodnight to me, too. Most nights. He comes in all stompy-fast and gives me a big hug. He says, "See you in the morning" and, "Listen to your mom." Then he walks away stompy-fast and pulls the door closed. I can hear him through the door, but his voice sounds funny.

"I want to hear it lock."

I lock it. *DONG*.

His feet go stompy-fast down the hall. Then down the steps. And it's music time.

One time, I asked them why I can't see my night parents.

"Don't they like me?" I asked.

"They don't really like anyone, Honey," my day mom said. "They're cranky and scary, so it's best you stay away from them."

"How come I have to lock my door?"

"It keeps you safe," said my day mom.

"Isn't our house safe?"

"It is during the day, but not at night."

"Can't my night parents keep me safe?"

"No more questions!" my day dad said. He sounded angry. His voice was barky. Mom smiled at me, and this time her eyes crinkled. I wish my eyes were pretty blue like hers, but they're not. They're green like grass. Like day daddy's.

A different day, I asked for a picture of my night parents, but my day mom said they don't like pictures, so they don't have any.

Maybe someday I can look under the door and see my night parents. Nobody will know I looked. The only reason I haven't yet is because I get real nervous when I think about it. And when I walk near the door.

The kids at my school only have one kind of parents. I asked my best friend if they were day parents or night parents. Her face got all frowny and confused, and she said, "They're the same both times."

That's weird.

I guess not everyone gets two kinds of parents.

The basement door is like my bedroom door. I like to knock on it when I walk by, because it's daytime, and it's less scary to make it go clang-clang during the day. At night, that sound is too loud, and it makes me feel afraid. It's too loud in my room, but in the open wide kitchen it doesn't sound so big.

The lock is just like mine, too, but it has a key lock in the middle of the handle. Sometimes I touch the handle, all cold in my hand, and I try to turn it. It feels slippery, and it makes my hand smell like pennies, too.

My day mom doesn't know, but sometimes I poke things under the basement door. Not my fingers. That's against the rules. But popsicle sticks are not against the rules. Wrappers are not against the rules. Leaves are not against the rules. I can stick lots of things through the cracks without breaking the rules.

A yucky smell comes under the door sometimes. It smells like the garbage can if my day dad doesn't take it outside for a lot of days, mixed up with the smell when someone hits an animal and it stays by the side of the road until it's all big and swelled up. When I ask my day mom about it, she lights a candle. Her favorite one smells like cookies. Spicy-sweet. Then she tells my day dad, "It's time to clean the basement." Her face is very serious and frowning when she says it. He puts big black plastic bags, paper towels, and a white spray bottle by the door, but he never goes down there when I'm home.

Today I went to my best friend's house. Laurie's basement had a great big TV set, with a shelf full of cartoon movies. We could watch whatever we wanted. She had toys down there, too. Lots of them. We played jump rope and checkers and dolls and dress-up. I wish I had a box full of neat dress-up clothes. She even had princess dresses. Mine was pink and shiny, and I kept it on even when we played jump rope. The crown fell off my head, but it didn't break.

Maybe my day parents don't want me to get to watch the big TV in our basement. I bet my night parents would let me. They don't tell me to read the rules. They don't yell at me or ground me.

I bet my day parents want me locked in my room because they're afraid I'll like my night parents better. My night mom is probably super beautiful. My day mom is pretty. Her hair is shiny black, and her skin is like milk. I like to touch it, because it's smooth and soft. She smells like flowers. But my night mom might be even prettier.

My night dad could be strong like Popeye. Or the Hulk. If he was all big muscles like that, he would carry me everywhere. He would build me a treehouse. My day dad has muscles, too, but they aren't as big as my night dad's might be.

Maybe when I hear them making noises at night, it's because they're playing fun games. Yes! I can't look because I'll see they're not scary, and I'll open the door. And my night parents will let me play with them. Then my day parents will be jealous, like my friend Beth was when I got the silver sparkly shoes. She got stompy just like my day dad does at bedtime.

Since my day parents won't tell me about my night parents, I have to open the door tonight. I want to play with my night parents and see what they look like.

First, I have to make a plan.

~~

It's almost time to go upstairs for bed now. The tea kettle

whistles. Tonight is a hot chocolate night. I can already taste it, sticky-sweet with marshmallows and chocolate. I bet my night mom would like a cup for her, too. I'll save her some.

My day mom gets the hot chocolate ready in a pot. She adds two big ice cubes. *Plop, plop.* I get the bag of marshmallows and put some in a little bowl. They're soft like sponges, and I squish one. Day mom isn't looking, so I pop it in my mouth and smush it between my teeth.

"You ready to go upstairs?" she asks me.

"Mm-hmm." I don't open my mouth.

She picks up the tray, and I follow her. The marshmallow is sugar-melty in my mouth, and I poke it with my tongue. It's still squishy, but it feels different.

In my room, she puts the tray on my table. We sit on my bed, and she brushes my hair. "What are you going to listen to tonight?" she asks.

"I don't know. I think maybe 'Road Trip Songs.' I feel like singing 'Clementine.'"

"That's a good one."

When she's all done, she puts the brush in its drawer and smooths my hair behind my ear so she can kiss me on the cheek. "I love you," she says.

"I love you, too."

"Remember the list."

"I do."

Then she gets up and moves to the door. Day dad comes in. *Stomp, stomp, stomp.*

He gives me a hug and says, "See you tomorrow morning."

"See you," I say.

Stomp, stomp, stomp goes day dad. Smiley-smile goes day mom. They pull the door closed.

Day dad's voice says, "Lock it."

DONG.

Stomp, stomp, stomp down the hall.

I turn on my music and play "Clementine" two times. I sing with it and twirl around. It's a sad song, so I put my hands together like I saw in a movie once, so I can look sad, too.

My hot chocolate is super chocolatey tonight. I float it around in my mouth before swallowing. It's so good I almost forget to save some for my night mom, but I pour it back into the pot before it's too late.

Now I've listened to ten songs. I bet my night parents are awake.

It's time for my plan.

I turn off the music first, and sit down to read a book. If my day parents are still awake, they'll come yell at me, I bet. This is my test to see if they're awake. See, I'm not a stupid baby.

I read three picture books. No stomps or yells yet. My day parents are sleeping, I know they are.

There are no night parent sounds yet. I take my nightgown off and put it on my bed for later. Then I put on my sparkly purple shirt and long pants. It's a little bit cold, so I get my sweatshirt with a cat face on it, too, and I zip it up. My hot chocolate is still kind of warm. I pour it into the cup and drop a couple marshmallows in. They don't melt fast like they usually do. I put a flower next to the cup, so it's pretty for my night mom.

Then I walk up to the door. I put my ear on it, even though it's cold. No sounds. I knock, and my knuckles make a *clang-clang*.

I put my ear to the door again. The door goes *clang-clang*, and I feel it shake. At first I'm scared, and I run to my bed and hide under the covers. I'm shaky scared and my breath is hot under the blanket. It gets hard to breathe a little bit, so I take the covers off.

Clang-clang goes the door.

Something sniffs a lot at the bottom of the door.

I bet my night parents have a dog! No wonder my day parents didn't want me to meet them. I always ask for a dog, but my day parents tell me no. "A dog would not be happy in this house," my day mom says.

"I'd be nice to it. And I'd pet it and take it outside."

"No," my day dad says.

Fine.

But my night parents have one.

I run to the door and get on my hands and knees. There is a big crack at the bottom, and I stick my eye to it, so I can see the hall. The lights are off, but there's a night light out there, so I can see a little bit. At first, there's only the brown carpet. But then something moves by real fast, and I can't see what it is.

There's sniffs again, and then a nose. But it's not a black nose like my friend Melanie's dog's nose. It's creamish like mine. It twitches and sniffs. Then there's a mouth. It looks familiar, but weird.

I stand up and unlock the door. It's always a little bit hard to unlock it, and I have to turn super hard, but it comes loose with a big *screech.*

Clang-clang-clang on the other side.

The handle is cold in my hand. It's not smooth anymore. There's a rough spot on the very top. I put my other hand on the wall and I take a big, deep breath that makes my stomach get big. I twist the handle and pull the door open.

Nothing there.

It's dark. The night light isn't working. It was a minute ago. I turn on my big bedroom light and it makes the hall yellow-white bright, so I can step out of my room. I can't see anything to my left or to my right. Not inside the light.

A growl comes from my left, toward the stairs. I look that way and make my eyes squinty, but I can't see anything.

Something growls from my right, and I turn that way instead. What's that? I can see a shape, but I don't know what it is. It's near the floor.

"Doggy?"

It whines.

"It's okay, Doggy." I get down on my knees and hold my hand out. "Come here."

Pomp, pomp, pomp go the paws on the carpet.

And then it's there, but it's not a doggy.

Pomp, pomp, pomp behind me, too. I don't want to look. I don't want to see this anymore.

I back up toward my room speedy-fast, but my butt hits the wall. The door is next to me. They *pomp, pomp, pomp* toward me. My day dad and my day mom. They're crawling like dogs, and their mouths are long. They have claws and big teeth, and their arms and legs are different shaped, like they broke them. They both twitch their noses and sniff at the air. I've never seen them without their clothes on before, but they aren't wearing anything. Their skin is white and wrinkled.

My scary mom gets close to me. Her nose is moving when she sniffs. It puffs air on my face. She smells weird, like Melanie's dog when it gets wet. Drool slides out of her mouth and drips on my knee, warm and wet. Her eyes aren't blue anymore. Just black. I can see myself in them.

A squeaky sound comes from my throat, and I slap my hand over my mouth so I can't make noise again. My hands feel burned from the carpet like my knees get sometimes if I crawl on the floor.

My scary dad's mouth opens and he growls mean at me. His teeth are super big, and I'm so scared I can't breathe. He gets close to the ground and his back legs move. I've seen kitties do that before they jump.

I put my hands down and crawl until I'm all the way inside my room. Scary mom doesn't follow me. Scary dad keeps growling.

I stand up, and grab the door. My scary dad jumps, and I scream. But the scary mom jumps in front of him and knocks him down. She snarls like a wolf did once in a movie, all big teeth and frightening sounds, her lip curled up. Scary dad tries to run around her, and she bites him.

I slam the door with a big, loud *CLANG*.

DONG.

The door is locked, and I lean my ear against it. I hear whines and growls, scratching. All I can smell is pennies. I taste them, too.

I turn on "Clementine" as loud as it will go. It makes my ears shake inside. The music feels like my heartbeat, and I think maybe my heart is beating to the song now. I try to breathe slow, because my head feels black inside, and it's hard to breathe.

I climb into bed and pull the covers up over my head, but I leave a crack so fresh air can come in.

Tomorrow I will follow ALL the rules.

Root of All Evil

Lily had spent a lifetime tamping down her irritation when yet another person told her she was astoundingly pale or asked if she felt okay. With skin the color of fresh milk, hair white as snow, and eyes a light crystalline blue, she was accustomed to drawing looks and attention everywhere she went. As a child, her classmates couldn't get over the fact that her veins were visible beneath the surface of her skin, a walking visible circulatory system.

The thing about spending her life as a freak was that she learned to let things bounce off her. Sadly, as a slender young woman with terrible taste in men, it had frequently been fists doing the bouncing. The bruises were always massive, the faintest taint of blood outside the vein a dark blossom of evidence for all to see.

Her first husband had talked her parents into pulling her out of school and giving her over to him at the age of fourteen. They'd been poor farmers who saw an opportunity to hand their creepy daughter over to someone else and make a few bucks in the process. Van had been fascinated instead of horrified. He'd also been nearly thirty years her senior and living in a small, rural town meant no need to hide his sick desires. Or his abuse of her. People in the town were accustomed to looking the other way, a side effect of knowing too much about their neighbors.

Van's farm was small, but he knew his way around a field and a cow, which was enough to turn a tidy profit. Unlike her parents' farm, his stood within a bounty of trees, which meant he could make some extra money on selling bundles of firewood along with his crops and dairy products. The cattle were free range and he treated them far better than he treated his wife, which was great for the cows, but not so much for Lily. As she had with her childhood bullies, she quietly took whatever abuse

Van meted out. Her lack of tears frustrated him, often causing him to beat her all the harder for it. If she could have forced them, she would have, but she'd trained herself to not cry, blush, or show any sign of the mental agony that others subjected her to. They could cut or bruise her, but they could not force her to show it any other way.

When Van went into town, Lily was left behind to clean the house, tend the cows, and do whatever jobs Van had assigned her. Sometimes she finished early enough that she could wander in the woods, enjoying the cool shadows and spongy moss. She learned the plant life, its names and uses, and collected small sprigs of the various plants to press between the pages of her bible, where he'd never bother to check.

It was on one of these walks Lily found a plant that would forever change things for her. Near the back of the property, where the cattle never wandered, a plant stood in the late-day shadows, the small, white, tufted blossoms beckoning to her, along with a mild, pleasant fragrance. More of the plants lined the edge between the trees and the meadow of the neighboring property, a sporadic dotting of the pure white flowers amidst the more colorful flowers of the meadow. They stood out in their pale simplicity, much as Lily always had.

Lily picked a small sprig and took it home, pressing it between two fresh pages in her bible. When she looked it up, she discovered it was toxic to both cattle and humans. The white snakeroot, as she learned it was called, had once erroneously been considered a treatment for snake bites. Well, she had a hell of a snake bite needing cured. She took her time studying the plant and its uses until she had the perfect plan.

The countdown toward the end of her beatings could now commence.

It would take time, she knew, but she had endless amounts of that.

The first step was to inoculate herself to the snakeroot. It would kill a cow within a week or so when ingested, but Lily figured giving minute amounts to Maisy, their main family milking cow, would cause it to be excreted in her milk without actually killing her. After all, livestock usually died after eating a significant amount of the plant. If done well enough, at least

Maisy might last long enough to produce the tainted milk for Van.

First things first, Lily had to be able to ingest it without dying so she wouldn't be seen to be avoiding the dairy products that came from Maisy. Van was a suspicious man by nature, as he'd proven repeatedly by making insane accusations about her cheating or otherwise trying to wrong him, despite her being trapped on this farm with no other human interaction. Too pretty, too ugly, too quiet, too talkative, too stupid, too smart. One iota of difference on any given day raised his suspicions and set his fists flying.

Unfortunately, the process of adapting herself to the plant caused her to become somewhat weakened, with vomiting interspersed throughout the days. Lily reduced the amount she ingested accordingly, and ultimately reached a point where the symptoms went away. The side effect of her weakness and vomiting was that Van assumed she was pregnant, and that it couldn't be his. Turns out he'd been told long ago with his first wife that he couldn't impregnate anyone. This must, of course, mean Lily was a cheating whore. The only solution was to have the baby beaten out of her.

Luckily for Lily, as soon as the symptoms passed, he assumed he'd successfully murdered the baby, so he left her alone. For a time.

Figuring out the dosage for Maisy was a higher risk, because Lily didn't want to kill the old girl, only get her to pass along the tainted milk to Van. A mistake would kill the cow and likely get Lily blamed. Given, for once it really would be Lily who had committed the sin. The thought of being punished for something she'd actually done was an odd one. She'd long been made to feel responsible for anything that went badly, for someone having a bad day, or simply for being in the wrong place at the wrong time. Recently, she'd been beaten for looking at her husband in a strange way.

She started with a very small amount of the plant and continued to milk Maisy and feed Van with the products of his favorite cow. The other cows were to provide dairy products to the idiots in the town, as Van said. Maisy was special.

Now she really was. Special.

It turned out the tiny amounts were perfect. Maisy showed no symptoms, continuing her patient and happy life. Van, on the other hand, got sick quickly. First he started vomiting, and he dragged through his days, growing weaker and weaker. Then he complained of being thirsty all the time. After that, the muscle spasms hit. He was miserable and ultimately confined to his bed. This man, who had made her every waking moment a misery, went out like the whimpering, pathetic child Lily knew him to be deep down. When the coma finally came, it was as big a relief to her as it must have been to him. Because she'd kept the dosage low to avoid hurting Maisy, it had prolonged his death beyond the usual few days it took snakeroot to kill someone.

Shaking, Lily called an ambulance to come get him. She said she'd thought it was the flu, but that he'd fallen asleep and wouldn't wake up. Oh, how she cried on the phone, though no actual tears fell. Her timorous voice and rampant sobs were enough to convince them that the little girl on the other side of the phone line was suffering and frightened. Innocent.

When the paramedics arrived to whisk him off to the hospital in a neighboring town, they thought Lily was Van's daughter. She allowed them to call child protective services for her and sat silently until a kindly woman came to get her and take her away. Being around other children was scary, though, and as soon as they threw her into a room full of her fellow minors, she convinced one of the adults to call her parents. Believing she'd kept silent due to shock, they did so.

Her parents weren't happy to see her. In fact, it took only a month for them to find yet another man to marry her. After all, she was of legal age in her state, and this man was just as happy as the last guy to take on a new wife who was young and tender. And completely at his mercy.

Lily had a process now, a plan. It was just a matter of finding a way to carry it through. The new husband, Carl, wasn't a farmer and didn't have any livestock. This time she'd married a banker. It didn't take long to figure out that he was a banker with a weakness for alcohol. When he drank, he hurt Lily, just as Van had, but he was more delicate about it. He tried new ways to keep from bruising her, because he didn't want anyone to be able to see it. But unlike a normal woman, Lily showed every mark on her body.

This meant Carl needed to do something different to take his anger out on her. Instead of beating her, he locked her in a closet and filled it with frightening things: spiders, snakes, roaches, rats, moths. At first, she screamed until her voice became hoarse. Then she got used to it, just as she had everything else in her life. She allowed the creatures to crawl over her skin. All it took was closing her eyes. The animals didn't want to hurt her. They were afraid, too. Ultimately, their tiny feet on her body became a comforting massage, a showing of support from the other creatures equally trapped by Carl.

It made Carl angry when she befriended his implements of torture. Bored and upset, he returned to beating her, but only where her clothing would cover. Never her face. That was the one place that couldn't be covered at all or explained away so easily. But a sock with an orange in it applied liberally to the torso was a reward in its own right. He was fascinated with her bruising, often stroking a finger along the outlines. When he risked appearing too tender, he'd dig that finger in so the bruise ached that much more, a darker spot welling up with fresh blood so that it stood as a black oasis amidst the purple and red.

Without a cow handy, Lily put the snakeroot into his homebrew. He treated home brewing like it was a calling, some amazing ability that placed him above other people. It was easy to add the snakeroot during processing, as she was home while he went off to his office.

He died more quickly than Van, because she was able to put in significantly more. Plus, she didn't have to inure herself to the poison since she never drank his homebrew. The smell always put her off. He didn't really want to share it with her, anyway, which saved it from being a reason to beat her. Most of the time.

Back home with her parents, there was already talk of finding her a new husband. At now sixteen years old, she offered to get a job and help support the family instead, but this was now their go-to method. She begged, she pleaded, but when her father proudly pronounced he'd found her a real good husband this time, one who wouldn't do something stupid like expose his cows to toxic plants or make a faulty home brew, she grew quiet again. Ice cold.

Without their own cows, her parents usually traded corn or potatoes for milk from other farmers. But they made their own dairy products from the milk they got, and Lily was an old hand at helping with that. A little snakeroot extract added to the cheese, and all she had to do was wait.

Tailgating

The car slid into the forest on the Pacific Coast Highway, occasional winks from the moon visible above the canopy.

Inside the car, the travelers grew quiet, the hush from outside contagious. This part of the highway was sheltered, with far fewer businesses open. They'd picked dinner up from a questionable gas station convenience store, which now appeared to have been the final bastion of civilization.

"Maybe we should be looking for a picnic table or rest stop," Sarah said.

"I really want to get to Newport tonight," Layla said. "I figured we'd eat in the car."

Sarah sighed, scratching her arm. Her skin felt tight and dry. "Okay." She turned up the heat.

"Besides, it's dark now that we're in the trees. In here we have music! And no bugs."

They drove on in silence, Sarah noting the shuttered old businesses they passed. The road curved here and there, making for a peaceful drive. She'd be lucky to stay awake to Newport. Good thing they'd decided not to try for Portland tonight.

Layla flexed her fingers on the steering wheel. They'd been on the road for seven hours, with her driving the last three.

"You ready for me to drive?" Sarah asked.

"No, I'm good. Just working out the stiffness."

Sarah's gaze drifted to the trees beside them, where she noticed something high in the branches. She only got a quick glance, all glowing eyes and bulky fur, but it looked to be an animal. "Did you see that? Are there wolves in Oregon? I thought I saw something in the woods as we passed, but it was in a tree. Do wolves climb trees?"

Layla laughed. "Not that I remember. Bears do."

"Could have been a bear." Or something worse. Sarah reached over and turned the radio up, trying to convince herself she'd imagined it. She took her seatbelt off and twisted around in her seat to fish through the bags for their dinner. When she'd arranged it all on two plates, she frowned. "How are you going to eat this?"

"Put the plate in my lap. I'll eat it from there."

Sarah carefully balanced the plate on Layla's thigh, shoving a fork into the potato salad so it wouldn't fall. She popped open a can of Coke and placed it in the cup holder for Layla. The luscious smell of fried chicken filled the car, making her mouth water. She picked up the drumstick and took a bite, savoring the salty crispness.

The trees grew closer together now, darkness smothering the road. Layla turned on the brights, which illuminated the trees nearest the road. Shadows danced as the lights moved over the trunks. One shadow in particular appeared to leap with a pattern of its own, defying the headlights.

Sarah squinted at it, heart pounding. It kept pace with the car, sometimes falling slightly behind, sometimes getting ahead, but always near. The headlights didn't reach high enough for her to see what it might be.

"Okay, there's something out there," Sarah said, squeezing Layla's arm. "In the trees. That's no bear."

"What are you talking about?" Layla leaned forward to look out past Sarah, eyes darting between the trees they passed and the road ahead. "I don't see anything."

"It's jumping through the trees!"

Layla sighed. "Maybe you were right about taking a break. We need to get out and walk around. I'll stop at the next rest stop."

"I'm not hallucinating."

"I'm not saying you are. But we're both tired and could use a rest."

Silence fell between them. Sarah looked out her window, body tense, arms crossed, jaw set. She continued to watch the shadow, irritation at her friend's disbelief battling with the trepidation she felt about giving this thing a chance to catch up to them. She sensed Layla's eyes on her and knew she was being studied, but couldn't bring herself to return the look.

Headlights appeared behind them in the distance, the first set they'd seen since entering the woods. Each time the road curved, the lights disappeared briefly, reappearing when both cars hit straightaways. The lights grew closer with every curve, creeping up on them. Seeing evidence that other people still existed made Sarah feel somehow safer.

At first, anyway.

Sarah broke her gaze away from the trees and looked back as the car rapidly approached. Within a matter of minutes, it pulled up within a car length of them and stayed close, the headlights flooding the interior of their car.

Layla looked in the rearview mirror and squinted against the eye-searing brightness reflected there. "Why are they so close? I can't see ahead of me." She adjusted the mirrors, brow furrowed.

Sarah watched the speedometer move up as her friend pressed on the gas. No matter how fast they went, the car kept the same distance, glued to them as if connected by some link. She squinted against the light, trying to see the driver, but all she could make out was the vaguely round shape of a head.

They continued in this way for twenty minutes. There were no open stores or gas stations, no passing lanes, no other cars. Sarah could feel the tension wafting off Layla, matching her own. Each time a break in the trees appeared, they both leaned forward, straining to see some other sign of humanity. The beauty and peace of the Pacific Coast Highway had become a trap of solitude. There was nothing they could do to shake the car trailing them.

Another break appeared ahead. Sarah's shoulders slumped when she saw that it was yet another abandoned, boarded-up building. A single ancient pump stood out front. There were no lights, and the parking lot had almost as much foliage in it as the woods.

The car slowed, and Sarah jerked her head around to stare at Layla. "What are you doing?"

"I'm pulling over so this guy can go around me. I can't keep this up."

"What if he doesn't pass you?"

"He will."

Layla pulled into the overgrown parking lot. The tires crunched over broken asphalt and gravel. She put it in park and took her hands off the wheel to shake them out.

The other car pulled up behind them and stopped.

"What the hell?" Layla asked. She rolled down her window and stuck a hand out, waving the other driver forward. "Pass me! What are you doing?"

The headlights continued to shine into their car. Sarah still couldn't make out the driver. What she could make out was the panic etched in her friend's face, forming lines around her mouth and between her brows. Her hair stood out in a golden halo. Layla looked like Sarah felt. Somehow, knowing her friend was as frightened as she was made it all worse. More real.

Sarah's entire body felt stiff as iron, her tension pulsing through it. How could Layla just be sitting here, her window open? "Just go! He's not passing us!"

Layla put it in drive and clenched the wheel, knuckles whitening as she stomped on the gas pedal. They took off, spitting gravel behind them. They fishtailed briefly before finding purchase on the solid road and straightening out.

Sarah grasped the door handle and looked behind them. The other car grew larger in the rear window, getting closer. It sped to its former position behind them and adjusted speed to pace them once more.

"He's there again!" Sarah's chest tightened, her pulse throbbing. "What does he want?"

"Maybe he's just trying to scare us."

"It's working."

Sarah realized they'd both spoken in hushed tones, as if the driver would hear them if they spoke too loud. She swallowed against a suddenly dry mouth. It felt clunky in her throat. They both stared ahead, fixed in place. She could see Layla in her peripheral vision, eyes wide, mouth a tight line. Thoughts of everything that could happen out here on this isolated road ran through her head. For such a popular road, it was dead right now. How could they have not passed any other cars? Why were there no gas stations or rest areas? There were signs warning of being in a tsunami zone, but nothing helpful in a situation like this.

As they passed another tsunami warning, a large branch bent down just beyond the sign, weighed down by the shadow creature. For a moment, the psychotic driver had distracted her from the animal leaping through the trees.

A new sense of panic fluttered in her chest, sending another shockwave of adrenaline coursing through her. She put her face close to her window, trying to catch a detail that might tell her what it was, but it slowed, disappearing from her line of sight.

"How far to Newport?" she asked Layla, fear making her voice shake.

"Another hour, I think."

"How much longer until we're not in the trees anymore?"

Layla hesitated. "Until we reach Newport."

"Shit," Sarah whispered.

Her body buzzed. Who needed caffeine when fear did such a good job? She wondered if Layla remembered the thing in the trees, or if she had already dismissed it as nothing.

Checking behind them one more time, not sure what exactly she was looking for, Sarah stared at the shape of the driver's head. She couldn't make out the shape of a ponytail or anything, and the hair was short, from what she could tell. The car looked like a normal sedan. Not much different from their own.

Layla's tight whisper sounded. "Sarah."

She turned to Layla. "What?"

Why were they still whispering?

"The gas is getting low."

"Are you kidding?"

Layla shook her head.

"How low?"

"It's right above the red."

What the hell did Layla expect her to do about that?

"Maybe it's enough," Layla said.

"There has to be a gas station."

On other road trips, Sarah had seen signs marked "Last gas station for x miles." Did Oregon just not care if people ran out of gas in the middle of nowhere?

Sarah looked toward the driver's side of the road. The trees were even closer to the road now, no grassy bank between the pavement and the trunks.

It was then that she saw the shadow.

More than a shadow, it was a hairy beast, as big as a human, if not bigger. Dark in color, it jumped from branch to branch, astoundingly fast.

Sarah lifted a shaking finger and pointed, almost touching Layla's face with her quivering finger.

Layla looked at Sarah's finger, then Sarah.

Finally, she looked in the direction the finger pointed. Her face fell. "Holy shit!"

"Do you believe me now?"

"Yes. What is it?" Layla screeched.

"I don't know! Definitely not a wolf or a bear, though."

Layla accelerated again, but couldn't go too fast with the random, sharp curves in the road.

Sarah fumbled her cell phone out of the purse at her feet. She pushed the button, causing the phone to light up and illuminate her face. "I'm calling the police."

"I don't know what they can do."

Sarah dialed and it rang twice before someone picked up.

"Hello, 911 dispatch. What is your emergency?"

"We're on Pacific Coast Highway, maybe forty minutes south of Newport. We're not sure. There's someone following us, and..." Sarah paused. It all sounded ridiculous as she pondered what to say out loud. They would think it was a prank call if she said something was leaping through the trees. People never believed in monsters. Even when they were right in front of them. "And we can't get them to leave us alone or pass us."

"Are they doing anything other than following you?"

"No. I mean, we pulled over to let them pass, and they pulled over, too."

The other end of the line went quiet. At first, Sarah thought they'd hung up. "Hello?"

"Yes, ma'am, I'm here. Can you tell me more about the person following you? Are they doing anything threatening or dangerous?"

"Well, they're tailgating us. And like I said, they won't pass us. They're menacing us."

"Have they bumped you, honked, anything like that?"

"No."

"Do you know where you are on the highway?"

Sarah looked around for a mile marker, but didn't see any. "I don't know." Angling the phone away from her mouth, Sarah spoke louder. "Layla, have you seen a mile marker, or maybe a sign?"

Layla shook her head. "No. There's been nothing. We haven't passed any stores for a while."

Sarah moved the phone back. "We passed a closed gas station. One pump. That was half an hour ago or so. I'm not certain. And we're almost out of gas. We're not sure we'll make it to Newport."

"I'll see if there's a free unit that can head your way. I can't promise anything. With no overtly threatening acts occurring, there's not much we can do short of making our presence known. It might be enough to dissuade them. Do you have Triple A?"

"No."

"If you run out of gas, call for a tow truck."

"What if the car pulls over and they come after us?"

"Then call us back. Stay in your vehicle and keep the doors locked."

"Well, great, thanks. I'll call you if we're actively being murdered, then." Sarah hung up the phone, clenching it in her fist.

"What did they say?" asked Layla.

"They said there's nothing they can do."

"What do you mean there's nothing they can do?"

"She's going to see if there's a unit that can drive this way to check on us. Other than that she said we weren't being actively threatened."

"Why didn't you tell them about the creature?"

"Why do you think?"

Layla blew out a breath, body slumping. "What are we supposed to do?"

"Keep driving. We can make it." A glance showed Sarah the needle rested firmly in the red. They could have twenty miles left. Or two. No way to know for sure.

She asked Layla, "How long you have once it's in the red?"

"Highway miles, usually about ten miles, I think. For where it is."

"We aren't ten miles from Newport, are we?"

Layla shrugged. "I lost track. It's been years since I last traveled this road. It all looks the same."

It did all look the same. Tree after tree after dark and brooding tree. They hadn't passed any other abandoned buildings or other signs that civilization even existed. Sarah silently willed the car to keep going. She caught herself rocking slightly in her seat, as if she could rock the vehicle forward.

Up ahead, a spot of light peeked around an upcoming corner.

"What is that?" Sarah asked.

"God, I hope it's a gas station or something." Layla leaned forward and accelerated, body almost touching the steering wheel.

The light grew brighter. Another few seconds and it revealed a small building, almost perfectly square. Wooden shingles slanted out from the sides, a warm light showing from windows in the front. Two gas pumps stood out front.

"Pull over!" Sarah said. A sense of hope came over her. Civilization!

"I am, I am." Layla pulled up to the front of the building. She put the car in park and reached for Sarah's hand.

Sarah took Layla's hand in hers and turned to see where the other car was. She couldn't see it. It hadn't pulled into the parking lot; it must have passed them and continued on. "They kept going. Oh my God, Layla, they're gone."

Layla twisted around in her seat to check for herself. She looked everywhere, never letting go of Sarah's hand. "I think you're right. But where's the thing from the trees?"

Sarah tightened her grip. "I wasn't watching."

They both looked around, staring intently back at the other side of the road.

Something thumped against the car, and they both shrieked, turning as one in the direction of Sarah's window.

A face peered in, and Sarah screamed again.

It was the gas station clerk. On his grey shirt a nametag

hung, slightly crooked. It said "Holden." He had a hand on top of the car, and had leaned down to peer in the window at them. Late-day scruff decorated his cheeks and chin. His hair was slightly mussed, and his eyes drooped with exhaustion.

"Can I help you with something?"

A nervous laugh escaped Layla's lips, and she rolled down Sarah's window. "Hi, sorry. We need gas."

"Okay, pull on over to pump one and I'll get you some."

"Right. I'll do that." Layla rolled the window back up and pulled the car around until the tank side was aligned with the pump. "I forgot they pump the gas for you in Oregon."

"Can we leave him filling up the car? I need a pee break. Really, I need a sanity break."

"I just want to be somewhere bright."

The car shut off, Layla handed the clerk her card, and they went inside, leaving him to fill up the gas tank and clean off the windshield. The warmth made the last couple hours seem distant, unreal. Being in a gas station was so familiar and normal that thinking of psycho killers and monsters in trees made Sarah laugh. "Oh man, can you believe the night we've had?"

"It doesn't seem real, does it?"

"Not even a little bit."

They perused the shelves, grabbing sodas and candy bars, giggling and nudging each other. Sarah picked a bag of beef jerky, and Layla added sunflower seeds. Setting their snacks on the counter, they went to the bathroom, relieved to find it relatively clean. Sarah emptied her bladder, then splashed cold water on her face, still flushed from the preceding panic. She studied her face in the mirror, pulling her skin tight around her eyes to get rid of the bags.

The bell over the front door tinkled as they exited the bathroom. They rounded the corner from the hallway and found the clerk standing in the doorway. He cocked his head slightly to the side and studied them. Nervously, Sarah ran her hands over her hair, face, and clothes, tucking and straightening, wondering what had caught his attention.. Finally, he spoke, jerking his head in the direction of the counter. "You guys want me to use your card for this stuff?"

"Yes, please," Layla said.

He walked around to the other side of the counter and rang up their purchases. "It's $53.27 for the gas and the food."

"Okay."

He ran the card, then held it out toward Layla. After signing for their purchase, they took one more look around at the warm normalcy of the gas station, then headed back out to the car. The darkness sucked them in like a vacuum, sealing around them more with each step they took away from the building.

"We should have asked him how far it is to Newport," Sarah said.

"We can't be far. Besides, he was acting weird. I didn't want to stick around. At least we have a full tank of gas now."

"Yeah. You want me to drive?"

"Sure. My arms are tired."

"My butt is tired."

They laughed, Layla handing her the keys and settling into the passenger seat. Sarah took another moment to stretch the kinks out. She got into the driver's side and took off, jumping when the locks automatically clamped down. She cracked her window, preferring fresh air while she drove, then turned up the heat, aiming the vents at her face and chest so she could soak up the warmth. The trees seemed to be spreading out a bit more, moving back from the road. They could see the sky now, the moon off to the side, just barely above the trees. The salty-fish scent of the ocean drifted around them in the soupy air, and fog crept toward the road from between the trees to the west. The temperature had dropped, cool air drifting in the window.

A glow in the distance indicated a good-sized town ahead. Not much longer now.

Opening her candy bar, Sarah took a bite, moaning as the sweetness of chocolate and caramel coated her tongue. "I needed this," she said, speaking around the chewy mouthful.

"Me, too," Layla mumbled, mouth equally full of food.

The sounds of their smacking and wrappers crinkling filled the car with the music of road-trip snacks. Sarah drove forward, gaze fixed on the glow in the distance, growing ever closer. She felt carefree and excited, happy to almost be to the hotel. She practically bounced in her seat. After the tension of the last few hours, she finally felt like everything would be okay.

A loud pop sounded. The wheel of the car jerked.

Sarah wrestled against its pull until coming to a stop at the side of the road.

"What was that?" Layla asked.

"I think we blew a tire."

They got out, sandals rasping over the pavement. Sure enough, the passenger side front tire hung limp and deflating.

"I'll get the jack and the spare," Layla said, taking the keys from Sarah before heading to the back of the car. After a moment she brought Sarah the cross-shaped, metal lug wrench and jack, then returned to the trunk.

Sarah positioned the jack and lifted the car up until she could spin the tire. She fitted the lug wrench to the first lug nut and put all her weight on it in an attempt to move it. It took several tries before it finally shifted. The other ones went a bit more easily and she got the tire off, reaching for the full-sized spare Layla had rested against her legs. While she put the spare on, Layla put the flat tire in the trunk.

Layla called from the trunk, "Hey, Sarah?"

"Yeah?" Sarah grunted.

"There's something weird about this tire."

"What do you mean?" She now had the tire on, and was getting the first lug nut tightened.

"Come here."

"I can't right now. Just tell me."

"Okay. There are three slashes in the tire. Almost like—"

"Claw marks?"

"Yeah. Like something scratched the tire."

"Do you think—?" The bushes behind Sarah rustled as she put the second lug nut on. She froze. "Layla?"

"I heard it."

"Get over here and help me!"

Layla slammed the trunk and ran to the front of the car. She put the next lug nut on and started spinning it manually as Sarah finished tightening the one she was working on. They took turns looking over their shoulders at the woods. Rustling continued to emit from the foliage behind them, but nothing had yet appeared.

Similar sounds came from across the street.

Layla started lowering the jack even as Sarah tightened the final lug nut.

Across the street, a creature stepped out of the trees.

It was heavy and furred like a bear, but it stood upright, long arms dangling almost to the ground. Its legs were shorter than the arms, but both were thick. The fur stopped at the neck, an oversized bald head sitting atop its broad shoulders. The face looked almost human, except for an excessively wide mouth and eyes so large Sarah could see them across the distance that separated them.

The women jumped into the car and threw the tools into the back seat. Sarah shoved the key in and turned it, slamming it into drive and taking off without putting her seatbelt on.

The creature loped after them.

In the rearview, a second one joined it. Both were visible in the rearview mirror, running faster than they had any right to move. Their eyes reflected the red of the car's taillights, making them look all the more menacing.

As Sarah sped up, the creatures broke away from each other, each going into the woods on either side. Only a moment later, they appeared in the trees, moving even faster than they had on the road. She could see now that they both swung and leaped, using those long, strong arms to maneuver from branch to branch like apes.

She clung to the steering wheel as if it were a lifeline, pressing the gas pedal to the floor. There were no curves now. She could go as fast as the car would allow. Eyes fixed on the road, she told Layla to fasten her seatbelt, using one hand to fasten her own.

The trees started to close in again, bringing the creatures closer to the road. Closer to them.

No matter how fast Sarah drove, they kept up.

A bridge appeared up ahead, the glow of lights closer. She punched it, leaning in with her speed. The needle climbed the speedometer, surpassing the last mark and twitching in place.

The trees were long gone now and the dark ocean stretched off to their left. Lack of trees didn't stop the creatures, but it did slow them. There were now houses and other buildings, plus hills covered in grass and black stone.

Once on the bridge, Sarah had to slow slightly to avoid losing control. Fearful that the creatures would catch her, she looked for them in her rearview.

They'd stopped. Standing side by side in the middle of the road, the creatures stared after the car but made no attempt to step onto the bridge.

Sarah eased to a stop in the middle of the bridge.

"What are you doing?" Layla asked, voice high.

"Look. They aren't following us anymore."

Both women looked back, watching the creatures.

"Maybe they can't cross over the water," Layla said. "They can't get us!".

Sarah put the car in gear and continued forward, calmer now, though still shooting looks into the rearview mirror. As the car went around a bend, the creatures were still standing in the road.

She made her way to the hotel. After checking in, she and Layla went to their room, dropping onto their beds in relief.

"God, I'm so tired," Layla said.

"Me, too."

"As tired as I am, I don't know if I can sleep. I'm still freaked out. Why do you think those things were following us?"

"I don't know. Do you think your parents had something to do with it?"

"My parents? No. There's no way they knew where we were going. Then again, they've used trackers before. Maybe the creatures are the newest version." Layla sighed. "Speaking of lunatics, what about that car? That was scary, too."

Sarah shrugged. The move caused discomfort, reminding her how desperately she needed to wash up and change. It had been a long day. "I think he was just a jerk out to scare us." She scratched at her neck and wrists. "Do you mind if I shower first?"

"I think I'll wait to take my shower in the morning."

"I really need it tonight. If I can get off this bed."

It took her a few minutes, but Sarah finally grunted and pulled herself up. She moved into the bathroom, taking her bag with her. Her skin felt tight and uncomfortable, like it had shrunk about two sizes. She stripped out of her clothes and climbed into the shower. The shower head was low and she scrunched down to get her head under the hot water. After thoroughly washing her hair and soaping up her body, she slipped out of the human-skin suit and hung it over the curtain rod. A groan of pleasure escaped her. All that food had made the suit too tight. She scrubbed at her scales, relieving the itching the salty air caused.

When she'd finished drying off and brushing her teeth, she turned off the light and slipped into the room. Layla had sloughed off her suit and left it hanging off the end of the bed. She'd regret it in the morning, when she had to figure out how to both clean it and get it dry enough for them to head out. The quicker they got going in the morning, the sooner they'd be in Portland, where Sarah's cousins waited to whisk them through a little-known shanghai tunnel to a boat on the Willamette River and the freedom it represented.

Climbing into bed, Sarah let out a contented sigh and snuggled under the covers.

Outside, a sedan pulled up and parked. The headlights, aimed at the room inside which Layla and Sarah now slept, shut off and the motor silenced. A shadowy figure sat inside, staring at the room. Waiting.

Darkness of the Concrete Soul

Burton approached the building, running silent. The utilitarian rectangular building squatted like a bug against the geometric backdrop of downtown. A nearby factory puffed steam into the night sky, white clouds against midnight blue. The scents of oil and day-long baked concrete drifted in his window.

He typed a quick message to dispatch on the small laptop mounted on his center console, letting them know he had arrived. Studying the building, he noted no interior lights on, one vehicle in the parking lot. It was a rusty old Honda sedan, dents on the rear quarter panel. Most likely belonging to the security guard who'd called in the disturbance.

A walk around the exterior of the building revealed no broken windows, doors locked, nothing suspicious. Burton returned to the front door and punched in the code the guard had given when he called in. A light on the box turned green and a metallic click sounded. He pulled the door open, cold air and the smells of paint and industrial cleaners rushing out to meet him. The door shut with a soft snick behind him, and wall sconces in the lobby flickered to life, casting a warm, amber glow throughout the space.

Elevators lined one wall, with bathrooms on the other side and a large information desk at the end of the lobby. A black letter board with white letters proclaiming "DIRECTORY" had been mounted on the wall between the two elevators. It was otherwise blank, indicating no one had rented out the available office spaces yet. Considering this building had just been finished within the last month, this didn't surprise Burton. They probably kept a single guard on duty to ensure no vandals broke in.

The call had been about a possible break-in, but with no sign of a means of egress on his walk around the outside, chances were good he had a wigged out first-time security guard or one that had been getting into some pot, both fairly typical situations. Night duty could creep out a lot of people, especially in an empty building. Still, he needed to touch base with the guard and check around inside the building before taking off.

Burton thumbed his mic. "Dispatch, this is Unit Twelve."

Static. "Go ahead."

"Do we have a contact number on that possible break in at 57 Wahsatch?"

"Give me a minute and I'll connect you." After about a minute, his radio crackled again. "Unit Twelve, you there?"

"Go ahead."

"No answer at the respondent's number. Sending it to you via your phone so you can try."

"10-4."

His phone vibrated in his breast pocket, indicating a text had come through. He removed the phone and called the number dispatch had sent him. It rang five times before triggering voicemail: "You've reached Jim. Leave a message."

"Hi, Jim, this is Officer Gus Burton, responding to your call. I'm standing in the lobby, and need to touch base. Please give me a call back at 555-762-9487. In the meantime, I'm going to take a look around."

Tucking his phone back into his pocket, Burton got onto an elevator and pressed the button for the highest floor: three. It rose smoothly, as one would expect from a new building, quickly reaching the floor with a *ding* to notify him he'd arrived. The doors slid open without a sound. As with the lobby, it smelled of newly laid carpet and fresh paint, a pleasant scent.

He stepped out and called, "Hello? Jim?"

When no voice answered back, he moved down the hallway, checking each room before moving on. The doors all stood open, empty rooms waiting in expectation of whatever business might move in. These were single room offices, a square window in each, taupe on the walls and carpeting like every apartment he'd ever rented.

It didn't take long to clear the floor, so he moved down to the second floor. The offices were larger here, half of them suites with a reception-type room then a secondary room. Once again they all stood open and empty, no sign of the security guard or anything untoward. Getting back into the elevator, Burton looked at his options. Below the "L" button was a "B." *Great, a basement. Perfect way to end this waste of time.*

The elevator jerked to a stop, a "B" forming on the digital screen over the door. Only the loops at the front of the "B" were missing, which made it look more like a backwards three or a pitchfork. *Odd in a new building*, he thought.

He'd expected more of the new building smells, like paint, but down here all he smelled was the musty scent of damp concrete. He wrinkled his nose in response and stepped off the elevator. There was something underneath the initial smell he couldn't identify. Something unpleasant, yet familiar. The dim lights flickered like a staticky television screen, irritating his eyes.

Burton once again called for Jim. He had to be down here; it was the only floor left. Of course, he could have moved back to the lobby at some point during Burton's explorations, but he would have heard the elevator running or a door slamming in the stairwell. He'd check that out before leaving, just to be sure, but it looked an awful lot like this Jim guy had abandoned his station.

Across from the elevator stood a chain link storage area, which seemed out of place in this posh business venue. He would have expected something enclosed, something that hid the random smattering of items now standing behind the links. There were band saws, a roll of carpeting, tool chests, paint, a desk, three different chairs, a television, a large stuffed duck head, and various unidentifiable bits and pieces. Other than the built-in desk in the lobby, there'd been no furniture anywhere else in the building.

The lights went out entirely for a few seconds, and Burton placed a hand on the flashlight at his waist, attempting to draw comfort from it. His shoes scuffed over the concrete floor, echoing off the cement walls. "Jim, are you down here?" When no answer came, he took out his cell phone and once again tried to call.

Music played, faint, but echoing as his footsteps did. He

froze and listened. The music continued, the ring trilling in harmony from his phone.

Voicemail picked up again, so he hung up, gave it a minute, and redialed. This time he followed the music, gun drawn, index finger resting along the barrel.

Wooden framing created a warren in the basement, plastic sheeting hung up in spots. Cautiously, Burton peered into each space, seeking the source of the music. Each time voicemail picked up, he called again.

He felt exposed, with no actual walls to keep at his back. Anyone could step through at any time. Attack could spring from any direction. He should call for backup, but something kept him silent, afraid to break the eerie silence surrounding the music. His throat clenched with the urge to call to Jim again, to will his response.

Rounding a corner, he saw a pair of shined black shoes, heels against the ground, toes pointing toward the ceiling. The flash of the lights created a strobe effect, the feet almost seeming to move with each successive blink.

One step more, and a man's ankles came into view, covered by thin, dark socks, and leading to navy blue pants, an expanse of pale skin covered with hair visible between the two pieces of fabric. Still the lights flashed in a visual cacophony.

Blood. The familiar scent when he'd stepped off the elevator had been a mixture of blood and other bodily fluids.

Darkness fell as the lights went out. Burton stiffened, holding his breath. Without the lights flashing, his own eyes mimicked the strobe effect, shapes materializing in the blackness before him.

The phone stopped trilling, the security guard's voice coming from his phone along with the faint light of the screen. He pushed the end button and shoved the phone into his breast pocket, fumbling for his flashlight. When he turned it on, he shone it directly in front of him onto the feet. One now slumped to the side, pointing at an angle toward the wall, rather than the ceiling. A good sign that the guard was alive, but unconscious.

Gun held out before him, he approached the guard, scanning the flashlight from side to side. He listened intently for any sound, anything that might indicate another person or a movement.

The flashlight stuttered, blinked. It went out.

Panting in panicked breaths, Burton shook the flashlight, willing it to turn back on. Light teased him briefly, a dull glow exuding from the bulb before going out for good. He shook, but nothing came of it. These were fresh batteries, put in directly from the charging station when he left today.

With only two hands, he had a choice: use his phone as a flashlight while keeping his weapon out or stand in the darkness while he radioed for backup, because there was no way in hell he was putting that gun away, and he needed the phone hand to press the button at his shoulder.

His hands shook as he slid the phone into his breast pocket.

A swirl of air caressed his neck. He spun, putting both hands on his weapon and holding it out before him.

Something scuffed behind him, and he spun again in the direction of the sound, stepping forward into it, finger on the trigger now.

A dragging sound to his left, plastic flapping on his right. He aimed toward each sound, no concept of where he stood now, where the body was located. He'd lost his bearings in the pitch black. A second infusion of adrenaline pumped its way through his veins, heart filling his chest in its attempt to escape.

A touch on his ankle caused him to yelp and jump away from it. All of his training disappeared. It took everything in him to keep from running blindly into the darkness.

When some time passed without more disturbances, he reached up to his radio, depressing the button. "Dispatch—" His voice in the silence startled him, and his thumb jerked off the button.

Bracing himself, he tried again. "Dispatch, this is Unit Twelve. I need backup at the Wahsatch call. I'm in the basement. Possible 10-54d. Location of perp unknown." He choked on his panic.

The hairs stood up along the back of his neck, and he threw an elbow backward, afraid someone stood directly behind him.

Where was the body? This wasn't his first body, not by a long shot, but the thought of it down here, possibly inches from him, hidden from his sight, scared the living shit out of him.

The squawk of the radio made him jump. Had he not had a death grip on the gun, he might have dropped it.

"This is Unit Five, 10-76."

Burton knew that voice. Sargent Sheila Harvey was on her way. Thank God.

"10-4."

The radio call finished, he took his phone out and pressed the button. Light illuminated his hand, but little else. He aimed it around him, trying to get his bearings. It didn't reach as far as his feet. No way he'd be able to locate the DB until he got some more light.

Phone and gun held out before him, he moved ahead slowly, sliding each foot forward without lifting it from the ground. He moved the phone around, thumb pressed to the screen to keep the light active. The negligible light hit a solid surface just ahead of him, a faint white circle showing him the way. He lifted a finger from the phone, reaching out toward the surface before him.

It rippled at the same time something nudged his shoulder.

Burton jerked around, gun held out before him, but stumbled. He fell backwards, expecting to hit a solid wall. Instead, he fell directly through, thick material sliding along his back. A solid *thwap* sounded, followed by a loud clatter. He hit the ground and immediately crawled backward, away from whatever had touched him before he fell. His tailbone hit something short, but solid, and a sharp pain shot up his spine. The same thick, cool material now stretched behind his back.

He reached back and touched the object on the ground, his hand tracing something flat and grainy. A new sharp pain slid into his fingertips. A splinter. He'd hit the framework for one of the rooms, the thick material obviously plastic sheeting like he'd seen earlier.

With nothing solid around him, and no light, he felt completely exposed, vulnerable. He still held the gun, for all the good it would do with no visibility. He scrambled away from the plastic sheeting in the hopes of being in the center of the "room," well away from the plastic on either side of him. If only he'd examined these areas more before the lights went out, so he could tell how close he might be to a wall, the exit, anything.

A chill slid up his back, expanding into goosebumps that covered his arms, legs, and neck. Whatever shared this space with him could be anywhere. He didn't even know how many there were. Or if it was all his imagination. Maybe the guard had experienced a heart attack. Maybe nothing living shared this space with him at all. Maybe.

It sure as hell felt like someone was down here. Something.

He strained his ears for any hint of a sound. The nerves on his exposed skin buzzed lightly with his concentration, an almost electric sensation. He felt naked.

His backup had to be close. He'd lost all sense of time. It could have been five minutes...or it could have been an hour.

A light touch fell upon his ear. He jerked forward, spun his arm around, and fired. The quick, bright light of the muzzle revealed nothing behind him. The bullet punched through something solid a distance away. Not a body. He knew that sound all too well.

The first thing he needed to do was get where he could have a solid wall behind him. Something moderately defensible. He crept forward, every movement telegraphed in the dead silence. A shoe scuff sent his pulse racing. Whatever lurked in here with him, it knew exactly where he was, and he had no idea where it might be.

It could be circling just out of reach.

Could it see in the dark? Was it watching him? Or did it scent him, his sweat and fear?

He reached out, terrified that at any moment something would grab his hands.

Feeling for a surface, he moved his hands in front of him and to his sides. He slid his feet forward, searching with them, as well. The rooms hadn't been so large that he shouldn't have hit a wall by now. Maybe he had exited the room without knowing it, which left him in the open space again. He just needed to find a wall.

Whispers sounded all around him and a shock of colder air caressed his arms and neck. The pitch of the whispers rose until they became muttering voices then screams. Male and female. Everywhere. Overwhelming.

He crouched, covering his head. The cold air swirled over

and around, sliding under his clothes like elongated fingers that poked and nudged. It felt as if someone stood close to him, inches from making contact.

He threw a hand out, but didn't come into contact with anything. Now more presences arrived, pressing close to him. Solid bulks, hovering. Yet when he swung, he still touched nothing. He was at once suffocatingly surrounded and desperately alone.

Burton screamed, folding in upon himself until in a tight fetal position, cheek pressed to the cold concrete of the floor. A great weight fell upon him. The air squeezed out of his lungs.

Silence. The screams stopped, the air stilled. The presences pulled back.

For the first time since arriving in the basement, Burton felt truly alone.

In the distance, the elevator dinged.

The lights turned back on.

Burton gasped in a breath and lifted his head. He lowered his arms, blinking against the sudden, glaring light. It took him a moment to get his bearings, but it turned out he'd been right—he was in the open space of the hallway. A few more steps and he would have reached a wall.

He stood up and moved to the wall, just in case. If the lights went out again, he'd just need to follow the wall to his left until he reached the elevators. Glancing over to check on the body, he saw only a bare floor. No body. No blood. Nothing.

"Forget this."

He followed the wall, one hand against its rough, unfinished surface, the other holding his gun at his side, pointed at the floor, finger along the barrel.

"Sheila?"

She should have said something by now. The elevator had signaled. Either way, as soon as he got to the elevator he'd be going up, far away from that basement. They could send someone else down to find the guard's body.

Distantly, he wondered whether his hand left a snail trail of sweat on the wall at his passing. He felt soaked through. It surprised him his shoes weren't squelching. He'd been so scared his underwear probably bore telltale signs.

Rounding the final corner, the cage of construction equipment came into view, only the door now stood open, lock dangling. Gaze on the cage, he continued toward the elevator. Nothing would keep him from getting out of the basement. Not a damn thing.

His hand hit the button, and he pressed it without looking. Then he hit it several more times to be sure. The elevator hummed to life, machinery clinking behind the wall. Odd. He'd thought the car would be down here. Maybe it automatically returned to the lobby. But this again raised the question of where Sheila could be.

"Sheila, are you in with the equipment? Why aren't you responding to me?"

He thumbed his radio, but nothing happened. His radio couldn't be dead. Thumbing it again, he looked down at it as if that would show him why it wouldn't work. It felt wrong that no visible sign of its brokenness presented itself. It should be torn up or shattered. Instead, it hung there, a dead piece of plastic and metal. Useless.

Holstering his weapon, he pulled out his cell phone. Dead.

Frustrated and frightened, he turned back to the wall and hit the button multiple times, looking up at the digital display. Like his phone and radio, the display stared back, black and empty. He lifted his hand to hit the door, and that's when he realized the door was gone. Though the machinery still whirred and the display and button told him he was in the right place, all that stood in front of him was a blank concrete wall.

Behind him, the cage door let out a metallic shriek.

The lights went out again.

This time, the thing stalking him didn't bother with stealth. A *click-drag, click-drag* told him precisely where his attacker moved—directly toward him.

Right hand on the wall now, he took off, back where he'd come. No escape awaited him here. The best he could do is evade the thing hunting him until he had a defensible position. What he needed was a corner or a solid room, and he had no idea where that might be except that there had to be a corner somewhere along this wall if he just kept going.

The pace of the *click-drag* picked up, matching his speed. It sounded closer than it had before. Louder. Shivers cascaded down his spine, and he sped up.

The *click-drag* became a *click-click*. No hesitation anymore. It still kept up with him, and now the monotonous *click* beat with his heart, a metronome of fear.

Burton closed his eyes, trying to use his other senses instead of straining at the dark as he had been. Skin chafed where his fingers dragged across the wall, but he ignored the discomfort and kept his touch firmly glued to the wall. Losing contact with it now would mean losing himself.

A hot slice of pain shot through his back and pressure held him back, his collar choking him. Something had hold of him. In one swift motion, he drew his weapon and spun, firing at the top of the arc. The muzzle flash showed a grotesque, twisted face before the second of light disappeared. A thick, meaty *thunk* followed the loud crack of the report, telling him he'd hit his mark, yet it didn't release him.

He threw himself forward, tackling the form to the ground. It fought back, releasing his shirt to grab his face. Its flesh felt clammy and too cool to be human. Finding its neck with one hand, he used the gun to beat on its face. The fingers on his face squeezed, pressing into his skin with an incredible strength. His head felt like it had been caught in a vice grip. Any second now the bone would start to crack.

Afraid it might actually break through his skull, he rolled away and crawled toward where he hoped to find the wall again. The thing grabbed his foot, and he slid backward despite his best efforts. Once again, he brought his gun around and squeezed off several rounds in the direction just past his foot, praying he wouldn't hit himself. Each *boom* of the gun deafened him a bit more. His ears rang. Nothing deterred it.

Burton kicked out until he made satisfying contact. Then he kicked the same place repeatedly until it released his foot. He stood and stumbled into the wall. Placing his left hand against it, he ran back the way he'd come. Toward the cage and the elevator. If he could get into the cage and lock it, maybe he'd be able to hole up for a while.

The thing grunted behind him, and Burton figured he had no time to spare. It was probably standing. Any second now he'd hear its footsteps, feel it gaining on him.

He hit the button for the elevator before the first footstep sounded. It must have been hit more than he'd figured. The wall still felt blank to the right of the button, telling him the door hadn't reappeared. It might have been far-fetched to hope for that, but it wasn't any less rational than the door having disappeared in the first place.

With his back to the wall, he squared himself forward and ran toward where he remembered the cage being, hands out before him. The footsteps raced toward him from his right, and that entire side of his body buzzed with the awareness that any time now it would be on him.

His hands slammed into the metal of the cage, sending a shockwave up the nerves in his arms. He dropped his gun, listened as it slid away from him. Nothing he could do about that now.

Unsure where the gate might be, he decided to try to his right, remembering it hadn't been directly in front of the elevator. If he was wrong, he would likely be dead soon. Even if he was right, he had no idea if the cage would keep it out. After all, it had gotten into the locked cage to begin with. Still, he had no choice.

The footsteps passed him, heading toward the elevator. It wouldn't take it long to figure out he wasn't there. He'd thought it could see in the dark or sense him, but maybe it had to be closer for that to happen.

Feeling along the metal links as quickly and quietly as he could, he pleaded internally for the entryway to open up. Surely he should have hit it by now. It couldn't be this far. He must have chosen the wrong direction.

He pondered moving back the way he'd come, but decided to try a couple more steps this way.

The footsteps paused, shuffled.

Burton hit the gate, which stood open, the hinge on his side of the entryway.

The footsteps came toward him, running.

He felt his way around the gate and stepped inside. Or so it felt.

The footsteps got closer. The thing groaned, and it sounded

like pain and regret. Like a soul tortured.

He pulled the gate toward him. It clattered into place, and he reached through the links, trying to get to the lock.

The footsteps reached the other side of the gate and stopped. Lukewarm breath exhaled across his face, bringing a sour scent with it.

Burton got the lock and lifted it from the hole to try to align the two holes.

The gate shook. Burton almost lost his grip on it, so focused on keeping hold of the lock, but he managed to keep hold.

Once again, the creature screamed. This time, the wailing from earlier joined him. The screams rose in a crescendo of pain and fear, and Burton's body reacted with pure, ball-shriveling, instinctual terror.

The lock slid into place, and he twisted it until it slid home. Locked.

Sighing with relief, though he couldn't hear his own breath over the screams, he slumped to the ground, exhausted. He backed up until he hit the roll of carpet. Having his back against it gave him a tiny sense of solidity.

The cage rattled with a tinny clatter, just barely making it through the screams, and he wondered how firmly it was attached to the ground. He hadn't looked at that before. Could it simply be lifted or pulled out of the concrete, or had it been embedded? It had to be solid enough, or they wouldn't have bothered setting it up. But that creature had been strong.

He remembered the tools. There'd be items he could use as weapons, but he'd have to feel his way around. The last thing he wanted to do was stand up and search through the dark further, but he had no choice. He stood and set out, hands out once more, feet sliding so he wouldn't trip.

The screams stopped at the same time the cage stopped rattling.

Not sure if the return of the silence was good or bad, he urged his feet to stay steady, and held himself back from breaking into a run. There wasn't room for that. He'd knock himself cold.

Why couldn't he hear the creature anymore? Had it gotten inside? Was it standing just outside the gate listening to him, pinpointing where he moved?

It could be in here with him.

Something hit him just below his belly, and he stumbled forward, even as he tried to fall backward, away from whatever it was. He kicked out, making contact with something light.

It moved away from him with a steady whirr, slamming into a hard surface.

A rolling chair. His foot must have gone right under the bottom of it.

He tried to swallow down the fear that had crept up his throat, but his mouth was too dry. No saliva, no swallow.

Forward again, and this time he found the steady, boxy feel of a toolbox. He felt around for the clasps, unlocking it with the slide of metal against metal. The familiar scents of metal and oil rose from the box when he opened it. He shuffled around inside it until he found a hammer and a flathead screwdriver. The latter he tucked into his pocket, but he kept the hammer in his hand. He hefted it to get a feel for it. Solid.

He turned to head back toward the gate, surprised at how hard it was to keep his bearings in the dark. For all he knew, he was actually heading toward the back of the cage. He kept his empty hand out, moving in the air to feel for any obstacles. The first one he came to was a desk, which he hadn't found the first time, so he was definitely off course.

Correcting his direction slightly left, he started forward again. Cool air swirled around him as it had earlier, increasing in intensity, both motion and temperature. The wails began again, the cage shaking. A shriek started up, followed by another. The band saws had been turned on. The band saws that were inside the cage with him.

Burton froze where he stood. If he moved, he faced possibly walking into one of the saws. The sounds pounding away at him from every angle made it impossible to tell where they were coming from. The cold air took away his sense of his surroundings. The darkness still kept him blind.

He braced himself, hammer held aloft before him in a grip as tight as he could manage. He'd go down fighting. They couldn't take that away from him.

Only they could. Entities surrounded him, their malignant

energy overwhelming. They pressed into him from every possible angle, like hard plastic molded to his body. Then they began to constrict, to squeeze and immobilize him. It took a moment for the pain to kick in, but once it did it quickly elevated to a new level of agony he'd never felt before. He heard his own bones break, sharp pain filling his entire being. Bone punctured organs, and the air rushed out of his lungs.

The lights came on. The last thing he saw was the elevator doors sliding open.

The Killing Tree

The bump and rumble of the wooden wagon wheels soothed Martha, even as the motion worked at her tailbone. After two months and eight days on the trail, she'd become accustomed to the wear on her bones. Ache was her permanent companion on this trek to a new life in the west. She'd heard rumors that women's lives were different in the west, that they could hold positions of power in the community. At the very least, there were ways for women to earn a living. In addition, she would not be judged for being a single mother, as for all they knew her husband had been lost on the trail, rather than the truth of his having abandoned her, pregnant and with a toddler.

It had cost her everything she owned, save her son and a milking cow, to purchase the wagon, supplies, and the two oxen currently pulling her wagon. The cow strolled behind the wagon, connected to it by a rope. Every once in a while, she lowed to make sure Martha knew she was still back there.

Little James sat beside her, large eyes taking in the landscape with a toddler's fascination. He babbled here and there, some words clear, others nonsense. Martha gathered the reins in one hand so she could caress his soft, sweet cheek. He smiled up at her.

Inside her, the child she was sure would turn out to be a younger sister for James, churned. Martha had cut things close but was determined to arrive in Cripple Creek before the baby came. Still three-and-a-half months out, she had time. The trek should only be another month or two, barring trouble on the trail.

A small creek meandered by the deeply embedded wagon ruts. With the sun getting low in the sky, Martha decided this was as good a time as any to stop. She pulled her team up at a spot several feet from a large tree, its weak, heat-dried leaves sparse on the many branches. The presence of the creek should have meant lush, green leaves.

When she roused James with a gentle nudge of his shoulder, he yawned with a squeak, stretched, and sat up. He'd lost some weight on their trek, but Martha knew baby fat went away in these early years, so she wasn't sure whether it was the usual weight loss of early childhood or if it was the strict rationing of their food. She'd certainly lost weight, but not an unreasonable amount. Her belly grew at a rapid rate now, heedless of the limited rations. She hadn't killed any game in over a week, and they were overdue for fresh meat. She'd need to hunt tomorrow, possibly remaining in this camping spot for another day to get the meat processed. It wouldn't hurt to wash and change out their clothing either.

Smoke rose in the distance, a dark column against a lightly blushing sky. A wagon train. She took a moment to wonder if this was one of the ones that had turned her down for being a woman alone. They'd told her it was inappropriate, that she needed a man to survive this trail. She looked forward to proving them wrong.

Martha put James to work finding the pans and preparing the fire. He couldn't light it, but he could gather kindling from nearby. She got the cow and the oxen ready for the night by tying them to the tree in a spot that would allow them to drink freely from the creek, then she checked the bucket hanging from the wagon. The butter inside looked ready. A quick stir with her finger showed it to be nice and thick. There'd be butter with dinner tonight.

The evening progressed well, and James went down for bed in the wagon without argument, much to Martha's relief. She doused the fire and snuggled up with him to keep them both warm. Luckily, he was still small enough his curled form fit above the bulk of her belly.

His soft breaths helped her relax, and she soon fell asleep beside him, rifle at her back.

~~

Martha awakened, her bladder sending an urgent signal for relief. She unclasped James' hand from her nightgown with care and climbed ponderously from the wagon. Night bugs chirped around the camp, the creek chuckling beyond the oxen. Her footfalls were loud in the night, and she made haste toward the spot she'd marked out earlier.

Her back had cramped up, tweaking as she walked. She stopped to stretch. A series of pops brought a measure of relief. Nights like this, she pondered sleeping on the grass instead of in the wagon. There'd be rocks, but it had to be more comfortable than the hard, wooden surface. It always circled back to safety. At least in the wagon she had a measure of security and distance from the wildlife.

Something moved in the opposite direction of the animals. She felt the movement, heard a crackle in the grasses. The animals woke up and snorted, alerting her to their unease.

Martha backed toward the wagon, eyes straining against the darkness. The slivered moon shed only sparse light on her surroundings. Shadows moved but did not coalesce into anything recognizable.

Her back hit the sharp corner of the wagon. She gasped at the abrupt pain shooting through her shoulder blade like a bolt of lightning through her nerves. Freezing, she strained her ears for any sound.

Nothing stirred. Nothing made a sound. Even the crickets and other night insects had stopped their chirping.

Martha held her breath.

One of the oxen huffed, followed by a quiet snort.

Steps crackled through the grass, quickening, running.

Martha clasped her hands at her throat as the steps approached. She still couldn't make out anything useful in the dark.

The steps stopped.

Hairs on the back of Martha's neck stood up. Fear kept her glued to the spot. If she moved, it might pounce. Whatever *it* was.

She'd been warned of Indians on the plains. Newspaper articles spoke of savage men murdering settlers, stealing their goods. Sometimes even taking women and children captive. But a man she'd spoken to for advice had told her these reports were greatly exaggerated. While there was a possibility of danger, he'd said most of them wanted to be left alone and would, in turn, leave her alone. A single wagon held very little interest.

Maybe that man, as knowledgeable as he'd seemed with his sun-squinted eyes and rough skin, had been wrong. Maybe they'd circled her camp, intending to murder Martha and James in their sleep, and she'd ruined their plans by getting up to pee.

Gathering her courage, she moved sideways slowly, the cloth of her dress snagging along the rough wood of the wagon. Even with her back to its hard surface, she felt exposed. Anything could come at her from the front, the sides, or even underneath. Goosebumps spread up her legs at the thought of something grabbing her, and she picked up her pace, racing around to the back.

Getting inside proved to be a struggle. It was always hard with the orb of her stomach before her, but her panic didn't lend itself to graceful movement. She scrambled at the lip of the wagon. A fingernail ripped into the quick, followed by another, but she ignored the sharp flashes of pain and fought to get inside. The air at her back was a physical sensation of exposure to whatever might lurk in the dark.

Panting, she landed on the floor of the wagon, shielding her stomach and taking the brunt of the hit on her side. Her elbow smarted. She hurried to close the canvas cover, pulling the drawstrings and securing them. She crawled to her son, his soft breaths reassuring her that he still slept.

The footsteps began once more, this time coming all the way up to the wagon. Breaths puffed on the other side of the thick canvas from her. Had the canvas been lighter, she would have felt the air on her face. Something scratched at the wood in insistent repetition.

Martha's heart pounded in her chest. She fought to control her breaths, to silence them. Without conscious thought, she moved her hand over her mouth, breaths from her nose warming her index finger. She choked back the whimpers threatening to escape.

What do I do?

She couldn't leave. Without her oxen, the wagon was useless, a boulder on the prairie. The canvas wouldn't keep anyone or anything out for long. She grabbed her shotgun and pulled it toward her, the feel of the cool metal soothing against her palm.

The breathing moved away from her, toward the back of the wagon, the soft crackle of crushed grass accompanying it.

Darkness made everything worse. The sealed canvas kept even the scant moonlight out, and there was too little of that outside to cast a shadow so Martha could see what stalked her. She yearned for light. They already knew she was here, so the light shouldn't make it worse, and it would help to be able to see what she faced. She felt her way to the front where she kept the tinder box. It proved easy to find, her hand landing on the hard surface of the lid. The candle lantern stood beside it.

Martha pulled these to her and shifted to face the rear of the wagon, eyes glued to the canvas. It remained closed tight. For now.

Working quickly, her fingers accustomed to the motions and the items in the box, she took out her flint and steel. She opened the port of the lantern and struck steel against flint repeatedly. Each spark sent out a pallid light, exposing the back of the wagon. Martha switched her eyes between the lantern and the canvas, desperate for a spark to take.

The canvas bulged inward, something slim and dark extending through the slit.

Martha hurriedly struck the flint again, staring at the canvas. She couldn't tell what had been stuck through. A rifle? No, it appeared to come to a sharp point, closed and solid. It was rounded, so not a knife. It was dark and reflected each spark.

The candle took with a soft *puff*, the smell of fire and wax rising. Martha closed the glass and thrust the lantern toward the rear of the wagon.

The pointed object withdrew, as did the presence pressed against the outside. The canvas flattened.

Candle smoke drifted within the confines of the wagon, a pleasant smell now, but she knew it would become irritable to their lungs and eyes after a while. She had to figure out what was going on before then.

She considered her options. Without being able to see

outside, she couldn't tell what time it was, or how long until morning. No one would be traveling at night, which meant no rescuers could happen across them. She was good with her weapons but had no clue how many awaited her out there. If she fired the gun, the camp she'd seen evidence of in the distance might be able to hear it, but she had no idea how likely they were to investigate, and they were too far to help her in time. As far as she could figure, her options were to try to wait them out or to go out blasting, but neither plan necessarily kept her and James alive until daylight.

Here she was assuming daylight meant safety, but she had no way to know for sure if that was a possibility. There might be more out there by daylight. The chances of anyone rolling up on them even then were spare, as she'd seen no nearby smoke back the way they'd come. They'd have daylight to work by, while she'd be trapped in the dark, vulnerable wagon.

Outside, one of the oxen snorted, huffing out a breath then lowing. The other two animals joined it, stamping their feet. The sounds became increasingly stressed and frantic. She couldn't let them kill the animals, or she and James would be stranded, which meant death just as surely as tangling with whatever stalked her outside this wagon.

The question remained what exactly awaited her out there. People or creatures. Surely, people would have spoken by now. Made some sort of sound. But she wasn't aware of a wild animal that would behave this way.

A meaty *thunk* sounded, followed by a horrendous high-pitched call from one of the animals.

A spike of adrenaline shot through her. Time to take action. If she stayed in here to wait things out, everything would be lost. She wrapped a leather thong around her upper arm and slid a knife through it, the cold of the metal radiating through her night dress. She maneuvered herself around James, still sleeping, bless him. She allowed herself a second to move a curl off his forehead.

James let out a small sigh and rolled onto his side, the curl flopping back onto his forehead.

The adrenaline had awakened the baby, and it kicked.

Her babies were depending upon her. Only her. No one

would show up and save them. Through the difficulties of this journey, she had never felt as alone and frightened as she did now. If something happened to her, they would both die before they had a chance to live. Leaving James in the wagon would take all her strength, but it had to be done.

Strength flooded through her, and she moved to the back of the wagon with determination, dragging the lantern with her. She didn't need a husband or a wagon train. She'd never need a man again. This was her moment to prove she knew what she was doing and could take care of not only herself, but her babies, as well.

Loosening the tie of the wagon cover, she eased it open, taken aback by the bitter darkness outside. Her eyes had adjusted to the lantern light, rendering her blind to anything beyond the sallow light that now crept from the wagon. She climbed down as delicately as she could, set the rifle and the lantern at her feet, then tightened the cover as much as possible from the outside in hopes that James would remain safe inside.

Breathing became a struggle, her heart pounding against her ribs. The baby seemed to dance in rhythm with her pulse, kicking and rolling. Her stomach visibly shifted. Normally, she would have placed a hand on her belly to calm the baby, but one hand held the rifle, the other the lantern. She'd just have to do this with the tiny acrobat having her way.

Martha moved around the wagon, eyes straining into the darkness toward where the animals were tied. The cow moved at the edge of the light, and Martha set the lantern on the ground, figuring this was as good a place as any. Its light kept her eyes from adjusting all the way, and it was better as a beacon by the wagon than blocking her vision going forward, though she yearned to carry it with her, wooed by the false security its warm glow offered.

The crisp grass crunched under her feet. She stopped.

The sound continued, coming from all around her.

There arose a clicking from somewhere beyond the lantern's glow, and she stepped forward, ensuring the light stayed behind her. She could now make out the tree to which she'd tied the animals, its bare branches a looming threat in the dark.

The tree looked strange. Lumpy. Large shapes roosted

around the branches. She took another step toward the animals, rifle held before her. The cow stared dumbly in her direction, eyes rolling. One of the oxen stumbled sideways, bumping its partner. Its mouth foamed, and it swayed. The other ox strained backward, pulling at the lead keeping it tied to the trunk.

"Shhh, it's okay," she whispered. "It's just me."

They all now faced the tree, yanking at the ropes. It didn't appear they'd even heard her voice. An ox pawed at the ground.

She continued forward until she stood among the frightened animals. The foaming ox's side shone, and she touched it. Her fingers came away dark and sticky with blood. She had no way to tell how bad the injury might be, but if the animal was still standing, she had to hope it could pull the wagon.

If she could get them untied and hooked up to the wagon, they could leave. At least they'd be moving targets. Speaking of which, where had the attackers gone? She stared up into the tree, but the shapes didn't move. They must be shadows or odd branches she hadn't noticed when it was still light out.

A twig broke with a snap, and she jerked around, the momentum of her belly taking her too far, almost making her fall. She corrected her position, sighting down the rifle, which she raked across the shadows. Light flashed near the wagon, reflecting off a moving surface until the figure disappeared under the wagon.

"Stay away from there!" she yelled. "Come this way."

But it was gone, swallowed by the darkness beyond the lantern's reach.

A branch creaked above her. She peered up, directly into a chitinous face, the features as black as the face itself. Three eyes clustered on the narrow face, which extended out on a long, slim neck that looked to be armored. The creature appeared to be nearly her height, with a hunched, rounded back. It had two legs firmly grasping the branch beneath it, with two more hanging limp at its belly. A long, scaly arm reached forward, a spike extended from a finger, elongating toward her. This was what she'd seen breaching the canvas of the wagon.

Repulsion filled her at the sight, an instinctual fear taking grip. She stepped backward, this time stumbling over a twisted root that had grown out of the hard-packed earth. Before hitting the ground, she dropped the gun and put her hands behind her, trying to cushion the fall. Even so, the impact rocketed up her spine, through her belly, and into her head.

Gasping, she looked up at the creature. The spike continued in her direction, even though the creature remained in the same position, the tip thinning from the initial width, just thicker than her thumb, down to maybe a pinkie's width. She scrambled away, but the spike moved faster. It reached her stomach, nudging against the bulge. She slapped at the spike, but it didn't budge, so she wrapped a hand around it and tried to push it sideways to no avail. It was hard and smooth, unbendable.

The baby kicked, raising her belly to the spike, impaling Martha's skin upon its tip for a second. A quick, hot pain shot from the cut, moving outward in a wave of dull, sick hurt. A dark stain appeared on the white of her sleep clothes, spreading slowly.

The spike withdrew.

She couldn't tell if it was the branch or the creature that creaked.

More creaking sounded, followed by clicking. The things in the tree stirred, shifting closer to the creature that had poked her. One leapt onto the same branch as the first and shot out its own spike.

This time she wouldn't allow it to get to her.

She grabbed the gun from the ground, pulled the right hammer back, and squeezed the forward trigger. The gun bucked against her shoulder, and the shot went wide. She pulled the left hammer back and squeezed the rear trigger, this time hitting the second creature. It screeched and dropped from the branch, making a sickening crunch upon impact with the ground. It didn't move.

The others moved faster now, this time away from her rather than toward her. They leapt higher into the tree, the branches bowing with their weight. Though thin, they had to weigh more than James.

With the gun now useless, she used it to help her stand. If the creatures stayed high in the tree long enough, she could get the animals loose. She pulled the knife from the thong and forced herself to go to the tree, where she rested the shotgun against the gnarled trunk. The knots came loose easily, but now she had to decide whether to keep the knife out and leave the shotgun against the tree or put the knife away and bring the shotgun with her, leaving her virtually unarmed.

The tree filled with chittering, high pitched and terrifying. She had the urge to cover her ears but resisted it.

Making the decision, she slid the knife back into the thong and grabbed the shotgun.

Eager to get away from the tree, the animals came with her easily. Every step she and the frightened animals took was loud, crackling thunder, covering up the possibility of hearing movement from the insect-like creatures hunting them.

She pulled them along rapidly, to the front of the wagon, hitching them as quickly as she could, despite the limited visibility. The lantern's light from beside the wagon caused dancing shadows to strain out ahead of the animals, their bodies blocking light from where her hands worked frantically. The chorus of cicada-like chittering assaulted her ears, forcing extra panic by virtue of the frantic sound. Her back itched with the feeling that at any moment one of the creatures might come up behind her.

Martha got the first ox hooked up with little trouble, but the hoop on the yoke of the second got caught. She struggled against it, panting with exertion, the baby shoving at her from the inside. Something crunched beyond the oxen, on the other side of the wagon, and she froze, though her stomach did not.

When there was no further movement, she continued, finally getting the hoop free to slide it up the yoke. She attached the yoke to the wagon tongue then checked both oxen to be sure they were tightly hooked up, all the while wondering when the creatures would attack.

Rather than take the extra step of bringing her cow to the rear of the wagon, she tied her to the front, hopeful the old girl would figure out how to stay out from under both the oxen and the wheels.

She grasped the gun with her left hand and pulled the knife out with her right before heading back toward the lantern and the rear of the wagon. Why the creatures hadn't left the tree yet was a mystery. Were they really that afraid of the gun? She could still make out the vague shadows at the edge of the lantern's light, chittering in the branches. Were there fewer now? She couldn't tell.

With her knife hand, she reached for the lantern, so close now to the rear of the wagon and possible safety. She needed to get inside the wagon to completely secure the rear in order to ensure none of the creatures climbed inside as she rode off. James would be back there, exposed and alone; she had to take precautions.

Just as her hand brushed the lantern, something cold and hard punctured the back of her ankle, sending her to her knees as sharp pain shot up her leg. The cold withdrew, but the pain increased, now burning white-hot.

Keenly aware of how vulnerable she was, Martha scrambled forward, once more trying to reach the lantern. Maybe it was the light keeping the creatures up in the tree instead of approaching her. Her middle finger hooked around the handle, her other fingers still clutching the knife. The lantern was heavy, pulling painfully at her finger.

Just as she got to her feet, it stabbed her once again, this time through the meat of her thigh. She didn't fall, instead yanking her leg sideways to disengage from the spike. She stumbled forward, leg and ankle holding, and broke into a sprint. Hot pain lanced across the skin of her back, but she didn't falter.

Her hands were full when she reached the back of the wagon. She set everything at her feet, the lantern warming her toes. It took a moment to get the back open, and there was her baby boy, still sleeping, just visible in the scant light the lantern provided. A moment's relief flooded through her at the sight of his chest moving peacefully up and down in the flicker of lamplight.

She squatted down to get the lantern and weapons. There, beneath the wagon, was the creature who had been stalking her, mere centimeters away. Their faces nearly touched, cold radiating from its body along with a vague, musty smell. Its glassy, black eyes stared back at her, empty and soulless, the lantern's glow reflecting off its dark shell of a body. Small mandibles opened, and it chittered, loud even against the racket of the others in the tree. When it stopped, they stopped, the prairie silent. The silence was stark and shocking after the constant sounds of before.

Martha held her breath, afraid to move. She stared back at it.

Neither of them moved.

She released her breath, fogging the shell. It jerked its face away from her. The spike appeared again out of the darkness, this time heading for her face. She rolled to her side, grabbing the knife as she went. Bringing her hand up as far as she could, she slammed it forward into the creature's head. The knife pierced with a crunch, and it shrieked, high pitched and frantic, disappearing under the wagon, the knife still stuck in its shell.

Martha grabbed the gun and stood up, throwing it into the wagon. It landed with a clunk, causing James to stir and whimper. There was nothing she could do about that now but hope he stayed asleep.

Off to her right, leaves rustled as if in a heavy wind, though no wind existed.

The chittering began again.

They were coming.

Desperate, Martha grabbed the lantern and ran in the direction of the tree. The lantern bounced with her steps, casting startling shadows. She slowed once the tree was in view. One of the creatures stood at the base. The others moved about over it, descending from the branches.

She threw the lantern, grunting with the effort. It arced though the air as she watched, heart in her throat, terrified it would miss entirely, that it would hit the creek and fizzle out. But her aim was true; it struck the ground in front of the creature standing there and shattered. At first, the darkness remained around the sickeningly small flame, which flickered, weak against the grass. Horror filled Martha as she saw it fading, sputtering, about to go out.

Then the flame caught the summer-parched grass and burst outward in a wave of heat and light, spreading rapidly. The creature lit up, looking almost humanoid in the sudden brightness. It reared back, standing on the rear set of legs, the others tucked at its sides. Its center mass was slim, surrounded by the larger, rounded shell and a plated armor of chitin that traced its torso and limbs. Shrieking as its cohort had, it ran in the direction opposite Martha. Flames licked up the tree trunk, climbing at a terrifying speed to where the others perched.

Martha didn't wait to see what happened. She turned and fled back to the wagon, climbing into the back. She closed it tight. Shrieks rent the air outside the wagon, slightly muffled by the fabric surrounding her. She took no pleasure in their pain.

With the creatures hopefully kept busy, she took the time to load the gun and strike her only other lantern, fearful that at any moment one of those spikes would pierce the canvas. The nerves around the injuries on her ankle and thigh were raw and screaming, the tacky blood covering her leg, but she had no time to tend to her wounds.

The baby's movements had become sluggish, and she patted her stomach, hoping this little one would fall asleep now, too. The calmer she was, the calmer it would be. The baby moved beneath her hand in a slow roll.

Outside, one of the oxen huffed in alarm. The wagon jerked then began to move. Perhaps the oxen were fleeing the fire. She could only hope that was it.

Stumbling, she worked her way forward. She hung the lantern on a hook just at the front entrance and leaned the gun there. Part of her wanted to remain inside the wagon and let the oxen continue forward, but the risks were too great. She had to go back out there to steer the team.

Martha took a deep breath and worked at the opening, afraid of what she might find on the other side.

Warm, orange light burst in as the cover opened to her. Climbing out was tricky with her swollen belly and the rickety motion of the wagon, but she got out onto the wooden bench and settled herself. Only then did she allow a glance back at the tree, now engulfed in flames. The fire had caught more of the grass and spread.

She took up the reins and urged the oxen forward. They could only go so fast in the dark, and the fire had them scared, but any additional speed she could get from them would be worth it. They shambled forward at a steady gait, the cow keeping up beside them.

Up ahead, a light bobbed in the air. She strained her eyes, trying to determine what it might be.

The light grew closer, changing shape.

One of the oxen let out a drawn-out moo. The other animals joined it with their own vocalizations and came to a sudden halt. The lantern behind her swayed, once again casting crazy shadows. Her own form bounced around before her in its frenzied light. She grabbed the gun and held it before her, aimed at the light that frightened her animals. It had to be the remaining creature, firelight bouncing off its reflective shell.

Squinting into the dark, Martha made out its form just before it leapt. It cleared the animals, chitinous body coming at her at a great speed. She pulled back the right hammer and pulled the front trigger without aiming. Ammunition met creature, and it jerked to a stop in mid-air, falling between the two oxen with a high-pitched, multi-toned squeal that sounded alien to Martha's ears. Slapping the reins, she urged the team forward and to the side. She heard and felt, more than saw, the still squealing creature being trampled beneath their hooves, its hard body crunching underfoot, the animals struggling over it. They let out frightened huffs, but continued forward, good, steady animals that they were.

The wagon bumped and heaved as one wheel ran over the body. The screams stopped. The only sounds were the huff of the oxen and the rumble of the wagon.

Looking behind her at her son, she saw he'd rolled to his side and put a thumb in his mouth, fully asleep.

Martha drove her team forward, ready to get to her new life and a safe bed. The ache of her bladder reminded her she'd never gotten the chance to pee. It could wait a bit longer. Though only as long as the baby slept.

Sweepers

The neon lights in the alley made it all the more tawdry, a bright glow shining on decay and ruin. Trash cubicles jutted from the walls, broken, garbage overflowing onto the plastic cubes of the street. Cybernetically engineered rats scurried through the dark, laser eyes gleaming in their eternal search for cockroaches.

Malina pulled up her collar to hide her face, darting toward a metal door that sported the Underground symbol, a "U" in a circle. It was only visible to those like her, who had been modified by the Underground. Her right eye phased in then out, her vision blurring and putting a green tint over everything. She flicked the eye, triggering a metallic *tink* and clearing of her vision, then moved closer to the flat screen next to the door, disguised as an antique mailbox. Sensing her presence, it briefly lit up with blue light and scanned her eye. A slight buzz sounded, followed by the *click* of the door unlocking. Malina did a quick scan behind her in the alleyway to seek out body heat. Not finding any, she pushed the door open and slipped inside.

The door sealed behind her, vacuum making her ears pop. They, at least, were still her originals. The only light in the stairwell came from LEDs lining the path, which she followed now, careful of her footing. It smelled of melted plastic and sulfur in the enclosed space, a possible sign of shorting modifications. Someone wasn't having a good day. This particular shelter was strictly limited on who could access it, so there were few who would have come this way.

When she'd gone down several flights of stairs, a repetitive rasp echoed off the walls. It was almost like a person's voice, but an octave lower than it should have been for even a deep voice. Malina slowed, peering over the railing, but all she could make out was the seemingly endless trail of LEDs. As she pulled back, something caught her eye: a dark spot where there should have been LEDs. Something blocked the sparse light.

Pressing a button behind her ear, she tapped into the Underground signal. Instantly, a distress signal sounded, the blare of it loud inside her brain. She forced herself to ride it out, hoping for more information, but the shrill screech of the signal was relentless. Malina shut off the receiver with another press of the button.

Something was wrong.

She could go back the way she'd come or she could continue forward. Leaving would mean she was exposed on the streets once again where the Sweepers might find her. They were always out searching for Mod-Freaks like her, but no one could say for certain what happened once they were caught. Some said they were forced to work for the shadow government, while others said all their mods would be removed, leaving the freak sans any sense, limb, or organ that had been replaced. Ultimately, that would be torture, death preferable.

Outside were known enemies, but in here, there was no way to know what had happened without going forward. If there were someone hiding below, they'd probably heard her coming. These passages were meant to be completely safe, unbreachable. She hadn't been quiet. Malina had to assume they knew where she was. If they had someone outside, they'd be waiting for her there. She decided to press on.

Unlike some of her fellow Mod-Freaks, she'd never had weaponry built in. The penalty for weapons was harsher than the penalty for other types of mods, and that was in the public version of the law. What they'd do to someone with weaponry after they scooped them off the streets and disappeared them would likely be even worse than the longer imprisonment of a surface sentence. Plus, Wep-Freaks were more likely to be picked up in the first place.

What she did have was a chip that allowed her to turn up her senses. The switch for this was hidden on the roof of her mouth. She pressed her thumb to the metal plate on her hard palate and activated the heightening of her senses. Instantly, the repetitive rasp became clearer and the darkness dissipated, the corners and steps now much more vivid and visible. The smell of burned rubber was stronger, and she could sense roasting flesh behind it, a very human scent and a bad sign.

Once more, she peeked over the railing. The darkness was still there, but she could now make out a human form. It slumped against the wall, head tilted. A slim beam of red light that hadn't been visible before flashed at the same pace as the rasp. The enhancement wasn't strong enough for Malina to make out a face, but she was at least certain that the person down there wasn't a threat. They wouldn't be going anywhere.

Her head started to throb, the enhancement taking its toll. She swallowed the pain and proceeded down the stairs, tuned in to her senses for anything out of the ordinary. It took only a few minutes to get to the figure. Up close, the left eye socket gaped, the red beam coming from within. Someone had torn out an eye mod. Malina knelt in front of the person and took their chin, moving them to face her.

It was Karim, one of the leaders of the Underground movement. She felt for his pulse, finding it thready, but present.

His hand came up and grasped her wrist, startling her. "There's been a breach." His voice was weak, as was his grip.

"Let me help you up," Malina said.

"No. You need to notify the rest of the Underground. The Sweepers know who we are. Where we are." He coughed, and something covered his lower lip, neon in Malina's vision. Blood. "I'm not going anywhere."

She pulled back and opened his coat—the neon of his blood shone from his torso. They'd done more than take his eye mod. She didn't know how he was still alive.

Squeezing his hand, she turned away and started for the stairs. It hurt her to leave him behind, but there were other lives at risk. The only way to warn everyone was to get to the communications booth and override the emergency signal. This was the only shelter in which the distress signal could be both overridden and forced, turning on the distress signal in anyone who had the mod.

The throbbing in her head increased in its persistence, but she once more pushed back. She needed the enhanced senses even more now. Sweepers didn't have mods the way she and the Mod-Freaks did, but they were trained to hunt people like her, and were nearly inhuman in how keen their senses had been developed. Most of them were natural born killers, those who had been taken from their mothers' wombs and raised by the shadow government when genetic testing showed extreme psychopathy was part of their genetic makeup. They had no conscience and little sense of pain, which made them the ultimate weapons.

For Karim to have been taken out in this way, when he was one of their strongest fighters and a Wep-Freak to begin with, meant there was probably more than one in here. They must have gotten him as he was entering, but he would have been able to sense their heat patterns.

Unless they didn't have normal body heat patterns.

She'd never seen a Sweeper, let alone read a heat signal from one, but she'd always assumed that they'd have regular, human body temperature. Whatever awaited her down this stairwell had clear advantages over her.

Malina pressed behind her ear and tapped into the distress signal once more, but found there was still no message. Karim must have been able to activate the signal due to his wounds, something Malina wasn't modded to do, but no one had been able to send out a warning message. It meant Karim had been alone or no one with him had made it to the signal booth.

Taking a deep breath, Malina continued. There were only two more flights of stairs remaining before she hit the entryway to the shelter. Behind her, the rasping stopped. Karim had died.

The two flights went by quickly, and Malina found the door open. Karim's eye mod lay on the ground just inside, his blood neon yellow in her enhanced sight. The cable was long, about nine inches. She'd never seen an eye mod free of its socket. Stooping to pick it up, she slipped it into her pocket to ensure no one else could use it for access.

A musty, stone hallway stood before her, a remnant of the Old City that had existed before the Reaping and Rebuilding, where undesirables had been cleared out, the New City built on top of the previous one. In some areas, old wooden structures still stood underground, but not here. This had been a tunnel system to begin with. Moisture dripped down the walls to form shallow puddles on the walkway. Wet footprints led the way down the hall, and Malina followed.

She wished they'd make a sound, something to alert her to where they were or how many she might be about to face. There was nothing. Her head now screamed with agony, and she knew her enhancement wouldn't last much longer. The most she could hope for was for it to shut off instead of shorting and taking her with it.

The passageway curved up ahead, and she knew the split would follow. She'd have to take the left passage and hope the Sweepers had taken the one on the right. Anything that might buy her enough time to warn everyone that their sanctum had been violated and it was time to scatter.

When she reached the split, a single wet footprint showed the Sweepers had preceded her down the path to the signal booth. Fear and disappointment flooded her, drying out her mouth and sending her heartbeat into overdrive. With a tweak of her left index finger, she slowed her heart rate and forced herself forward. The heart mod wouldn't last long. Between that and her sense enhancement, she didn't have much time at all.

There was no one visible in the booth when she reached it. She'd been told long ago that the strange, tall rectangle had been something called a phone booth in the Old City. Phones were no longer a thing, but it seemed strange that people had spoken into plastic and the voice had traveled through lines to arrive in someone's ear. She couldn't comprehend how that might be possible.

The Sweepers must have passed the booth without recognizing it. Malina allowed a sigh of relief before opening the bi-fold door. Inside, the old phone still hung, but now a circuit board was mounted beneath it. Malina pulled out Karim's eye and rubbed it against her coat to clean off most of the blood. A flat, red light shone on the eyeball when she held it up, allowing it to be scanned. Purple light projected a screen and a keyboard onto the floor, and Malina knelt and typed rapidly: *Underground violated. Evacuate all shelters and go into hiding. Sweepers...*

The blow came out of nowhere. Her head slammed into the base of the phone, and she reeled, turning in the compact space to look behind her.

Its heat signature was brighter than normal, contradicting her earlier thoughts. It stood tall and large, too big to fit into the booth, a hunched, but humanoid, figure. Looking out the glass to her right, Malina watched as more heat signatures appeared, standing from behind something that blocked them from her gaze: heat shields.

As the Sweeper held up its iron-gloved fist to hit her again, Malina smiled, agonizing heat filling her head as her enhancement shorted. "You can't hurt us," she whispered. The smell of her own burning flesh filled her nose and a wet trickle came from her nostril.

She reached behind her and slid her hand over the "enter" key, beaming the message out to her fellow Mod-Freaks. Her own signal receiver turned on, the message playing in her head as her eyes dimmed and her heart ceased beating.

Psychosis

Joy wasn't sure when the hunger had started. Whether it was before or after everyone had been confined to their homes. All she knew was that her belly ached as if it would never be filled again. No matter what she put into it, it rumbled and growled and beseeched her for more.

More.

Her sole defense against the cramping agony of her insides was to sleep as often as possible, waking only to stuff more food into her mouth, to push it toward her miserable stomach. It was as if she could hear the echo as the food reached its destination. Only instead of sound, the waves moved through her entire body in an ecstacy of pain. Her body rejected it. Nothing appeased her hunger whatsoever.

Food no longer had any flavor. It tasted of dirt, of air, of things that shouldn't be eaten and couldn't satisfy. With no other options, she ordered whatever she could get the most of. It had to be cheap and plenteous. She no longer attempted to be healthy by eating fruits and vegetables. Instead, she ate the cheapest cuts of meat, most of them canned. Spam, tuna, ground beef, bulk chicken. Rice and bread were cheap, and she ate them hoping they would expand in her stomach, make it feel full for just a moment. Anything to feel as if she'd done something right.

Her abdomen bloated while the rest of her body shrunk. When she looked in the mirror, it was in horror. She'd become so thin, so hollow. Dark circles bruised her undereyes. Her sallow skin sagged, wrinkling as if she were eighty instead of twenty. It jiggled when she moved, a billowing cloud of flesh that strived to be set free from its starving cage.

The change in her appearance was easy to track, courtesy of the images she'd posted on her social media accounts. Before the lockdown, she'd been able to go out with friends, to dine at restaurants, to run to the corner store on a whim. She'd enjoyed life. It showed from the smiles, the fullness of her skin, the brightness of her eyes. She'd had energy, and been able to eat whatever she wanted without gaining any weight. Or losing it, as she was doing now.

Once she couldn't leave the house for anything, it was like she'd devolved. Work switched to remote only. She ordered groceries online to be delivered to her. She couldn't go near her friends in case they were infected without knowing it. Going around other people could mean her death. Or theirs.

Joy hated talking on the phone, and meeting up online was weird and depressing. She wanted company, craved human touch. Without a doubt, she was as hungry for these things as she was for sustenance, and there was no way to satisfy any of these needs anymore. As it was, she wandered around the confines of her home, knowing what a caged animal must feel. Outside there was sun and wind and rain. There were trees, birds chirping, wildlife scurrying about, flowers bobbing on their stems. Outside there was life, though seldom human. Food deliveries were left on her doorstep, as if magicked there by some sorcerer. Contactless delivery, they called it. Contactless everything. What a nightmare.

So now she wasted away, hungering for food that couldn't sustain her, hungering for interpersonal connection that came direct with body heat and warm breath. She'd never thought of herself as an extrovert, but now it registered that she needed the company of other people. Her street looked like a zombie wasteland, cars abandoned in driveways, no children playing in their front yards. The postal worker came through once a day like clockwork to drop off the mail. Her garbage cans sat empty at the end of her driveway when she got up every Tuesday morning. She couldn't help but want to keep something back from the garbage, to hold onto something that had touched the outside world more recently than she had.

Just the other day, she'd stepped out onto her porch wearing a mask, hoping it would provide the double duty of protecting her from germs, but also hiding her frightening appearance from everyone. When the postal worker walked by, she'd waved and called out a rusty, "Hi!" He'd touched his mask as if to check that it sat where it was supposed to before throwing her a quizzical look and a mask-muffled, "Hello." It had taken every ounce of self control she had not to run after him, to grab him and force him to look at her, to talk to her. Anything. But that single hello would have to do for now.

Only, she'd felt something else in that moment, watching him walk away from her in his dark blue shorts and light blue shirt. Something that scared her more than the hunger, more than the wasting away. Alarmingly, what she'd felt was a new stirring of hunger. An anticipatory hunger. As he'd gone on his merry way, unconcerned about her presence other than to question why she'd called out to him, she'd coveted him. Not in a sexual way. No, the appetite he had awoken in her was one more simple than that for sex. Something even more animalistic.

He'd looked delicious.

She'd caught herself replaying the interaction with him and licking her lips, saliva flooding her mouth. His browned arms and thick calves. So much meat. She'd been hungry this whole time because she wasn't eating the right thing.

Ever since that day, a fantasy had played in her mind over and over. How she took him mattered less than the fact that she did take him. She wrestled him to the ground and ate his raw flesh as he screamed, warm blood pumping into her open mouth in a sensual dance of predatory fulfillment. Or she lured him into the house and slit his throat before chopping off pieces to feed into the oven. Or he willingly brought her a slice of his juicy, well muscled thigh and coaxed her to eat it however she liked. Or she gutted him and dove in, consuming the soft organs, those delicate sweet meats.

There were so many scenes. The gist of every single one, though, was that she craved the flesh of her postman. It was the only thing that could sate her hunger.

Of course she fought it. There was no possible way this craving could be real. She had groceries at her fingertips. Never had she even thought about cannibalism.

Then someone knocked on her door when she wasn't expecting any visitors.

Joy put her mask on before she went to the door, an almost automatic reflex now, and peered through the peephole. At first, the sight of a stranger on her doorstep brought trepidation, but as she studied his face, distorted by the glass of the peephole, it came again, that mad hunger. This hunger was different, because it carried a promise with it: eat this and you'll feel better. The other kind was pure emptiness, a black hole that couldn't be filled. This sensation, though, could be appeased. How she knew wasn't important. She just did.

Any fear at the mysterious presence of a stranger dissipated. She opened the door to find a slightly overweight young man on her sun-bleached porch, his cheeks pink with exertion. He squinted through lightly tinted sunglasses, a wide smile on his face. Though he wore pants and a button up white shirt, she could make out his heft beneath the clothing. His sunburned, freckled arms alone could feed her for days. When he clasped his hands together, his fingertips dimpled the doughy flesh.

She was so fixated on his hands that his voice caused her to jump. "Good afternoon, ma'am, how are you doing on this gorgeous summer day?"

It took great force of will to tear her eyes away from his hands and meet his eyes. In fact, she was so distracted that only now did she realize he'd come to her door maskless. "I'm good. How are you?"

Normally, she resented any unplanned interruption. No matter what, this young man had to be peddling something, whether it was a product, a service, or a religion. Even before everyone had been shoved into the forced isolation of these last few months, she'd hidden when someone had knocked on her door, heart pounding at the anxiety caused by the possibility of having to talk to a stranger. Today she welcomed it. His plump, virginal appearance told her this was most likely a religious pitch, and his lack of a mask only reinforced the idea. After all, as she'd repeatedly been told, God was more powerful than the virus.

She eagerly awaited his reply. He didn't make her wait long. "I'm wonderful. Have you received the word of the Lord?"

There it was. She looked around with a smile beneath the mask, seeking acknowledgment of her successful guess. It took her a moment to realize her loneliness had made her maybe a teeny bit loopy. There was no laugh track in real life; it existed only in the shows she'd been binge watching while stuck at home.

"You know what? I'd love to hear what you have to say about the Lord. Come on in." She stepped back and gestured toward her living room. "I'm Joy."

Surprise flitted over his face, but he quickly modified his expression and stepped inside, holding out a hand for a shake. "I'm James." A whiff of soap trailed behind him. He looked back at her for direction as to where to go next. When she waved her hand at the nearby sofa, he dutifully strode over and sat upon it, waiting for her to join him.

She realized she'd made her decision the moment she'd chosen to allow him in the house. Something had to be done about her misery, and this was the only way. Everything else had been tried. Everything else had left her starving, desperate.

Hungry.

It sucked to feel like nothing could fill you up, like you could never be full or even momentarily satiated. This desperate feeling of emptiness must be eradicated. However, a litany of doubts and questions flitted through her mind at lightning speed: Can I kill a person? Can I eat a person? How do I even do this? What the hell is wrong with me? What have I become? Do I cook the meat or eat it raw?

At this last, her stomach rumbled loudly. So loudly, in fact, that surprise registered on the young man's face in a widening of his eyes and a mild double take. She smiled at him and shrugged her shoulders. "Sorry. I seem to always be hungry these days." She settled into the easy chair across the coffee table from where he sat. "Where do we start?"

He took a deep breath and launched into what was obviously a rehearsed spiel. "I'm here to share the word of our Lord. Jesus long ago told us to bring the word to all people, as in Matthew 28:19. We believe that all can be saved. When—"

"Oh, I'm sorry, but I should have offered you a drink. Can I get you some water or juice?"

He hesitated, but a deep swallow told her his answer before his voice did. "Yes, please. It's hot outside, and I'd love some water."

"Great, I'll be right back."

She hopped up and sped into the kitchen, where she stopped to look around for ideas. He didn't exactly look strong, but any person could pull up the strength to fight for their life against an aggressor. Her knife block stood on the counter beside the sink, shiny black handles poking out of it. The butcher knife would do nicely. It was long and thick, and she'd recently sharpened it. But a knife might be easy to wrest away, or she might cut herself if it slid. They addressed that in true crime shows all the time.

She slid various drawers open, seeking inspiration. Most of it was useless. Each thing that seemed a possibility was placed on the center island. So far, she'd found a meat tenderizer, a frying pan, and the base of her blender. Poison wouldn't do, because it would take time, but also probably poison the meat, which could be deadly to herself.

This last thought made her pause. It was inhuman to think this way. She couldn't really be pondering killing and eating this poor, innocent idiot. Any minute now her stomach would revolt. She kept waiting to feel nausea or a true, physical reaction of horror at what she planned. It hadn't come yet, aside from the conscious thoughts she kept forcing on herself. It was the fact that her subconscious seemed entirely fine with it that bothered her now. As if only her intellectual side had an issue with it, but no emotional inhibitions existed.

It was amazing what hunger could do to a person.

"Can I help with anything?" he asked from the other room.

"Nope, sorry about that." Crap, she was taking too long. "I'll be right there."

She grabbed a glass, filled it with ice then water, and grabbed herself a small glass of orange juice. A quick eyeballing of the items on the counter showed they wouldn't make any sense, because it would look weird when she walked into the room holding them. Surely he wouldn't just sit there and watch as she approached him with a butcher knife or the base of a blender. If she'd been thinking ahead, she would have sat him with his back to the kitchen so she could come at him from behind. Instead, his position sat him squarely facing the doorway she'd be going back through.

An idea hit her, and she set the glasses down before scuttling over to the refrigerator. She pulled out some pre-sliced snacking cheese that didn't look moldy, setting it on the counter. She also grabbed a heavy decorative platter and some crackers. Arranging everything on the platter, she removed her mask long enough to drink down her juice, picked up the platter in one hand and his water in the other, and headed back out to where he sat.

"I realized I was hungry, so thought a snack might be a good idea." She set the water down in front of him, then set the platter beside the glass. "Help yourself."

He'd set a bible on the table, which he now picked up in a tight grip, his hand shaking. The fact that he was getting more nervous instead of less so made it appear this might be the first time anyone had taken him up on his proselytizing. Her mouth went dry, which, as soon as she thought about it, made her feel a little better. The fact that she felt guilty meant she wasn't as bad as she'd started thinking she must be. That slight twinge in her stomach backed it up. She wasn't evil, just desperate. Surely there was something in the bible that would confirm that was a legitimate thing.

His voice squeaked. "Do you have anything specific you're curious about?" He cleared his throat. "Any life questions you want answered?"

Actually, she did. "What if you're about to do something wrong, and you don't feel guilty enough about it?"

He opened his mouth and drew in a breath to speak, but she continued on.

"I mean, you might feel a little guilty about it, but you know you have to do it, that you don't have a choice. If it means your survival, if you'll die if you don't do it, doesn't that mean you have to do it?"

He cleared his throat again, looked at his bible, looked at her. "Uh..." He opened the bible and started flipping through it. "Okay, um..."

She waited, thinking that if he came up with the right thing to say it might save her. If not, at least it might make her feel better about what she had to do. Maybe religion was worth it when you needed to make hard decisions. She saw people praying for help for all kinds of things all the time, to win a game, to get something they really want, to help them with making choices. They wouldn't do it if it didn't work. Someone who was fifty and doing that would have learned by now that their prayers were never answered, which must mean they did get answered.

So she waited and watched him as he continued to make little noises and thumb back and forth in the bible. A wave of red crept up his neck and into his face, his cheeks blazing with it. He kept licking his lips, and he darted looks at her.

Finally, his eyes widened and his posture relaxed. "Here it is. Second Corinthians 13:7. 'But we pray to God that you may do no wrong—not that we appear to have met the test, but that you may do what is right, though we may seem to have failed.'"

She sat back, only then realizing that she'd been leaning closer and closer to him as she awaited his response. "What?"

"It means that if you have faith, you need to test yourself to make sure you're doing things the right way. If you do the right thing, even when you want to do the wrong thing, you pass the test. If you know it's wrong and you do it, you've failed."

"What if I don't have faith, though? What am I testing myself for? I can't fail a test for a class I'm not taking."

"Well, um, I mean, you know what's right, right? You know what you're thinking about doing is wrong?"

"Yes."

"So it's still a test of yourself. You know you should do the right thing."

"But what happens if I don't do the right thing?"

"You..." he started looking through the book again.

Her hunger now gnawed at her entire inside. She'd been distracted by her inner struggle and nerves about the situation, but he was boring her. No longer distracted, all she could do was return to obsessing about her own physical torment. Now that she was paying attention to it, she found her skin even ached. Her nerves were on fire, every single one of them. It felt like she would burn to death, with not even a lick of flame nearby.

Without thinking, she stood up and grabbed the platter in

one fluid movement, the food flying into the air only to land on the carpeting in the same instant the platter met with the side of the young man's head. She felt the *conk* of the contact as much as she heard it, along with the *pomp, pomp, pomp* of the food. The hit was so solid it hurt her hands and spread up her forearms.

He fell forward, but didn't pass out. She'd fully expected it to knock him out completely. Blood pumped from his head where it had split like a seam. He put a hand to it, looked at the blood, and started an insanely high-pitched scream that didn't stop.

She screamed, too, and hit him in the head again. Blood pattered onto her mask in a tiny parade of droplets.

His screaming stopped, but he remained conscious, blood now pouring from his mouth in a viscous ribbon. Another seam appeared, splitting slowly from his temple and back through his red hair. It formed a bright white chasm in an arc along the side of his head, but then that split filled with vivid red blood. His scalp peeled down in slow motion, flopping over the ear.

Equal parts horror and ire surged through her. This wasn't how it was supposed to go. He was supposed to die with one hit from the platter. It should have been easier.

God damn it, she was so *hungry*.

With a feral snarl, Joy dove for him and slammed the platter into his head repeatedly until he finally slumped the rest of the way to the ground. One of his eyes remained fixed open, the eyelid torn and hanging down the bridge of his nose. The other had already swollen closed, the blood filling every line. There was blood spatter everywhere, including the ceiling, and a small clump of scalp had landed on the couch arm like a small rodent. Blood pooled beneath him, soaking into the carpet.

She sunk to her knees and tossed her mask to the side, warm blood seeping through her pants. Unsure of what to do next, she picked up his hand and put two fingers where she thought his pulse should be. Nothing there. He must be dead. Just to be sure, she shoved his shoulder to see if he'd react, but that one eye remained fixed on her and his body shifted right back to where it had been. It smelled like he'd crapped himself, which definitely wasn't appetizing.

Yet she salivated when she thought about eating him.

First things first, she needed to clean him up. It took her an inordinate amount of time to drag him into the bathroom. Getting him into the tub took almost as long as the rest of it. By the time she'd finished, her entire body ached, she reeked of every possible human body fluid, and she had worked up an even bigger appetite.

She took off his clothes and stuffed them into the garbage can, then she washed him until his skin showed white and clean. With the last dredges of the filth gone, it was time to figure out how to eat him. There was no way she'd be transporting his entire body anywhere else. This had been hard enough. Which meant she either had to eat him here or cut him up. Cutting something off made the most sense.

Joy went to the garage and grabbed a saw. It had belonged to her dad and had sat there rusting since his death five years ago. She wasn't even sure what he'd used it for, but it should work fine for this job.

Back in the bathroom, Joy started with a leg. She felt it would be nice and meaty, like a steak or a roast. Just thinking about it made her mouth water more, and she went to work with the saw. It went through the meat easily enough, but when she got to the bone she couldn't make any progress. It rasped and scratched in a way that gave her goosebumps, like nails on a chalkboard, but it didn't go through.

She pulled the flesh back to look, but she'd only made a small scratch in the femur. This wasn't working.

Obviously she wouldn't be able to get the whole leg off.

Instead, she sawed sideways, slicing the meat off the top to form a steak-sized cut. She was surprised at how little blood there was. A small amount seeped down from the slab she held in her hand, but nothing welled up out of the thigh where the chunk had been removed. Somehow that made it easier to deal with. She wasn't looking at a human being anymore. It was meat. The same thing available at any store. All meat had once been life.

She walked into the kitchen and slapped the meat down onto her cutting board. Red hairs rose from the freckled thigh skin, and she figured it would be best to trim the outer layer of skin off. As far as she could tell, the muscle part was the equivalent to a steak. She should have cut deeper, but for her first time a thin steak would have to do. She'd know better next time.

The filet knife cut through the meat pretty well, though there was some resistance, and the cut wasn't straight. Once the skin and hair were removed, it looked...normal. She sprayed the pan down and set it on the stove to pre-heat. Sweat poured down her back, sides, and forehead. The foul stench of body odor rose in a bouquet of nerves and physical exertion. Fear, too, she realized. Fear of what she was doing, of what would happen if she didn't do it. Fear in every moment she had to make a decision and follow through on it.

Fear of wasting away from this hunger.

The scent of hot metal brought her back from her thoughts, and she plopped the steak into the skillet. It sizzled loudly. She seared it then added seasonings while it finished cooking. The rich smells of garlic, meat, and thyme mingled together and her stomach rumbled yet again.

Outside, darkness had fallen. This had all taken hours, an entire day. She opened some windows to allow cool air into the house. Voices from someone's television drifted in, filling what was an otherwise lonely night with distant company. All this time, and she'd never put on music or turned on the television. Cutting meat was a fairly quiet thing to do except when the saw had hit the bone. The body itself had made a variety of noises while the gases settled within its guts, disgusting noises most of them. Yet she'd ignored them while she worked, lost in some distant part of her mind, various thoughts swirling.

She got like that sometimes. Lost. Plunging deep into her own head.

The steak finished, she plated it, grabbed utensils, and sat down at her table. Finally, she would have relief. She would feel full. As her hope climbed, so did her excitement.

She cut into the tender meat and slid it into her mouth. It tasted gamey. Like deer she'd once eaten when a neighbor gave her some of his kill. Each successive bite tasted worse, but at least she could sense flavor again. Her stomach grumbled angrily, pushing back at the food she forced down her own throat.

This was the answer. This would work.

Only it didn't.

She gagged and threw her fork down, pushing the plate away. Something had gone wrong. She gagged again, but this time it brought vomit up into her mouth.

Joy clapped a hand over her mouth and ran for the bathroom. Kneeling beside the man's body, she threw up every ounce of his meat. The smell sickened her, made her gag again, and she flushed the toilet to get rid of it.

Looking over at the dead body, she realized it must be the raw meat she had to eat. Weakened by the day's exploits and her vomiting, she crawled over and leaned on the edge of the tub. She studied his body to figure out what looked the easiest to eat and the most appetizing. His upper arm near the shoulder looked firm and mostly hairless. The thought of hairs tickling her tongue while she tried to eat made her gag again, and she went for the shoulder.

It was harder to break the skin with her teeth than she expected. She bit as hard as she could and tore at it, bringing a small chunk of flesh with her. It was rubbery and springy, but she chewed nonetheless until it became mashed up enough to swallow it without choking. When she went to take a second bite, she couldn't even sink her teeth in before her stomach forced her back to the toilet to throw up her last bite.

She continued to vomit until nothing remained, not even bile. Then she passed out on the bathroom floor.

~~

Joy woke up to a room that reeked of vomit and death, and a mouth that tasted the same. Pooling blood had colored the lower parts of the corpse purple. The skin looked to have shrunk, sunken over the joints. The redhead was even paler than before, and Joy's bites stood out starkly.

She climbed to her feet, feeling weak and hungry. Everything hurt, including her stomach. She went to the refrigerator to look for food, but the sight of it left her feeling ill. Maybe this was her punishment for killing someone and trying to eat them. Maybe she'd never be able to eat again, and she'd die from lack of nourishment. She felt so strange, so out of it, like her body wasn't her own. Every movement cost energy she didn't have. Her limbs felt elongated and clumsy. When she held up her hands in front of her face, her fingers looked thinner and maybe a bit longer, but she couldn't tell for sure if she'd changed more.

The doorbell rang. She walked to the door, fighting the fatigue and discomfort draining her body. Through the peephole she saw the postman she'd waved at the other day.

Her stomach growled, her mouth filling with saliva.

So hungry.

She put on her mask and opened the door.

"Are you Joy Desmond?" he asked.

"Yes, that's me."

"Package for you." He held a large box, which he pushed in her direction.

"Can you bring it inside for me?" she asked. "It looks heavy."

"No problem."

She closed the door behind him and locked the deadbolt.

One more try.

A Darkness That Evades the Eye

Within the bounds of our natural world lie many wonders that most people can't see. They don't exist on a different plane, nor are they invisible. Like with some people, they are simply so unassuming, so boring to the human eye, that we look past it without registering it. Just as a person's brain fills in missing gaps when looking through a damaged eye, so it also erases the things we aren't meant to see.

Which is why I find myself seeking the tiny church within the walled historic city of Cartagena that no one knows exists save for a few of us dedicated souls who spend our lives revisiting the wretched events of the past. If I can locate *la iglesia de oscuridad* perhaps I can set the spirits free and remove the darkness that lies over the building, finally bringing it into the light.

Before the church came to my attention, I'd only heard of Cartagena, a small, but beautiful city in Colombia, because of a certain romantic adventure film starring Kathleen Turner in her prime. Nothing in that movie prepared me for the actual city, which I approached by boat. Nestled in the Caribbean Sea, first appearances are deceptive. High rises and resort hotels reflect the over-bright sun, causing an almost blinding radiance at a certain distance, especially with the sea doubling the sun's power.

It wasn't until I reached the walled city that the true power could be felt. Snuggled in between two contemporary arms of civilization, the ancient walls stand as a guard against those who would have stolen the riches from the flourishing city of *Cartagena de Indias*, where the Spanish had discovered treasure buried with the dead of the indigenous peoples who'd lived there before. Pirates attempted to get in for the treasure, while other invaders saw it as a way into Colombia, but the residents managed to keep those inside safe most of the time, even through a bloody battle between England and Spain.

Many of the buildings are reminiscent of those in Havana and various cities lining the Caribbean, with bright stone fronts, arches, and grand porches. Towering Catholic churches rise above the walls, the fortress still standing atop a hill, its aged gray boundaries a stunning sight. It speaks of battle with its scars, but also of strength and fortitude, of victors and riches.

A *limonada de coco* in hand, I sip the cool beverage from a coconut shell and stand in an alley behind a seafood restaurant and a touristy shop. Nobody bothers me back here, shadows my only company. The air is cooler than out on the main streets, but sweat still swaddles my body, an oddly comforting density to it. Before me, there stands what looks to be an old wall. Nothing special. Another minute, though, and I'll see the church. Or so I've been told.

I've only met one other person in our group. We call ourselves the Society of Seekers. Mostly meeting online in chat rooms, we study the old urban legends and wives' tales for glints of truth, brainstorming and researching until we find somewhere that sounds likely. This one has been in the works for about two years now. I almost didn't get the assignment, but a bad bout with the flu eliminated John, the original recipient of this particular honor. I can't say I was disappointed. He, however, was pissed. Something I'll deal with later.

The coconut and citrus flavor of my drink dance around my tongue and I finish the last swallow just as a ray of light breaks through a decorative bit of grillwork between the buildings. When it hits the lower section of the wall I've been staring at for the past twenty minutes, an arched door appears, heavy dents in the wood, some manner of rusted metal for the hinges, bracings, and handle.

I set my empty coconut on the ground and approach the door. Heat hits my back when I step into the sun, and it feels like I just secreted a tub-full of sweat down my spine. The handle is cool to the touch, but when I press the latch, it opens easily. Cold air swirls out around my ankles, defying the sun to quash it. A musty smell exits, as well, along with a series of moans that die out the moment my foot crosses the threshold.

The floor, the walls, everything inside here is made of wood, meaning this church had to have stood before the city was burned down by invaders in 1552. How it remained standing when the entire city had been obliterated is a mystery for another time.

Behind me, the door swings shut with a *creak* and a resounding *thud*.

Whatever remains inside this building knows I'm here.

I carry only a single cross-shoulder bag. From it I pull out a flashlight, shining it around me in every direction. The inside is much larger than the exterior space indicated, meaning the other buildings around it are oddly shaped. How many have worked or lived inside those buildings and wondered at the strange setup? There's no way to know, but in other buildings we've discovered that people often have an awareness of the spatial disparities, though no amount of investigation leads them to the answers they seek. One man in New Orleans actually broke through the wall of his condo, only to forget what he was looking for. He sealed it back up and couldn't remember what he'd seen. Instead, he told himself it had led outside, that everything was as it should be. In actuality, an old asylum stood on the other side of the wall, a place where many horrors had been perpetrated. The ghosts stood inches away from him, pleading for a salvation he couldn't provide.

My steps cause a floorboard to squeak, initiating a flurry of movement off to my right. Following the sounds, I come to a narrow, winding staircase that leads up to a dark second floor. Shining my light ahead of me, I ascend, careful with my footing. The lack of people in this building for so long has probably protected the interior, but I don't feel like taking any chances. Wood rots. Stairs fail.

The curve of the staircase is tight, making it so I can't see where it leads or what lies ahead of me. The beam of the flashlight reveals the rough wooden walls that brace the stairs. A smear runs around at waist height, a deep, brownish-red. Panting breaths twist down the stairs toward me, "no" whispered here and there, along with *"por favor."*

There's an impact, a grunt, screams.

The hair on the back of my neck rises. Between climbing the

stairs and the tension of walking through a history of death, my heart tries to jog straight through my breastbone. It's one thing to know these haunts can't hurt me, another to ignore the sounds of violent death and not have an emotional reaction.

Pushing through my discomfort, I finally reach a level floor that opens into a large room, perhaps a nunnery of some sort. There are no bodies, no spirits, just myself and ancient furnishings. Ratty curtains drift in a wind I can't feel, an arched window standing against the far wall. There are rows of broken beds, simple in their original forms. Splintered wood and straw-packed mattresses host teeming masses of insects. Perhaps they were initially drawn by the remnants of death. Now they're stuck here for eternity, or until I find something of power to bring the church into the present.

Wails and the sharp sound of lashings hitting flesh push me through the room. I step around the remnants of furniture and what appears to be a nail-studded kneeling board, covered in brown, dried blood. A small, wooden door rests in an alcove, hanging crooked from its hinges. A blast of cold air rushes over me when I push through it.

I'm on a balcony that appears to have once been covered with some sort of netting, perhaps to block those below from seeing who stood up here. The wall is short, about knee-height. Through the tatters of netting I can see the chapel below. The pews are dull and scarred, some toppled over. On the dais stands a podium and what may be a large bible atop it. Against the wall is a cross, and on that cross…

My mind stumbles, my eyes refusing to see. I blink against blurry vision.

On the cross is an incomplete skeleton. The bones are only white in glimpses, the rest covered in darkened skin that hasn't fallen off or rotted away completely. Strips of fabric hang off the body, a priest's collar intact around the throat of the corpse.

With the rest of the building free of bodies, I must assume that what I seek is in that chapel. I'm not eager to enter it, but I don't see an alternative.

The trek through the nunnery and back down the stairs goes without incident. As my shoe touches the aged wood of the main floor, the church comes alive. Air moves in purposeful swirls around me, through me. There are screams, wails, sobs. At one point I hear laughter, an evil chuckle that bounces from the walls in waves.

Even more frightening are the sounds that indicate violence. The thuds and wet, meaty impacts. A whip cracks. Metal slides across metal. There are gasps, grunts, and last breaths.

A woman's voice rises in prayer, quickly joined by others. The prayers become a murmur, a susurration of voiceless panic and pleading. The people in this church died violently and never received their last rites.

The force of the fear and pain around me makes it hard to walk across that floor to the large arched doors that await me. Every step feels as if a thick substance fills the space, invisible to the naked eye. I cover my ears, try to block it all out. No person should ever hear such evidence of violence, especially not all at once.

The noise rises to a crescendo that abates with the same suddenness as it began. All at once, I go from being pummeled with it to aching for something to fill the empty space. No air moves. My footsteps don't elicit even a creak from the floorboards. It feels as if I'm in a vacuum. My ears pop.

Placing my hands on the rough surface of the door, I push as hard as I can. It swings open, sound rushing back into the vacuum with the introduction of its *creak*.

This is the first I've smelled death, despite my journey through the rest of the building. It's an amalgamation of scents I've never smelled all at once—blood and feces, urine and sweat, fear and pain made palpable—yet one I recognize immediately. Down here, within the chapel, I can now see the evidence of violence that must have occurred. Though there remains only the priest's body, residue of the many lives that must have been within this church over the years covers the floor, the walls, and the pews. Bloody handprints, thick puddles of bodily fluids, a shoe, bible pages, a tiny cross fallen from its neck chain, a baby's bottle. These are just some of the detritus I witness in my slow walk up the aisle.

When I get within a few feet of the stage, my eyes are drawn to the priest, who I've tried to avoid looking at until now. His face is frightening, a dark sinew and what looks to be hardened flesh, lips stretched into a grimace of agony. He has been mounted to the cross, nails through his hands, which are now mostly skeletal. At some point, the femurs separated from the hips, the leg bones lying on the ground, suspended by the nailed feet. Fragments of his robes lie around the dais, and even on the floor beneath the front pews. They look to have been torn, not aged off him.

I hear a trickle of water behind me and turn to look. The fountain at the back where parishioners would have crossed themselves upon entering once more flows, though it was bone dry when I passed it coming in. With one more look at the priest, I go to the fountain.

The water is clear and looks clean. I cup my hands and dip them into the cool liquid, bringing it up to smell it. There is no odor at all. The water is pure.

Searching the chapel, I find a pitcher, which I take to the fountain, filling it as full as I can. I dip my fingers into the pitcher, wetting the tips. This, I flick along the pews on my walk back up to the dais. Sighs fill the chapel, a peaceful sound as of rest.

At the dais, I seek out the stairs and climb them. The stage feels surprisingly sturdy beneath my feet, and I make my way to the priest upon the cross. Though I will never be able to take back what he and others in this building may have suffered, I can give him rest now and hopefully free this building from the age-old torments that have been repeated within its walls.

Dipping my thumb in the water, I swallow my trepidation and press it to his forehead. The skin is dry, mummified, and crackles as I run my thumb down along the dip at the top of his nose, then side to side along his brow.

"Our Lord in Heaven, please accept the souls of those in this church into your kingdom. Forgive them their sins and allow them to be without pain and torment. Amen."

I'm not Catholic, so it's the best I can do.

I stand on the dais, unsure of what to do next. Nothing's happening. I've obviously done something wrong. My heart sinks at the thought that I haven't done right by the priest and the others trapped inside this building.

Setting the pitcher on the floor, I walk around and examine

the rest of the dais. There isn't much up here, and I don't find any mystical items that offer up a magic solution. There is cloth, dust, and other bits I don't recognize that I imagine have fallen off from the ceiling, walls, and such throughout the buildings' many years.

A crackling sound begins, and then it's like a million ants marching along a hard structure. The tone changes, softening.

I turn, and there, standing before the empty cross, is a young, dark-skinned priest, his brown eyes smiling along with his restored mouth. He nods and mouths, *"gracias."* Holding a hand over his heart, he fades from sight.

Then all around me, the building revives. The chapel brightens, the pews righting themselves. The windows clear, allowing a stream of sunlight inside. The fountain positively gurgles.

Up in the balcony, the netting heals as if being formed before my eyes. And looking down at me, I see a group of nuns, all of whom smile softly. They fade as the priest did, leaving behind nothing but peace.

Running out into the lobby, I gasp in wonder at the beauty of this tiny church. Many of the windows look directly onto the walls of the neighboring buildings, but I can make out the colorful stained glass, all the same. The stairs are smooth and bright, as are the walls.

Taking one last look around, I open the door and step out onto the street. The church is now visible to anyone who would walk back here. Soon it will be discovered. Will people remember that it wasn't here for so long, or will it slide into their memories as if it had always been whole and welcome? While I'm tempted to stay and watch, to see how people react, my ship home awaits me. The only ghosts within these walls will be the happy energies of those who worshipped and were comforted. Perhaps I'll come back again sometime to enjoy the released spirits who might have stuck around to greet any who might want to meet them.

Watched

"Hey there, Kim. Did you get the Neighborhood Watch email about the suspicious car?"

Ned stood on his porch, peering over at Kim. He wore khaki shorts with multiple pockets, a pair of sandals, and a t-shirt with the emblem of his old security company on the chest. A toothpick stuck out of his mouth, the end twitching as he fidgeted with it. Sunlight reflected off his mostly gray hair in a bright halo.

"No, I haven't checked my email yet today. I'll look when I go inside."

"Pretty shady. Kept moving to different areas, no lights. Milt thinks they were casing houses."

"Great, just what we need." Kim wiped away a trace of sweat before it could run off her forehead into her eyes, careful to use the back of her wrist so as not to get any dirt on her face.

"Yep. Just wanted to make sure you saw it."

"Thanks, Ned."

His sandals scuffed as he went inside and shut the door.

Ned and his wife Deb were nice folks, and Kim was glad to have them as neighbors, but now that Ned had retired, he had become a busybody, intent on keeping the neighborhood safe and up to par. He'd been elected president of the Homeowner's Association recently, solidifying his place as head of the Neighborhood Police. If she so much as left a corner of her lawn looking unkempt, a citation appeared in her inbox. While she could appreciate the boredom of unemployment, it would be nice if he'd get a hobby that didn't involve policing everyone else.

Deb agreed wholeheartedly. She sometimes invited Kim over for a cup of tea while Ned was out golfing. "That man's going to drive me crazy if he doesn't settle in retirement soon."

She was actually considering finding a job at a craft store or something that would get her out of the house to leave Ned to his devices.

The couple was always happy to watch her house when Kim was on a business trip, and they helped her feel safe as a single woman in the neighborhood. No one would sneak up on Kim with Ned on the job. He was a tough old bird, who had retired right at sixty-five. He looked maybe a decade younger than he was, as did Deb. Kim often wondered how they stayed so youthful. Deb claimed their grandchildren kept them young.

Kim dusted off her hands and stood, tugging her shorts down where they'd bunched on her legs. Her hands were dark with soil and smelled of rich loam and the acidic stench of freshly pulled weeds. Her back ached from having been bent over for so long, and her knees popped with her first step. Yep, at thirty-seven years old, she was desperate for the secret behind Ned and Deb's fountain of youth.

Once inside the house, the cool air-conditioned air quickly dried the sweat on her back and forehead. She sighed with relief and grabbed a glass of ice water after washing her hands. Thin lines of brown still showed beneath the nails, even after scrubbing them.

Sure enough, when she checked her email there was the watch notice about the suspicious car. It had been reported by her neighbor to the other side, Brady, whose wife Stacy went for late night walks. Brady and Stacy had two elementary aged children. They had a harder time keeping the appearance of their house up to Ned's stringent standards, what with the kids having toys outside, and both the adults working full-time. There'd been a couple verbal duels between Ned and Brady, but nothing major, and they got along overall. Kim kept waiting for a war to break out between the two of them, her stuck in the middle.

There were several more emails in her inbox, and she perused these, marking two as spam, setting aside a work-related one to read later, and dispatching with the others. The last new email, which had been sent at seven o'clock this morning, had the subject line "Sleep Well?" She opened it, figuring it was another piece of spam about sleep medications.

You looked comfortable when I checked in on you last night. Hope your dreams were delicious.

Definitely spam. She deleted it and shut her screen off, ready for that shower.

~~

Monday, a thunderstorm rolled in over the course of Kim's commute home. The ominous clouds blew over the mountains, sinking down to squat over the west side of town. Lightning flashed in the distance, thunder following behind a few seconds later. No rain had fallen by the time she pulled into her garage, but the thick smell of ozone told her it was on its way.

Aggressive male voices rumbled across the street toward her when she got out of the car. Ned and the guy whose house was directly across from hers—Carlos she thought—were embroiled in a debate. Carlos probably hadn't watered his lawn right or something. She pressed the button to close the garage door, and went inside. They'd sort it out. Everyone dealt with Ned's hypervigilance the best they could.

Of all her direct neighbors, she knew Carlos the least. He was a long-haul truck driver, single, and his house was often empty. He and Brady sometimes chatted out in the street, occasionally sharing a beer. His yard got shaggy when he was on a haul, and it drove Ned crazy, but Carlos always maintained it when he was able.

She poured herself a glass of white wine to help her cook dinner. 90s rock poured out of her radio, and she turned it up to drown out the patter of rain on her roof before commencing the chopping of vegetables.

Twenty minutes later, the smell of roasting vegetables and chicken filling the house, she checked her email. A subject line caught her attention. "Don't Ignore Me." When she opened it up, the message read, *When I send you a message, I expect an answer. Last night seemed more restless. I could have helped you sleep.*

Kim frowned, checking the sender's email address. Jbx32@hotmail.com. It wasn't one she recognized, and she hadn't checked the email address on the weird one from the day before. Her computer was set to dump her trash each night, so that one was gone. She'd save this one, just in case. If another one came in, it would be good to see if they were coming from the same person or if they were some new type of spam. Maybe the foreign spammers were getting better at checking their English grammar.

She shut down her computer and went to grab another glass of wine.

~~

Over the next week, she got more emails, all from the same email address. They ranged from cajoling to threatening, asking her personal questions, like what she'd had for dinner, did she masturbate, was she seeing anyone. She didn't erase them, but still didn't reply. From what she could tell, the police couldn't do anything but document it, so she left it alone for now. So far the sender hadn't used her name, indicating she was a random recipient, rather than a known target.

Even so, her stomach ached whenever she saw an email from that address lurking in her inbox. Reading the emails instantly made her mouth go dry. They were not only inappropriate and deeply private, but ominous. They had an increasingly threatening tone to them.

Now it was Friday, and she sipped a cold beer after work. A new email lurked in her inbox, and part of her didn't want to open it. Not being afraid was one thing, but subjecting herself to these bizarre emails was another entirely.

Her curiosity won out, and she clicked on the email with subject line "Excellent Choice."

Saw the new panties. Or maybe they aren't new, and I just haven't seen them yet? I couldn't tell exactly what color they were, but the lace was sexy, and you look good in dark colors. Brunettes always do, don't they? I wanted to touch you so badly, run my hands over that smooth skin. Soon.

Ice ran through her veins, gooseflesh dappling her body.

How did this person know she was a brunette? Lucky guess, maybe. But she had also been wearing new lace panties last night. Black. The sender hitting on one accurate coincidence seemed possible, but two?

Her heart pounded, mouth dry. This wasn't something she could ignore, even scoff at, anymore. She'd told her best friend Lacy about the emails, and they'd laughed at them.

It wasn't funny now.

She dialed Lacy, who picked up on the second ring. "Hello?"

"Lacy? Feel up to a lady's night tonight?"

"I thought you wanted to take it easy this weekend."

"I changed my mind. I'd rather not be alone."

Lacy's tone changed from cheerful to wary. "What's going on? Are you okay?"

"I got another email."

"You want me to come over? I can grab nachos and a six-pack."

"Sounds great."

"I'll be there in thirty." Lacy hung up.

While she waited for Lacy, Kim walked around the house, peeking out the windows and making sure they were locked. How had this person seen her underwear? She wasn't exactly an exhibitionist, but she had probably walked through the house in bra, panties, and an open robe. She usually closed the blinds in the evening, well before changing into night clothes. The front door had a thin, full-length window she'd never gotten around to special ordering blinds for. Had she walked in front of it? Possibly.

She made sure all the blinds were closed then went into the garage for some cardboard. It was time to order blinds for that window, but in the meantime there were other ways to cover it up.

The electronic lock on the front door beeped, an indication that Lacy had arrived and was letting herself in. The lock made it easier to give people access when they watched her house, as well as making her feel safer since it automatically locked each time the door closed. Kim had given the code out to her close friends and family, and they knew to let themselves in when she expected them.

"I'm heeeere!" Lacy called out. A plastic bag rustled, glass clinking together.

Kim called, "In the kitchen!"

The kitchen window didn't have blinds, but it did have decorative curtains. She pulled these closed, dismayed at the gap in the middle. She'd have to order blinds for this one, too.

Suddenly, she felt exposed in her own home. Her house had gone from feeling secure to feeling like the display window at a shop.

Lacy plopped a plastic bag on the counter, the scent of seasoned beef wafting from it. She opened the fridge and placed the six-pack inside, pulling out two beers. Air released in a spritz as she popped the top off each bottle, handing one to Kim before taking a long drink of hers. "Show me the latest email."

Kim walked into the small main floor office and leaned over her desk, grabbing the mouse. When she opened her inbox, a new email popped up. "Cute" read the subject. Kim sunk into her chair and opened the email, while Lacy stood behind her, leaning over to see the screen.

Your friend's cute. She could never be as beautiful as you, but I'm not big on blondes.

"Holy shit!" Lacy said. "Whoever did this saw me come in. You need to call the police."

"I don't think they can do anything about it. It's got to be a neighbor. He saw me in my underwear last night, knew I was wearing a new pair."

"How long has this asshole been watching you?"

"I don't know. The emails just started this week."

"Did you give your email out to anyone in the neighborhood who didn't have it before?"

"No. Not that I can think of. For the most part, I just know folks to say a passing hello to. I travel too much to be part of any of the social gatherings."

"Well, who DO you know?"

They moved into the living room with the nachos, crunching away while they discussed Kim's neighbors.

"I know the ones on either side of me. You've met Ned and Deb. I've spoken to the couple behind me. Most of these houses have young families in them. The only ones who don't are grandparents and the guy who drives trucks."

"The cute one?" Lacy had seen Carlos out packing up his truck one day and taken interest. He was tall, dark, and wiry. A man accustomed to putting in hard work.

Kim wondered if he worked out; she had a mental image of truckers that involved guts, not abs. "Yes, the cute one."

"You know how many horror movies involve truckers? I can think of two off the top of my head. One's Australian, I think."

"Okay, it's feasible it could be him, but he's never shown any interest in me. We've barely exchanged a word."

"Just like a psycho to act shy and disinterested in a person, then send creepy emails in secret."

Kim rolled her eyes. "I'll add him to the list of suspects. I don't know who else would do it. I've caught the guy behind me looking at me, but he and his wife seem to have a good marriage, and she just had another baby two months ago."

"Isn't that when husbands cheat? When their wives have gained weight from having babies?"

"Only shitty ones. And he seems pretty involved with his family."

Lacy hopped up and left the room.

"What are you doing?" Kim called after her.

"We need paper and a pen. I think we should write down the most likely suspects for the cops. They can trace the emails. Call your service provider. I'm pretty sure, anyway." Lacy came back into the room, settling on the floor next to the coffee table. She set a lined pad and two pens on the table in front of her and crossed her legs before pulling her long, blonde hair back into a sloppy bun.

Kim envied both the ability to sit cross-legged on the floor and how good the sloppy bun looked. She'd never been able to pull the bun off, looking like a slob instead of stylish, and it had been years since her knees and back had allowed comfortable floor sitting, let alone criss-crossed legs.

"Alright, I'm writing down the cute trucker and the creeper behind you. Who else?"

"Honestly, I don't know. I'm friendly with Brady to my left and Ned to my right. There's Stan, Charlie, and Alec, all married. They live on this street. The guy kitty-corner from my backyard is never home, and his wife is the weirdest one of the two. She sits on her back porch for hours, smoking and staring at everyone."

"There's no rule saying this has to be a guy. It could be a freaky chick neighbor."

"True, but she's not staring *that* way."

"I think we should include other acquaintances, not just neighbors. Someone else could be watching you."

Kim remembered the suspicious car that had been seen driving around the neighborhood. Maybe she should have paid more attention to the warning. Maybe they weren't so much casing houses as spying on single women. She had lacy add the stranger to the list.

The women worked for several more minutes, each downing a second beer. In the end, the list took up three-quarters of the page, but Kim didn't have a strong suspicion of any of the people on it. She set the list aside and proposed a movie. "A comedy, okay?"

They finished the nachos and the six-pack, busting out a bag of popcorn. After the movie, Kim felt more relaxed, distanced from the threat. It was after midnight, and she was tired.

"You want me to stay the night?" Lacy asked.

"No, I'm okay. Doing something about it, even if it was just making a list, helped."

"All right, I'm going home, but I'll keep my phone next to the bed and the ringer on. You call me if you need anything, even if it's something as simple as the wind making weird noises. Got it?"

Kim laughed. "I got it. I'll call you if the house creaks wrong." She walked Lacy out, making sure to lock the deadbolt and slide the chain lock into place. She did a final set of rounds to be sure every door and window was locked.

Sleep was fitful, but she finally got some rest. In the morning, she did everything other than check her emails, casting glances at her office each time it came into view. The emails preyed on her mind all day, knots sliding down her throat. When evening began to creep in, she sat down in her office to check the emails. Not knowing if anything had been sent or what had been said was harder than letting herself read the email. The nerves twisting her stomach made it impossible to eat.

"Bummer" was the newest subject.

I was hoping there'd be a slumber party. Does she have

lace panties, too? You should bring her out tonight, so we can have a little fun.

She couldn't take this anymore. With rapid keystrokes, she shot back a reply. *Who the hell is this?*

The reply came in less than a minute. *No need to be rude.*

I'm not the one being rude.

Each response came as quickly as the first had, and they went back and forth.

I'd watch my tone if I were you. Being rude comes with a price.

Stop writing me. Stop watching me. I'm going to the police.

What do you think they can do about it?

Why are you doing this?

You interest me. I want to know everything there is to know about you, to feel you beside me.

Leave me alone.

I will never leave you. This one was accompanied by the image of a rose.

Kim stared at the screen. Did he think this was some kind of romantic gesture? Either way, talking to him was getting her nowhere. She reached for the mouse to shut down the computer, but a new email came in.

Don't turn the computer off. I'm not finished.

She shut off the computer, clasping her hands to her mouth, staring at the black screen. She was dealing with someone insane. She thought about the two men at work she'd added to the list of suspects. Josh had asked her out on a date. She'd nicely let him down, telling him she didn't want to date in the workplace, that she'd had a bad experience in the past. He'd taken it well, or so she'd thought. It was possible he'd been acting and was now got his jollies from stalking her. The other guy, Rick, was just weird. He tended to speak to her breasts instead of her face. He'd show up behind her when she took a coffee break or went to grab office supplies. He never spoke to her, just looked. While it was strange, everyone there acknowledged how odd he was, and she wasn't the only one he stared at. Maybe the only way he could talk to a woman was through a keyboard.

She jumped when her cellphone buzzed. There was a new text from an unknown number.

I told you not to turn off the computer. Do I need to come over and teach you some manners?

A whimper escaped her throat. She grabbed the cordless phone off her desk, loath to touch her cellphone, and called the non-emergency number for the police.

"Police Department, how can I assist you?"

"I--I'm not sure. Someone's stalking me. They've been emailing me, and now they're sending texts. They can see me."

"Slow down. Can they see you right now? Is there someone around the house that you can see?"

"I don't know. He knew what I was wearing to bed the other night. He knew when I was about to turn my computer off just now. I don't know how, but he can see me."

"Do you feel you're in immediate danger?"

"Maybe? I live alone."

"I'll send an officer around to your house. Confirm your address for me, please."

"337 Peace Chimes Drive."

"Okay, an officer will be there as soon as possible. Are you secure?"

"Yes, the doors and windows are locked."

"Good. Do you have any other concerns right now?"

"No."

"I'm going to let you go then, okay? There is no immediate danger. The officer is on his way. Stay inside. Don't answer the door until the officer arrives. You have the right to request he show his badge when he gets there. Call us back if anything else happens."

"Okay. Thank you."

The dispatcher hung up.

The silence became oppressive. It had darkened while she talked on the phone, the last vestiges of light disappearing behind the mountains. She closed the few blinds she'd opened and turned on as many lights as she could, brightening the dim space.

Her phone buzzed again, followed by a series of buzzes. The texts were coming rapid fire, her phone shifting across the desk. She didn't want to look, but she had to.

Did you just call the police?
I saw you on the phone.
They won't be able to find me.
You shouldn't have done that.
This changes our relationship.
I can't trust you anymore.
No more giving you space.
I'm disappointed.

Shaking, she put the phone back on her desk. So he could see her, but not hear her. She attempted to look outside, but with all the lights on, she couldn't see. Someone could be standing directly outside her window, inches from her, separated by a sheet of glass, and she wouldn't be able to see them.

A chill climbed her spine, and she backed away from the window, feeling exposed and vulnerable.

She shut off the lights in the living room, leaving the others on, and peered out of a corner of the window, careful to keep her face along the wall. The moon was a sliver, barely illuminating the street.

Carlos' truck stood in his driveway. Lights shone from his living room window. His silhouette filled one of them for a moment.

She dropped the blinds back into place and turned the lights back on. She stalked into her office, grabbed a roll of black electrical tape from her desk, and taped over the camera on her monitor in case he was watching her from there. In the kitchen, she grabbed a butcher knife, gripping it in her right hand. She took the knife back to the living room, where she settled on the couch and turned on the television. The cop should be here any moment. It felt like it had been an hour since she'd called, but it was probably more like twenty minutes. She took a moment to calm her breathing, which was nearing hyperventilation at this point.

The lock on her front door beeped.

Kim froze and stared at the door.

The knob turned slowly.

She clutched the knife tighter and set the remote down

next to her.

The door pushed inward, catching on the chain lock.

Kim sprang up from the couch, clutching her shirt at her neckline.

The porch light shown through the crack, blocked in places by a shadowy form. An eye peered out of a pale face.

Her entire body shaking, Kim ran to the door and threw her body against it, closing it. She pounded her fist on the door and screamed, "The police are on their way! You need to leave!"

Tears streamed down her face. She stepped back from the door, waiting for what would come next, unwilling to move from that spot. Afraid to breathe.

She didn't know what to do, where to go.

No sound came from outside. The lock didn't beep. The knob didn't move.

Kim eased herself backward and settled on the bottom step, staring at the doorway. Her hand felt sore from her tight hold on the knife, but she refused to loosen or adjust her hold.

A knock sounded at the door, loud and sudden.

She jumped and let out a startled yelp.

The knock came again.

"The police will be here any second!" she yelled.

A muffled voice came through the door. "Police, ma'am."

She didn't trust that it was truly a cop. Her entire body quaking, she stood up and approached the door. "Hold your badge up in front of the peephole."

She pressed her body against the door and peered through the peephole. A metallic flash showed what looked like a badge. "I'm going to open the door on the chain. Hold your badge up again, please."

"Of course."

She touched the handle and hesitated, running through all the possible risks of opening the door. But she finally turned the knob and opened the door to the chain's limit.

A blunt fingered hand with traces of hair on the knuckles held up a shiny badge in a worn black case.

Sighing with relief, she shut the door and sprinted over to the table to put the knife down. It was probably best not to be holding a knife when she let the officer in. When she opened the door, an officer of medium height and broad build stood outside. His hands rested on the bulky belt around his waist. He nodded at her, face serious, but friendly.

"Come on in." She stepped back from the door and opened it wider, closing it behind him. She gestured to the kitchen. "We can sit at the table in there."

He waited for her to lead the way then settled at the table with her. "I understand you have a stalking situation?"

She told him about everything that had happened over the course of the last week. He asked questions, taking notes throughout. He took pictures of the texts and emails with his cell phone and had her forward them to him. He also walked around her house, checking the doors and windows as she had so many times over the past week. When they'd finished, he put the small notebook back into his pocket, pulling out a business card to hand her. It was a crisp white with the PD insignia on it. Officer Chad Bailey.

He gestured at the card. "My cell number is on there, so call me if you have any questions, or if anything else occurs. I'll be looking into that phone number you gave me. If you get any further emails, forward them to me. You can forward the texts to my cellphone, as well. I'd change the code on your lock, too. Do you have somewhere else you can stay tonight?"

"I'm okay to stay here, I think."

"Okay. If anything else occurs, just make sure to call right away. You want me to stay while you change the lock code?"

His offer brought her a measure of relief. She nodded and ran to grab the manual from her office. It took only a couple minutes to find the instructions and change the code. He waited while she tested it, then headed out.

She thanked him, feeling sick to her stomach. At least it was documented that something was going on, but she had been hoping to feel safer after calling this in. Hoping that there'd be a solution, though she knew that was unrealistic. Of course the police couldn't do anything about a few scary texts and emails. Hadn't she said that very thing to Lacy?

Speaking of Lacy, Kim picked up her phone to send her a text. Before she had a chance, her phone buzzed with the notification of another text.

You two looked cozy at the table. How was the coffee?

She jumped up and ran to the door, unlocking the chain and jerking it open. The street stood empty; Officer Bailey had already left.

Buzz.

Your friend's already gone. Now it's just us.

Buzz.

Come upstairs and find me.

She ran out the front door, not bothering to shut it behind her. Her legs pumped as she sprinted to Ned and Deb's. There was only one light on in the house, upstairs toward the back. She pounded as hard as she could, casting looks over her shoulder at her front door, sure that at any moment a figure would emerge and cross toward her. Goosebumps prickled along her flesh.

No one came to the door.

She looked over at her house again. He could have come out while she wasn't looking. Could, at this very moment, be moving toward her through the shadows. Golden light poured over a crooked rectangle of her lawn from the door. A scant amount of light etched its way around the blinds on her front window. Everything else was pitch black.

Her back tingled at the thought of him coming at her, the small hairs on her body standing up. She kicked the door, screaming, "Ned! Deb! Help me!"

Kim turned and put her back against the door, panting. Her chest was on fire from her panicked breaths. He could be anywhere.

She looked toward Carlos's house. His lights were off, but that didn't mean anything. Most of the lights in the neighborhood were off.

Grass rustled nearby.

Staring into the dark, she tried to make out a form, anything. Nothing stood out.

A moan escaped her throat.

She pounded on the door with her foot, afraid to move her body away from its solid surface.

A light turned on, the glow breaking through the darkness to her right, casting the shape of the window on the porch.

Somehow it made the space between her and her front door all the darker.

"Hurry!" she screamed.

A breeze caused the nearby bushes to rustle, the tree branches to sway. The rustling covered up all other sound.

"Please," she whispered.

Tumblers rolled and squeaked. The door opened, spilling her inside at Ned's feet. She scrambled up to her feet and slammed his door, locking it. "Oh my god, I'm so glad you answered. There's a man in my house."

"In your house?"

"Yes. He was sending me messages that he was in my house. I need to call the officer who was just here." She shoved her cellphone in her pocket, afraid he could be watching her through the camera on it. Tracking her via her own phone.

"Why don't you calm down first. You're safe here. Want a shot of whiskey?"

He stood there, the picture of calm, ready for bed in silk pajama pants and a matching belted robe. His hair had been neatly combed, and he smelled of whiskey and cologne.

"Where's Deb?" she asked.

"She's at her mom's. Gloria isn't doing too well right now."

"She didn't say anything about it earlier."

"Call came in this evening. She left straightaway."

"I'm sorry to hear that." She looked through the peephole at the yard, but couldn't make out much of anything. "Listen, can I use your phone to call that cop? I don't want to use my cellphone."

"In a minute. Come in the kitchen with me and I'll go get it." He led her into the kitchen, flipping on the light switch. "Would you at least like some water? Wine? I know you enjoy a bit of wine."

He was acting weird, eerily calm. Like he didn't believe she was telling the truth.

"I'm not kidding about this. There was someone in my house," she said.

"I'm sure there's been a misunderstanding. Want me to go check it out for you?"

"I'd rather call the police."

"Suit yourself." He walked toward the stairs, pausing at the base, one foot on the bottom stair. A blade of grass stood out on his slipper. "I'll be right back with that phone. The one down here's dead. I forgot to put it back on the base earlier." He continued up the stairs, disappearing from her sight.

The piece of grass was odd, but maybe she'd tracked it in and his slipper had picked it up from the carpet. It didn't make sense for it to be on top of his slipper if that were the case, though.

Her phone vibrated with an incoming call. She pulled it out to check the caller ID, which read Bailey.

"Hello?"

"Kim? This is Officer Bailey. Listen, do you know an Edward Swanson?"

Voice quiet, eyes on the stairs where he'd disappeared, she responded. "Yes, why?"

The cellphone that texted you belonged to him. I couldn't investigate it through official channels, but I called in a favor."

She didn't speak, couldn't. All she could do was listen for Ned's returning footsteps over the pounding of her heart.

The officer's voice startled her. "Ma'am?"

She swallowed against her dry throat and whispered, "I'm at his house right now. He's my neighbor."

He'd sounded laid back before, professional. Now there was a hard urgency to his voice. "Get out of there right now. I'm on my way. I'll meet you at your house."

Kim hurried toward the door, quiet on her bare feet. She stopped at the wall next to the staircase and pressed her back to it before peeking around and up. No sign of Ned yet, other than the spill of light from one of the rooms.

She shot across the gap, a chill climbing her spine. She felt exposed, vulnerable, in leaving her back open to the staircase behind her.

With shaking fingers, she fumbled at the locks. The very ones she'd used to lock herself inside this house with the man stalking her. Any moment now, a hand would fall on her shoulder. She could almost feel it coming at her, a buzz of energy across her back.

A stair behind her creaked.

She got the last lock open and threw open the door. It bounced off the wall with a loud crash.

Rapid footsteps sounded from behind her.

Kim leapt forward, foot heading toward the concrete stoop. Her shirt tightened, choking her, and she was stopped in midair. A seam tore, the sound abrupt against the silence of the night.

Her back hit the floor hard, the breath knocked out of her.

Ned stood over her. "What do you think you're doing? I was getting things ready."

Still unable to speak, all she could do was shake her head, mouth gaping open like a fish's.

"I was going to come over. But you messed up my plans tonight. Don't worry. We can still make it work."

Finally, her lungs expanded, allowing her to take a deep breath.

She scrambled backward, running into the back of the sofa. Looking around frantically for a weapon, all she could see was heavy furniture and a couple lamps. She pushed herself up to standing, eyes never leaving his.

He shut the door.

"Why are you doing this, Ned? You and Deb have a great marriage."

"That boring old biddy? I don't think so."

Keep him talking. "But she loves you. I can tell in the way she looks at you."

"I'm not going to discuss this with you. Marriage is a personal issue. Tonight is about you and I." He advanced on her, a wolfish smile on his face, no teeth showing. He undid his belt as he walked toward her, wrapping the ends around each fist with calm purpose.

She yelled, leaping sideways to the lamp. She grabbed it, tried to hold it up over her head.

It stopped short, causing her to stumble. The cord was too short.

She yanked at it, tried to pull it from the wall. Her movements were frantic.

He was upon her then, the belt around her throat, his hands hard against the backs of her shoulders, pulling her backward, choking her.

She couldn't breathe, but she held onto the lamp.

One more yank, and it came free. She thrust it backward, her throat painfully compressed, lungs burning.

He grunted, but didn't loosen the belt.

Her vision darkened, faded, blood roaring through her ears. Using all her remaining strength, she brought the lamp over her head, felt the contact, hard and abrupt. The cord slapped her in the face, a burst of hot pain across her eye.

This time, he let go, the silky material of the belt slithering down her chest. She didn't wait to see where he was, just ran, the lamp still in her hand.

He hadn't locked the door. She threw it open yet again, ran full-tilt, not sure where to go, blind with panic.

She ran into the street.

He roared wordlessly behind her.

The cord flopped around her, tangling around her feet. She dropped the lamp, heard it shatter. Pieces of it pinged painfully off her legs, but she kept running.

Ahead of her, blue and red lights. No siren.

She ran toward it, hands out in front of her.

The car stopped. Officer Bailey got out.

She collapsed at his feet.

~~

"His wife was unconscious in their room. He'd drugged her. We found tiny cameras hidden around your house." Officer Bailey paused for a second, the sound of shuffling papers filtering through the phone. "You said he housesat for you at some point?"

"A few times, yes." Kim cleared her raw throat. "The last time was about a week before the emails started."

"That fits with the timeline of the recordings. He must have installed them then. It would be easy enough for him to do with his previous work experience in security."

Lacy came up behind her, placing a gentle hand on her back. She set a mug of hot chocolate in front of her friend. Not too hot, since her throat was sensitive to the heat still, but warm enough to be soothing. She'd insisted Kim stay at her apartment until the crime scene folks and police told her she could go back to her house.

"Thank you, Officer Bailey. I don't know what would have happened if you hadn't shown up."

"You'd done the hard work. I think you would have been okay. The two hits to his head gave him a concussion. I'm just surprised the lamp didn't break earlier."

"Me, too. But deeply grateful."

"Of course. Well, you have my card if you have any questions."

"Thank you. Bye."

Lacy leaned against the counter across from the table where Kim sat. "So you disabled texting on your phone?"

"Yep."

"Ever going to enable it again?"

"Not a chance. Phones are for talking, not texting."

"Fair enough."

Neither of them said anything for a moment.

Lacy broke the silence. "He seemed like a nice guy the one time I met him. Not pervy at all."

"He had us all fooled, I guess."

"Have you talked to Deb?"

Kim shook her head. "She won't talk to me. I don't know if she's mad or embarrassed. I heard from someone else that she's putting the house on the market."

"I guess that's good news for you."

"Sure. Though I'm tempted to do the same. I just hope they found all the cameras."

"They probably have specialized equipment for that sort of thing. I bet they're all gone."

Kim's phone buzzed, indicating a text. They both stared at it, afraid to look.

It buzzed again.

Kim chucked it into the garbage can. "Nope."

Coffin Birth

The sound of her own blood pulsing inside her ears slows, becomes sluggish.

Her senses dull. The sights blur, the sounds mute, the smells fade. Even the pains lashing her body pull away, becoming background sensations. The taste of her own blood in her mouth, strong, almost unbearable before, sweetens and mellows, floating over her tongue.

She can no longer hear the voices, the raucous cries, the hateful words.

A sensation of weightlessness comes over her. She's gliding, sliding through the air. When she tries to open her eyes, the lashes are gummed together. Cracks of yellow light seep through, but the landscape is invisible. Briefly, a face floats into view. A fleshy blob with no discerning features except for the yawning darkness of a mouth.

Then the baby moves, a rolling flutter at her center, and she remembers why she fought so hard, who she was fighting for.

Her senses come crashing back. All at once it's too much. Agony, terror, sensory overload. The voices are quieter now than they were before. Gruff and low, arguing, panicking. The words they used before—squaw, trash, redskin, whore—have changed now to "the body," "this bitch," and "what do we do?" Anger and hatred to fear and paranoia.

Their hands are rough on her body as they carry her, drop her into the back of a pickup truck, the bed hard and rippling, hurting. A metallic rasp is followed by the slam of the pickup's gate.

Cold. Everything is frigid, from the air to the metal she lies on. It smells of soil, manure, metal. The baby moves again, restless, hungry. Suffocating. He rolls and kicks. Inside his mother, he fights.

Because she has stopped.

Her breath feels like syrup in her lungs. All she wants is to fall asleep, to give into the dark edges that creep in on her.

"Shhh," she whispers, lifting a hand that feels heavy like cement to place it on her roiling belly. "Shhh," she says again. Warm liquid spills onto her lips, her chin, and then she feels nothing.

~~

Upon waking, Rainey feels nothing. No pain, nothing. A person always feels something, like the surface on which they rest or the ambient temperature of the room. She exists in a vacuum of sensation. She attempts to move her hand, but can't tell if anything happens. All is dark, but she can't feel if her eyes are open or closed. The absence of sound, taste, and smell scares her. At least that can be "felt." Even as her fear swells, the comfort of having an emotion calms her. Somehow she perceives both things at once.

Just as she cannot put hands to her belly or discern movement, she senses her baby boy's presence. He's here with her, wherever here is.

Rainey tries to remember what led her here. At first, it's hazy, but the harder she concentrates, the more it comes back to her. At first there's a single voice. She can't quite make out what it says, but she can tell it's a man's voice. It's a higher male voice, more of a tenor than a bass. She ignored it at first, but now she focuses on it, here deep inside her head. He's yelling and laughing, encouraging shouts coming from other male voices.

"Hey there, pretty lady, why don't you come hang out with a real man."

He's behind her, so maybe he can't see her swollen belly from this angle. She keeps walking, hoping he'll take the hint or get bored, leave her alone.

He does neither, though. His voice gets louder, clearer, as he trails her. For now, his friends stay back. His footsteps crunch on the gravel and the scent of cigarette smoke catches up to Rainey.

She speeds up, takes out her phone. The screen pops on, bright in the low light of late evening, and she glances down long enough to enter her password and pull up the recent calls. Here, she selects her boyfriend's name, Stephen, and waits, the phone now to her ear. The ring tone is low, not loud enough to drown out the man's voice.

"Hey, squaw. I'm offering you an opportunity to try white meat. Bet you'll never go back to those long-haired savages you're used to."

The aggression in his voice is ramping up the longer this goes on. Rainey doesn't know what to do. The strip is quiet, no cars passing by. Dark storefronts stare back at her, closed for the night. She's in the middle of a barren strip of road, where there's no one who can help her. She'd just needed oat milk for the morning, the bag now swinging heavy at her side. It hadn't seemed like a big deal to walk to the little grocery store while Stephen was out with the car. This was a fairly safe neighborhood. She'd made the walk a million times with no issues.

They hadn't paid her any attention when she'd walked by, at first. Maybe they hadn't noticed her yet. They were loud, the smell of alcohol and cigarettes drifting on the air in a bubble of odor from them. They stood on the pavement of the parking lot, leaning against a large pickup truck. There was a bar in the strip mall; they'd probably come from there.

The phone continues to ring, finally going to voicemail. She waits for the beep, still walking forward at a fast clip. "Stephen, I need you to come pick me up when you get this. I'm walking home from the grocery store. There are some men. Please hurry."

Rainey ends the call and ponders what to do next. Icy fear pumps through her veins. Her breaths huff out faster than her pace calls for. Her adrenaline has woken the baby, sending him rolling around inside her belly. He lands a solid kick at the height of her stomach. She places the hand with the phone on it to comfort him, or maybe herself. He kicks her hand, but calms after a moment, though she can tell from his small movements that he's still awake.

"Think you're too good for me, you redskin whore? Can't even turn around and answer me?"

His voice is closer now, angrier. She can almost feel the puffs of breath coming from him. The stench of him is suffocating with her pregnancy-heightened sense of smell. She's afraid to turn and look at him, afraid it will spur him forward faster, be the final straw that sets him into motion.

Her street's coming up, but first she has to turn onto a connecting street and walk past a park. She's afraid of that part of the walk. Here, a car might come by. On her street, there will be other houses, people who might hear what's happening and help her. But the park is large and likely empty at this time of night. She should have waited. She could have eaten toast for breakfast instead of cereal. It now feels as if she had a million other choices she could have made.

It strikes her that maybe he'll leave her alone if she turns to show him her belly. That swollen belly had eliminated the male gaze once it grew past a certain point. Men didn't even give up their seats for her the way they'd offered before she was pregnant. They didn't hold doors for her. Her belly had rendered her invisible, and she hadn't minded that anonymity at all except for a bit when her feet hurt or her arms were full. It had taught her a lot about modern society, that was for sure.

She couldn't outrun him. She couldn't overpower him, especially if his friends chose to catch up and help him. These guys rarely went it alone once the action heated up. She'd seen Stephen pay the price of crossing a certain type of drunk white man. Her brothers, too. It was an American past time in some places. But as a woman she'd avoided violence. So far.

Rainey brings her phone back up and dials 911. She doesn't know what else to do.

"Who you calling now, you uppity piece of trash? I just wanted a little of your time. You could be friendlier, you know."

"911, what's your emergency?"

She keeps her voice low. "I'm being followed by a man. He's acting very aggressive."

"Where are you, ma'am? Do you know the man?"

"I don't know him. He's yelling at me. I'm on First, just up the way from the grocery store."

"Can you return to the store?"

"He's between it and me. And his friends are back there."

"Is there another business you can see that's open?"

"No. It's all dark here, just a bunch of closed businesses. I'm almost to Pine and then there will be houses, but no businesses."

"I'm sending a patrol unit your way. Chances are, when he sees a car he'll turn back right away. Do you want me to stay on the phone with you?"

"Yes, please. I'm scared. How close is the car?"

"I'm not sure, ma'am. It will be a few minutes, at least. You could let him know you're on the phone with the police, that we're on the way. That could be enough to scare him off."

"Okay."

Rainey takes a deep breath and stops, turning to face the man for the first time. He wears a ratty t-shirt with a flannel over it, jeans, and work boots. His hair is short, sticking up in the back in sweaty spikes like he's been running his hands through it. The sight of her pregnant belly elicits no reaction whatsoever, telling her he's known the entire time she's pregnant, yet still pursued her. He stops and stares back at her, a cocky grin on his face.

"You ready for a little fun?" he asks.

"I'm on the phone with the police. They're on their way here. You should leave." She waits for his reaction, phone still held up to her ear, breath held. Through the line comes the sound of typing. Other voices speak in the background. The quiet rasp of the operator's breathing rattles over the mic.

His expression doesn't change at first. Then he turns and waves to his friends, gesturing them to come his way. They climb into the truck and start it. When he turns back, he winks. "I doubt they'll get here in time."

"Ma'am, did he leave?" The voice on the phone makes her jump.

"No. His friends are coming with the truck."

He steps closer to her and tries to grab the phone.

She yanks it back from him and swings the cheap plastic bag with the oat milk in it.

The arc isn't sufficient, the milk pulling at it so it doesn't swing well. He easily deflects it, but now his expression changes, his brow furrowing, grin disappearing. He narrows his eyes and this time grabs the hand holding the phone, squeezing hard.

The operator's voice sounds distantly from the speaker. Rainey can't make out what he's saying.

The bones in her hand grind and crunch, and still she holds on against the pain. She knows losing custody of the phone will be the end of her. The phone is her lifeline, her chance at hope. It's the only thing keeping her from being completely isolated out here with this man and his friends.

Her hand gives out before her will, the phone falling to the ground. When the man bends to pick it up, she swings the milk again, this time doing it just right. It hits him across the head and sends him to the ground.

She drops the milk and runs. The truck isn't in the parking lot anymore. If she can get back to the store, maybe beat him there, she can go inside and wait until Stephen gets her message, comes to get her. Or have the clerk call for a cab.

It feels weird to be running with all that weight hanging off the front of her. She braces her belly with both hands and does her best. Behind her, tires squeal.

She's gotten farther from the store than she'd realized. The warm beacon of its lights, even the flickering one, shine out, the puddle of light so far away. Her lungs, already struggling to inflate fully on a normal day, ache and fight her all the way. The baby, at least, is still, probably lulled to sleep by all the motion.

Feet now pound behind her.

Rainey puts everything she has into a burst of speed.

The footsteps get louder, closer.

Headlights cast her shadow before her. The shadow lurches and shortens as the truck pulls up beside her.

The shriek of metal announces the opening of a door.

She leaves the sidewalk, trying to cut diagonally across the gravel and clumps of grass, to cut down the distance.

The ligaments on either side of her belly strain and ache.

Footsteps pound.

Rainey is almost to the outer reach of the parking lot lights. Just a few more steps. She screams.

One set of footsteps stops.

For a split second, Rainey thinks perhaps the pursuit has stopped. That the scream has scared them away.

Then a missile hits her mid-back, snapping her head back. The impact comes from behind her at an angle. Rainey twists just enough to not bear the brunt of the fall on her stomach. She tries to scream, to fight, but there's pain everywhere at once. Blows rain down on her. She kicks, strikes out, but when the blows hit her stomach, she has to protect it, rolling into the fetal position.

The man on top of her yells, but she can't make out what he's saying. Words bounce from his lips in a guttural onslaught. Pure rage pours from him.

Something harder than hands and feet slams into her head, making a sound like two rocks clacking together. She hears it both inside and outside her head, the exterior sound sharper, more like an eggshell cracking. Inside it's a dull thud.

It hits her several more times until she blacks out.

~~

Remembering brings sensation back all at once. It's still dark, but the darkness has a different quality, one that implies the existence of light nearby. She can't smell or taste anything, nor can she hear, but there are too many agonies to focus on.

Underneath it all, Rainey feels something different.

A deep cramping fills her abdomen. It feels as if her entire stomach is a rock, like it's squeezing hard all over at once.

These pains come one after another, picking up speed. There are sharp pains mixed in with the roiling, cramping pain. She remembers her Lamaze training, but when she tries to breathe through it, that's when she realizes she isn't breathing at all.

Rainey exists as nothing but pain.

The urge to push comes. Alone, afraid, she pushes.

As her son slides from her body, the cramping subsides. All the pain disappears.

And then she's floating outside her body, looking down at it. It's beaten and bloody, her head caved in. One eye stares up at her. Her long, dark hair is matted and full of leaves, white fragments, and blood.

Her body lies in some sort of culvert, the limbs twisted where she's been dropped. Between her legs, something moves, twitches.

A baby's cry rises to her ears.

As Rainey watches, a woman walks by. The woman stops, looks around. She moves over to the edge of the culvert and looks down, squinting. Her hand shoots up to her mouth and she's on her phone right away, calling in help.

Rainey hovers as long as she can. When her infant son is picked up by a police officer, swaddled in a jacket he's pulled from his car, she feels a pull she cannot resist. She goes willingly, knowing her baby is safe, the men long gone.

From death, life. Her story goes on.

Coulro-Psycho

My day started out pretty awful, but as it progressed it got increasingly worse until each moment I was in was spent wishing I could go back to the horrors of earlier and spend some time with them, maybe buy them a drink so we could laugh about how minor they'd really been.

It started with a paid gig, which is great on the outside looking in, but something which, in hindsight, I should have gone ahead and turned down. Kid parties suck, but they're what a clown specializes in. And in case that sentence didn't clue you in: I'm a clown.

This particular party was a big one, a bunch of rich kids who were expecting the Avengers, but would instead get, well, me. I admit I'm a bit sloppy, not being an expert at clown makeup and costumery, but I feel I deliver a great goofy magic show, which is really a two-in-one deal. Who needs a magician *and* a clown when they can have them both rolled into one? No one, I always say (as do my ads, which are in random places because I can't afford an actual ad, so I just print them up and stick them wherever I can). I am, however, no competition for superheroes who were supposed to show up in force and do crazy acrobatics and hero-type things. An acrobat or superhero, I am not.

But the Avengers, those absolute pricks, had cancelled at the last minute, leaving little Bruce (notice he was named after the *wrong* superhero team?), his friends, pets, and parents in entertainment limbo for the massive shindig the parents had put together to show off how much they lacked any real creativity and how much money they had to burn. There were door prizes in living animal form, for heaven's sakes! (No, really, each child got to pick a bunny, a parrot, or a kitten to take home at the end of the party. In the meantime, there were different types of droppings everywhere!) Each child also got a gourmet box of chocolates, a fancy step-counting watch and gym membership (so they could work off the chocolates, I suppose), and a remote-control car. I'd be lying if I said I wasn't hoping to make my way out with my own gift bag. The door prizes I could do without. After all, I was barely feeding my own mouth, let alone anything else's.

Yep, that's right, instead of the mighty superheroes a single clown showed up. It was a loss from the beginning. They didn't want magic, they wanted choreographed fights. They didn't want a honking nose, they wanted skintight lycra unitards. From the moment I clomped in with my giant shoes and oversized, polka-dotted jumpsuit with its frilly neckline, thirty children were plotting a coup. The malice in their evil little faces was terrifying. The balloons wobbled with my tremors born of fear as I tried to twist them into exciting shapes. When I did the never-ending handkerchief trick, one of them ran up, grabbed the line of hankies, and ran around me in circles until I fell, trussed up like a champion fatted calf.

Where were the parents, you might ask? Don't bother, because they didn't bother looking up from the never-ending free alcoholic beverages they'd been provided by the host family. The drunker you are, the more impressed, I imagine. Besides which, parents always think their kids are the most precious things and can do no wrong, so they wouldn't have stepped in, anyway.

One of the little creeps, who couldn't have been older than eight or nine, asked me if I dressed up in costumes to hide my sexual repression. How does a kid even know how to ask a thing like that? Another one straight-up asked if I was a pedophile. Then there was the little girl who threw her punch on me, screaming for the other child criminals to do the same. Food was next, and I was absolutely pelted. If I hadn't had a smile drawn on, they surely would have seen how angry I was.

By the time I had finished my last trick, I was sopping wet, dripping icing and ketchup, and saved from the embarrassment of my own tears merely due to the white pancake makeup on my face that hid the tracks so well. When one of the kids picked up a stick and screamed, "You suck!" leading a trail of tiny imbeciles with their own sticks and rocks after me, I escaped into the house, locking the door behind me, only to run into the inevitable mother with coulrophilia. I encounter a few each month when I'm fully booked, and I have yet to find a graceful way to exit if they're the one holding the check. Which she was.

This isn't an x-rated story, so I'll skip what happened next. I will mention, though, that she also apparently had a kink for being covered in food, so my deplorable state was a further turn-on for her.

I did get the check, but she didn't even tip.

Not even a goodie bag.

Because they were ankle biters, my wig and face weren't really messed up, meaning I just had to change my clothing. The shoes were easy to wipe off, a specification I'd learned early on in my clown career needed to be made. Clown shoes cost way too much to have to be replaced often.

For my next gig, my outfit was striped instead of polka dotted. Polka dots are for kids; stripes are for adults. This next one was at an office downtown, which was about a half-hour drive from the rich outskirts of suburbia in which I'd just been tormented. You might think this would lead to an easier time of it, but you'd be wrong. Adult parties are the worst. Luckily, I don't book many of them, as there's not a big call for clowns in the adult space, but this one was from my second business as a clown dancer. Don't judge. It takes all kinds. Plus, it's not that hard to cut apart a costume and add Velcro for easy removal.

I knew I was in trouble when a woman embraced me and yelled, "Bobo smells like fruit punch and sherbet!" before leaping on me. As she attempted to wrap both legs around my midriff, I lost my balance and we both tumbled to the ground. Instantly, I was dogpiled by people in business suits. An errant tie slapped me in the face, followed by a misplaced step sending a spike heel through my scrotum. One inebriated man tore the belt from around his waist and fastened my legs together. What happened after that is unspeakable. I hardly even got to dance.

However, they *did* tip. Score one for the office jerks!

My final gig for the day was supposed to be a simple one. Show up at 10 PM with a box of donuts and a dozen red roses to deliver to a woman who worked late nights with a small crew. It was some sort of warehouse or factory, so I had to be buzzed in by a security guard in a shack out front. He eyeballed me with a grim look as I pulled up, but the person who'd hired me had let security know I'd be coming. With a shake of his head, he opened the gate to let me in, advising me to park in the eastern parking lot and to go through the door there.

As I started to drive forward, he held out a hand and said, "Wait."

"Yeah?" I asked.

He paused, looking unsure whether he should continue or not.

"Well?" I might have been a little unnecessarily abrupt there, but I now smelled like hot dogs, fruit punch, aftershave, and desperation, and I really wanted to deliver the crap that had made my car smell like floral sugar and go home to enjoy a nice, long shower in which I would likely sob while lamenting the shitty financial position I'd gotten myself into. Who wouldn't?

With a raised eyebrow and a deep sigh, he said, "You might want to rethink going in there. The night crew is a bit...off."

"I get paid to deal with people who are off in all the wrong ways, but I appreciate your concern." And I did. I'd walked into some awful situations, and no one had ever warned me before. This was a delightful first.

He simply nodded and waved me through, watching me, unmoving, until I couldn't see him in the rearview anymore.

I parked in the east lot and climbed out. This suit was all silky and covered in zigzags of color. I'd switched my wig out for a miniature hat with a strap under my chin, my bald head painted with the same pancake white as my face. Wigs get itchy fast, and I'd been in one for nine hours by this time. Also, I was kind of concerned about a certain employee at the last gig who looked like she might have had bed bugs or lice or something, and I felt it was safer to leave the wig off for now. I had ways of sanitizing everything at home.

The building was tall, rectangular, and metal, with only a couple windows on what seemed like a second story. Even these were small and probably didn't let in much light during the day. At night it must be truly dismal inside. Grubby light showed through them, but didn't reach the parking lot. A single lamp post flickered on and off as I approached the metal door, a light buzz syncing up with each flash of light.

I knocked on the door with a sharp rap and waited.

The light continued to buzz.

From inside, I thought I heard a scream cut short.

Afraid someone had maybe cut off an appendage, I tried the doorknob. It opened easily, soundlessly. Someone knew how to use WD-40.

There was a small vestibule, with coat hooks hanging all around it, each with a short locker underneath, just about big enough for a purse or something around that size. Precisely five of the hooks held coats. Combination locks hung off some of the lockers, but not all. A single shoe lay on its side in the entryway to the hall. It smelled like musky body spray in the miniscule space.

Cautiously, I stepped forward toward the hallway. "Hello?" I called.

No one answered.

My shoes wheezed as I followed the hallway. There were offices on either side, but they were all closed. Light shone out from under one of them, creating a parallelogram on the concrete floor. The plaque on it read *Operations Manager*. It seemed odd that they'd be here at this time of night, especially with only a skeleton crew, but who was I to judge? Most people didn't expect to see a clown in the evening. Given, most people didn't expect to see a clown at any time of day unless they'd hired them. I thought about knocking, but I'd been given specific instructions, and they didn't include interacting with any of these doors.

Continuing forward, I listened for anymore strange sounds. Frankly, it was too quiet. Shouldn't there be machinery running? Whether they were making things or just packaging them, it seemed like there should be some kind of noise. There was, however, a low hum underneath it all. It raised the hairs on the back of my neck. I actually felt it more than heard it. Even my teeth ached.

There was a door at the end of the hall. It looked to also be metal, with a thin, rectangular window over the doorknob, like the ones at some schools. Dull light shone through, but I couldn't tell if that was the fault of the light or if the window was grungy. I certainly couldn't make anything out through the window as I approached. Then I realized the glass was reinforced with chicken wire or something similar in it, a small grid making visibility low. When I got to the door, it seemed to be vibrating, a secondary hum to go with the first one. I tried peeking through the wiring, but all I could see was maybe a doorway across from this door.

When I pushed this door open, I finally heard some machinery. There were *clicks* and *whirs*, *rattles* and *clonks*. A voice called out, "Mary?" There was what appeared to be a brightly lit break room straight ahead of me, and I went here first, hoping there would be someone there to direct me to where I needed to go. No dice. It looked like someone had just been there, though. There were two cups of coffee—one of them still steaming—on a small, round table with four plastic chairs around it. Half a cruller sat on a napkin, crumbs spilling onto the table. As I neared the table, I realized there was a chair on its side, and another cup of coffee spilled across the taupe carpeting. A fly buzzed around the spill.

Here's where I made the wrong decision. I should have left the donuts and flowers on that table and hiked my happy ass right back out that set of metal doors until I came to my car in the east lot and drove it home. I'd been prepaid for this visit. That's how singing telegrams work. (Listen, don't judge. I had to diversify to make any money). The donuts had the name *Desdemona* written on the box, so surely the right person would get them when she came into the breakroom.

But no, I had to be a nosy creep. Had to make sure no one was hurt. Plus, I depend on referrals for new business (need I mention my pathetic attempts at advertising again?), so my goal was to always deliver what I'd been hired for. In this situation, I had been hired to go down the hall to a machine that would be to my left, where I was supposed to find Desdemona, present her crap, and sing the breakup song. That's right, this was a breakup, complete with a clown, donuts, roses, and a song. Super classy. I hadn't even had the breakup song in the beginning, but there was surprising demand for it, and a fellow's gotta' eat. I was losing an entire chunk of the market until I came up with the clever ditty and slapped it on my website. They usually didn't send a clown, opting for other costume choices, but this person had specifically wanted one for this delivery.

Clutching the box and roses in my hands, I stood in the doorway of the breakroom and looked both ways. I was supposed to have turned right when I came through the door with the chicken wire. To the right of where I now stood, there was a pitch-black corridor, light only leaking as far as the bulb centered in front of the two doors. The light and sounds of machinery came from my left.

A shadow crossed the chicken wire window, causing me to jump. I waited, breath held, to see if anyone would open the door. My eyes fell to the doorknob, hoping it wouldn't turn.

Someone shouted in the direction of the machinery.

My heart pounded so hard I could feel it in my temples.

It was days like this I wished for a diaper or some kind of catheter to get through my shifts. Because right now, I was barely keeping urine in my bladder. The last thing I needed was to add bodily smells to the odd bouquet I'd earned myself today. I cinched up every sphincter I could control and headed left, glancing back repeatedly to make sure no one could sneak up on me. The door never opened, not that I saw, anyway.

The machinery got louder as I proceeded. I knew from my instructions that the ceiling would open up from the claustrophobic one I walked under right now, and that I'd find myself in a vast room. During the day it was a hive of activity, but at night they focused on a few specific things, corralling themselves in one small area.

Sure enough, the room opened up just ahead. I could make out monstrous metal machines, most of them still. The ones that ran all seemed to be to the left, which was exactly where I'd been told to turn. But when I stepped out into the larger area and turned left, there was no one there. Instead, I saw a pair of high heels, a smear of blood, and a single barrette with a clump of hair in it.

"Nope." This was too much. If someone was hurt, they wouldn't have gone farther into the factory. They would have headed toward the breakroom where I'd seen a First Aid kit prominently displayed over the sink. Or to the manager's office.

I turned to leave, but not before setting the flowers and donuts next to the heels, which I assumed to be Desdemona's.

Only...now there was someone standing in the hall I'd just exited.

They were on the other side of the breakroom doorway, which meant they stood in mostly shadows. But they were there. I saw what looked to be a pair of jeans-clad legs leading down to cowboy boots. A pale face emerged from the shadows, crazed eyes fixed on me.

I backed away.

"H-hello? I just have a delivery."

The person went from complete stillness to a headlong rush toward me. He opened his mouth wide and yelled the whole way. In his hands, he gripped an axe.

I turned and ran for my life. There had to be other people in here. If nothing else, there must surely be hiding places. I'd seen five coats. Assuming one belonged to this guy, there were four more people hiding somewhere in this building. Plus or minus a manager, who might have had their coat in their office. This could, of course, *be* the manager, but I was trying not to make too many assumptions. Assumptions didn't just make asses out of people, they also led to assassinations.

The bottles being filled on a conveyor belt to my left had gone cockeyed, with a bunch of them bunching up and splats of liquid on the belt instead of in the bottles. They clinked against each other as I ran full out, my shoes now full-bore squeaking with each step. Behind me, the dude still roared, his boots slapping against the concrete.

I veered off to the right, afraid to hide in moving machinery. If I could find someplace to climb in when I was out of view, he'd surely pass right by me.

Only he seemed to be gaining on me.

These shoes simply weren't meant for running.

I tried to think of a solution, but they were tightly velcroed to my feet. They often got stepped on, sat on, even pulled at, and I needed to ensure they stayed on. Thus, there were a bunch of complicated laces and bits of Velcro that I had to fasten each day when I put them on. Instead, I put everything I had into a burst of energy that propelled me faster for a few glorious, hopeful moments until my energy flagged, having been used up by the day that had come before. As I petered out, I once more turned, this time into a clump of machines that looked big enough to hide a clown with questionable choice in footwear.

I slammed into a man with a green vest, who took one look at my face and screamed, running the other way. I screamed with him and chased him, certain he must know how to get away from the psycho on our tails. He looked back at me in pure panic and ran faster.

"Wait for me!" I yelled, huffing and puffing to keep up.

Now there were screaming men in front of and behind me, and every time I stopped concentrating on keeping my mouth shut, I started screaming. My scream wasn't a flattering one; it was high-pitched and definitely not manly, but who needed to be manly in situations like this? I just needed to be able to run faster than this guy so he could get the axe.

He led me on a merry chase, threading through various machines, the axe-bearing psycho hot on our heels, until he came to a doorway. I was completely turned around, with no idea where in the factory I was. He opened the door and ran through, much to my relief. I was certain it would have been locked. I put my head down, pumping my legs and arms, and ran full-tilt toward that beacon of safety.

Only to slam directly into it when he slammed it in my face. I heard the lock click.

"Let me in!"

"Get lost, clown!"

Now that hurt, but I didn't have time to dwell. Besides, I *was* a clown.

I turned, flattening my back against the door. My eyes darted around as I tried to determine where to go, how to escape. He was so fast, and these precious seconds had used up any time I had to get out of range of that axe. I closed my eyes and waited.

When no blow came, I opened them back up. He stood maybe two feet away, axe held high. His stare was intense, chest heaving as much as mine. Then he said something that confused me. "I called the police. They're on their way."

"Great," I said.

He looked puzzled, face all scrunched up, which only confused me more.

"They'll be here any minute," he said.

"Fabulous. Maybe the guard will come, too."

"What?"

"What?"

"You won't get to kill anyone else, you freak!" Again with the hurtful remarks.

"For your information, I haven't killed anyone, and I assure you there were plenty of people who deserved it today. Even some kids that could have used the business end of a bazooka."

A woman in a red sweater walked up behind him. Her pace was slow, bare feet silent on the floor. She smiled in this really strange way, chin tilted down, eyes looking up at me. A clump of hair stood straight up, and I could see a small, bloody, bald patch on her head. She had one hand behind her back, the other held out in a weird, dainty way, palm flat toward the ground, wrist bent.

The axe wielder called out without removing his eyes from me. "Mary?"

With a set of smooth motions, she slipped up behind him, revealed the hidden hand and the knife within it, and slid it across his throat. It took a second for the blood to well out of the cut, but then it quickly became a torrent. Some sprayed toward me, hot against my cheek and chest.

He dropped the axe and clapped both hands to his throat. His mouth gaped, opening and closing, but no sound came out. When he turned to look at her, I rushed forward, picked up the axe, then took off. I imagine you're wondering why I didn't immediately put that axe through her head. Let me ask you this, would you be able to do that? Just axe someone in the head? Also, she was behind the guy, and there was no clear shot, so attribute it to whatever you want, but I wanted out of there. Maybe I could find my way back to the front. I just needed to follow the sound of the machinery.

Only the machinery now squealed, and the sounds bounced off all the hard surfaces. It was hard to hear where I needed to go without stopping to get my bearings, but there was no way in hell I was going to stop. I couldn't hear her behind me, but I had to assume she'd followed me.

I risked a glance back and promptly tripped over my ridiculous shoes. I smacked the ground and pushed myself up right away, but my right shoe had busted just past where my toes reached, and now I ran with a *squeak-slap* that required high stepping in order to get the whole floppy toe of the giant shoe ahead so I didn't step on it when my foot came down.

As I zipped around another hunk of machinery with unknown usage, I saw a woman peek out from behind a wall up ahead. She quickly pulled her head back, and I heard footsteps running away. "Hey!" I yelled. "Wait! Is there another exit?"

Running faster, I darted around the corner and stopped immediately. She had her back against a door. There was no window in this one, and it appeared to be chained shut. Her eyes were so big I could see the whites all the way around. In her hand, she clutched some sort of metal bar or rod. "Stay back!" she yelled.

"I'm not going to hurt you. I just want out."

"That's what a killer would say."

"I didn't kill anyone. You have to believe me! I don't know how to get back to the front door. Some woman just killed a guy with cowboy boots back there. I think he said the name Mary?"

Her face paled. "I'm Mary."

"Oh. Huh. People keep calling your name." I pondered for a moment, replaying that moment in my head. I tried to stop before we got to the cut and the squirting blood, but I failed. "Well, he didn't actually look at her, so maybe he thought it was you coming up behind him. Anyway, how do we get out?"

Without turning, she reached behind her and rattled the door, but the chains held fast. Tears ran down her cheeks. She sobbed loudly. "Why are you playing with me this way?"

"Playing with you? Are you kidding me? What are you talking about?"

Her face changed, and she seemed to become angry, mouth flattening into a straighter line, eyes narrowing. "You're not a killer, huh?"

"No!"

"Then why are you holding an axe?"

Oh, yeah. I'd forgotten I wielded an axe like some kind of

psycho clown. I lowered it, but there was absolutely no way I was putting down the only weapon I had. "I picked this up after the cowboy boot guy dropped it. You know...after..."

"And I'm just supposed to believe you?"

This conversation was going nowhere, and the longer I stood there arguing with her, the more time the actual psycho would have to catch up to us. I let out a giant sigh I'd been holding in and tried one more time. "If I wanted to kill you, I could have already run at you and taken you out with the axe."

She straightened and held up the rod. "Well, I've got this. Maybe you're afraid I'll hit you."

"I'm definitely afraid you'll hit me, but I'm way more scared of the woman with the knife." I sighed again, shoulders drooping. "Listen, how do I get out of here. If you just tell me where to go, I'll leave and we can split up. Though I think it would be smarter for us to go together so we have twice the chance of seeing her and fighting her off. After all, our weapons are bigger than a knife."

Mary looked at me a moment, and I could practically see the gears turning. Finally, she said, "If you go back out the way you came, turn left to continue in the direction you came from, then turn right at the machine with the red handle, and right again at the machine right after that one, you'll have a fairly straight shot at the main hallway."

"What about you?" I asked.

"I don't know you. There's no way I can trust it's not you, though you made some good points. So I'm not telling you my plan."

With a shrug, I called, "Fair enough!" and turned to go back the way I'd come, just as she'd instructed. I turned left, then seeing the red handle, turned right. Before I got to the next machine, a set of footsteps came from behind me. I panicked, afraid to turn to see who it was. Was it the knife woman or the rod woman? Either one could be trouble. For all I knew, they were working together, and *she'd* actually been toying with *me* when she asked me that question. I ran the best I could with my stupid, floppy shoe and braced for impact.

Mary raced past me, her shoes not an impedance. She rounded the next machine, heading right just as she'd told me.

"Hey, what are you doing?"

She turned her head just enough to shout over her shoulder, "I figured if you walked away instead of coming for me, you weren't the killer. Let's get out of here."

Sounded good to me, and follow I did. It had started to smell of smoke in the factory, and the squeak of the machinery had turned into a horrible ratcheting sound. Glass shattered on the ground up ahead. I could finally see that original machine I'd passed, but we still had the length of a swimming pool to get to the hallway leading to the breakroom and exit door.

Behind me, more footsteps.

Shit!

There was no way I could outrun Mary so the killer would get her, so I just had to stay ahead of the killer and hope for the best. Maybe the security guard would do his rounds. But as I thought of my brilliant escape plan, I once more tripped on the shoe and biffed it. I almost fell on the axe, but managed to throw myself to the other side and hold that arm out. Trying to get around the axe meant I hadn't fallen right, and I hit hard. (Still better than falling on an axe, but oof!)

The air was knocked out of me, the footsteps gaining, and Mary was long gone. Safety in numbers only counted if you were the fastest.

I stood again, stumbling, and righted myself. The footsteps were close.

I turned to face my attacker.

And it turned out to be that dick with the green vest who locked me out with the killer. "You!" I yelled, jutting a finger in his general direction.

He froze and stared at me. "You killed Ken!"

I stomped my foot in frustration, the floppy toe bouncing up and slapping again for emphasis. "The hell I did! You locked me out with a psychopath woman in a red shirt."

His head tilted the way a confused dog's will. "Are you sure you're not the one who killed Ken?"

"Damn sure."

"A red shirt, you say?"

"That's exactly what I said." Frankly, I didn't care if Green Vest believed me. He'd pissed me off.

"Desdemona was wearing a red shirt."

"Desdemona? That's the person I was supposed to deliver breakup donuts to."

"What kind of donuts?"

"Breaku—listen, let's have this discussion later. I'm going to follow Mary and get out of here."

Given, Mary was long out of sight. I knew where I was now, though, and I took off, high stepping like I'd landed on the moon. Green Vest gained on me, but I'd long since become used to the fact that anyone could outrun me. Next time I stopped to talk to someone, I definitely needed to try to get that shoe off.

The machine was completely backed up now, glass bottles having stacked against each other. They rattled, some shattering right there on the belt, others falling off like the ones I'd seen before. Smoke poured out from under the entire apparatus. It looked like it was going to blow, which would send glass and metal shrapnel everywhere. Somehow that sounded worse than being stabbed. I sped past the volatile chaos and into the hall.

And there was Mary. She stood in the hallway, partially in the breakroom entryway. Creepily, she just stared at us as we approached. "Let's get out of here!" I yelled, unsure what she was doing.

She took a step forward, stumbled, tried to right herself, then fell face-first onto the floor. The long-stemmed roses I'd brought had been shoved into her back one at a time like she was a pincushion, a donut ringing each one.

"This is why you don't split up, Mary!" I screamed, almost completely irrational at this point.

I veered toward the door that would lead me outside, terrified that Desdemona would lurch out of the darkened hallway at any moment. Grasping the knob, I turned, not really expecting it to open. Yet open it did, and I popped through into the hallway. The light was still on in the office, so I opened the door to warn whoever was in there that a psycho was on the loose.

In the middle of the room, there stood a desk. Behind that desk, sat a balding man, "Terminated" stamped on his shiny forehead in red ink. His face had been covered in staples and thumbtacks. His hands had been affixed to the desk by pencils, and two red pens jutted out of his ears. I screamed that high-pitched scream again and leapt backward, slamming into a warm body. This time I choked on the scream and tumbled sideways, big, red shoes up in the air as I hit the ground.

Green Vest stood there in the doorway, staring at the guy behind the desk. "Gary?" he asked.

"Gary's dead, man."

He helped me to standing and we exited the room, easing the door shut out of some misguided form of politeness. The entry was darker than it had been when I'd come in, so we both approached with trepidation. I still had the axe—which I had not fallen on the second time either—but he didn't have a weapon of any sort. I held the axe with two hands and approached the entryway where the coats had hung. Five coats. One for Mary, one for Desdemona, one for Gary, one for Ken, and one for Green Vest, whose name I still didn't know.

"What's your name?" I asked. It felt important to know.

"Matt."

"Hey, Matt, I'm Bob, but people call me Bobo when I'm in this getup."

"Bobo, let's get the hell out of here."

I couldn't have said it better myself.

I hesitated on the threshold of the coatroom, afraid to step out in case she was waiting for us there. There was a pretty good view of the room, despite the darkness, and there didn't appear to be anyone standing there. I crept to the front door. Just as my hand fell on the doorknob, a coat off to my right rustled.

Terror crept up my spine. My mouth opened in a rictus, all moisture instantly evaporating.

One of the coats shifted. A foot descended from the top of the short locker.

The coat dropped.

There stood Desdemona, the notorious woman in red. If this was how she behaved, it was no wonder she'd been sent an anonymous clown to break up with her.

Matt shoved up against me and yelled, "Open it! Open it!"

I turned the knob, but it wouldn't give.

Desdemona did that creepy down-tilted chin thing again

and approached us slowly, like Mike Meyers, but somehow worse. She held the rod Mary had been wielding. Then in two liquid steps she moved forward and thrust the rod straight through Matt's rib cage. The end popped out on my side, scraping along my own ribs, but not entering them.

Matt sunk to the ground.

I screamed and worked at the doorknob again.

"Sing me the song," she said.

"What song?" My voice was high and hysterical.

"You know the one. The one you were sent by Gary to sing to me."

The dots connected. It *had* been a Gary who'd hired me.

Slowly, I turned to face her full on, realizing I didn't have much choice. She'd maneuvered so she stood between me and the hallway. Reaching into the pocket of her jeans, she held up the knife she'd killed Ken with.

I took a deep breath and began:

"This is your breakup call, your little wakeup call.
It's time we end this thing, because it's lost its zing.
That's right we're done for good; I hope it's understood,
You're not the one for me: such instability.
Goodbye my ball and chain, let's never meet again."

She stood there in silence a moment, brows drawn together. Then she laughed. It started as a chuckle, but grew into a belly laugh. She even clutched her stomach and leaned over.

I reached behind me and tried the knob again. This time it turned.

Excitedly, I turned to the door and pulled with all my might. It started to open, and I was just shifting to get my body around it, when the laugh turned into a scream. I glanced her way. She lifted the knife above her head and ran at me.

Without thinking, I hefted the axe and slammed it into her chest. I probably should have gone with the brain, but it wasn't like she was a zombie or anything. Surely a chest blow with an axe would be enough to disable her. She sunk to the floor just as poor Matt had.

I didn't wait to see if it had worked, instead pulling the door open the rest of the way and dashing outside.

There was some grunting, then the scream started again,

along with heavy, clumsy footsteps.

I fumbled in my pocket for my car keys but couldn't find them. Instead, I veered to my right and ran for the security shack. If I had to, I would run all the way home. Only, when I got to the shack, it was empty. The gate was shut. I grasped the bars and shook them, to no avail. Once more, in what had been a long, long day, I turned to face the onslaught, my back against the bars.

Desdemona limped toward me. The axe stuck out of her chest, dark blood welling around it. She still held the knife.

I looked for somewhere, anywhere, that I could run to get away. My body was giving up, exhausted from a crazy day. The adrenaline had stopped surging. My side stung where the rod had scraped along it.

"You think you're funny?" she asked. "Do you enjoy delivering messages like that one? I'll have you know that I was beautiful once, valued. Gary said he loved me. What a liar. He promised me we'd do amazing things together. All we did was work and have sex. I cooked for him, cleaned up after him, gave myself to him. And what did that piece of shit do in return? Send a clown, one of my greatest fears, to dump me. With donuts. He knew I was diabetic!" This last part she shrieked at full volume, face blood-red. "I gave up my best years for him, only to—"

An engine roared, and the next thing I knew a black sedan with an emblem on the side flew out of nowhere and slammed into Desdemona. She flew up over the hood and slammed into the windshield, headfirst. The knife flew from her hand, and she went still, head flopping backward on a broken neck.

The security guard climbed out of the car, mouth agape, eyes wide. "Shit, man! Is that an axe?"

"Yeah."

"Did you do that?"

"Yeah."

"Don't you know you *always* double-tap?"

I sunk to the ground, back still against the bars. "Yeah."

"Man, I told you not to go in there. The night people are crazy."

"The night people are all dead."

An explosion rang out. Fire alarms sounded. Smoke crawled out of the front door and rose into the air.

"You've got a crazy job," the guard said.

"Not anymore. I quit. This clown thing is for the birds."

Hork

The raspy *hork* echoed off the walls, causing my heartbeat to surge. Sweat popped out on my palms and forehead, and I leapt up from my food-encrusted easy chair, stocking feet hitting the carpet. I slid as my socks came into contact with the scuffed kitchen hardwood floor, but caught my balance just in time to glide around the corner, my senses on high alert.

Where had it come from? I paused, trying to hear over my heart pounding in my throat. My entire body pulsed.

Hucka, hucka, wheeeeeze, hork.

Oh, shit.

The sound had come from my left. I ran like I'd never run before, heedless of my safety in the dangerous maze of the dining room, dodging chairs left and right with desperation born of experience. My little toe made contact with a chair leg and bugled pain up the nerves of my foot and ankle.

On soft, padded paws, the culprit walked by me, holding her tail disdainfully in the air. She didn't so much as acknowledge my presence. Instead, she came to a stop by her food dish and preened, tongue rasping through her fur, still ignoring me.

"Real nice, Sasquatch."

I scurried around the room, seeking the offensive pile of hair, vomit, and bile. It had to be here somewhere. The sound she'd produced was not one that left a dry, clean floor in its wake. Any second now, I'd feel the warm, wet, chunky squish of cat vomit between my toes, soaking my sock faster than a sponge in a rain puddle. I steeled my stomach for the inevitable task of soaking up hot bodily fluids with a paltry paper towel. This time I wouldn't gag.

But as I searched, confusion rattled me, and I grew dizzy with panic and puzzlement. No vomit under the chairs or the table, on the cat tree, or on top of the table. The plants appeared safe. Nothing stood out on the stairs. Grimacing, I bent down and felt along the carpeting that lined the steps, waiting for the thick fluidity of the bile to web its way between my fingers.

Still nothing.

Did she swallow it back down?

A whiff of cat-vomit smell, that raw mix of fish and intestines, drifted by, but disappeared before I could follow it to the guilty pile.

I turned and shot a glare at the stupid, majestic beast. Her charcoal-colored fur shone smooth and velvety in the light streaming through the dining room windows. She glanced at me once then proceeded to eat daintily from her dish. The gentle crunch of her teeth sinking through the pellets sent the odor of meat and whatever else cat food contained drifting around the room, gradually replacing the foul stench of her horks and hairball-fueled vomiting.

After looking around one last time, I returned to my chair and restarted my TV show where I'd left off. My heart returned to a normal pace, and my breath calmed.

False alarm.

Damn cat.

From the next room came the delicate lapping of water then her clicking claws on the wood, and she leapt up onto the back of my chair, causing it to shift slightly under her weight. Her purrs vibrated through the thick cloth, and she butted my head with hers, urging me to pet her. I massaged her head and scratched her neck until she'd had enough, at which point she nipped my hand and jumped off the chair, disappearing to nap elsewhere in private. Fed, watered, and petted, she wouldn't show herself again for hours.

Or so I thought.

About twenty minutes later, I heard her approaching. She sounded weird, almost like she was rolling across the floor. And the liquid *sploot* sounding intermittently told me she'd somehow gotten wet. Sometimes she drank from the toilet, but she'd never fallen in. Then again, as graceful as cats were supposed to be, I'd seen this little diva slip and trip in a variety of ways, always standing up immediately and acting like she'd meant to do it.

More concerned about the mess she must be making than her state of wetness, I stood up, but only halfheartedly. My eyes remained on the television screen, where experts discussed a famous serial killer and his methods. Horrified, yet fascinated, I couldn't take my eyes off the crime scene photos that flashed between snippets of talk. The things a person could do with a can opener and a hairbrush were absolutely terrifying and disturbing.

I stepped in something wet and went ass over teakettle, right foot flying into the air, left foot sliding backward. I landed in a split and pain tore up my legs, radiating out along my thighs. Adding insult to injury, the goo on the floor was soaking through my jeans.

I groaned, gripping my groin and rolling to the side to put both legs in front of me. Studying the moisture, I discovered it was a slime trail, grotesque in its viscosity. It looked like something Slimer would have left behind, only yellow and brown instead of green. Mixed into the slime were chunks of what appeared to be cat food, along with elongated rolls of charcoal-gray fur.

No healthy cat could possibly produce this much stomach purge and still be okay. Maybe she'd eaten something bad. I looked around for her, but she wasn't in the room. My fall must have scared her off, though I'd been too busy shrieking profanity to hear her scamper away.

Wincing, I stood up. The cold air hit my sopping wet crotch, and I shuddered at the unpleasant sensation that dripped down my legs. I limped around the room, peeking under the end tables, but Sasquatch was nowhere to be found. Tracking along the same path I'd followed earlier when seeking the furball, I checked every nook and cranny, careful to avoid the slime trail.

When I got to the cat tree, a muffled *merowp* sounded from within. A peek inside revealed one curious, half-lidded amber eye. She unfurled herself, came partway out of the hidey-hole, and stretched as far as she could, ears pulling back with the intensity of the movement. Then she yawned, turned around, and retreated into the hole, her back to me.

Reaching in, I touched the fur on her back then petted along her spine down to the tip of her tail. A quick scritch of her head and shoulders left her purring, but gave no evidence of slime or vomit. I rubbed her chest and scratched just beneath her chin. The purring stopped when I pushed forward and ran a hand over her belly. The energy she saved from not purring instantly transferred to her tail, which whipped around in irritation. It was amazing how much ire a cat could express with one part of the body, a tail dancing around like an irate cobra.

I straightened. Huh. She seemed fine, and her fur was dry. Not even a trace of dampness on her chin. The cat tree was also dry.

As I stood there, something else dawned on me. The slime trail hadn't even gone to the tree. How had I not noticed that before? Instead, it diverted around the kitchen table and into the bathroom.

I hadn't checked there for the hairball.

Tiptoeing around the sludge path, I approached the bathroom door. It stood slightly ajar. A ray of light fell through the crack, casting a narrow beam of illumination across the sink and cabinet and leaving the rest of the bathroom in shadow. The slime trail disappeared under the door. It wouldn't be the first time Sasquatch shut a door. But for this scenario to happen, she'd have had to vomit on the way in, nudge the door mostly closed, then manage to squeeze out through the crack. Even the most agile of felines—and agile, she wasn't—would have trouble pulling that off. Also her paws should have gotten wet. And in fact, there were no wet pawprints at all, in either direction.

Something had made this trail, and I didn't think it was Sasquatch.

Standing as far back as possible while still within reach of the door, I used two fingers to push at it. The cheap wood caught on a bundle of cat fur dreadlock, so I gave it another shove and the door swung open. This allowed more light in, but I still saw nothing other than the sludge. Once more I reached out, this time to turn on the light. My hand moved out of my sight, groping in the air for the switch. I leaned in farther, shoulder now inside the doorway, arm extended as far as it would go.

Goosebumps crawled up my arm.

As I flipped the switch, something soft and dry touched my

skin.

I jerked my arm back, expecting... well, I don't know what I expected.

That was when I looked down and got my first glimpse of the horrid cat sploot on the bathroom floor—if indeed the throw-up had originated from inside a cat. It was the foulest thing I'd ever seen. Oozing across the tiles were half-digested cat food pellets in a thick, slimy bile that looked like squashed jellyfish, only yellow, and a thin bit of red string. Plus what appeared to be blood. Fear for Sasquatch resurged, but the stupid cat had been fine and in her hidey-hole just a moment earlier.

On a whim, I stepped into the bathroom, careful to avoid the gut-splosion, and followed the stream of semi-fluids that disappeared behind the toilet. Furred strands of something lay beside the mostly white porcelain of the toilet pedestal. I squinted to make out what exactly lurked behind the toilet tank, in that shadowy crevice rarely touched by hands or sponges.

I leaned closer.

A gray-furred tendril shot out and wrapped itself around my leg.

Another one came for my face, dripping even as it flew through the air.

I threw myself backward and my head and shoulder slammed into the wall. The appendage just missed my face with a wet splat and rebounded. Bits of caustic stomach juice splashed onto my cheek. At the same time, something wet and heavy landed on the floor, sending out a wave of putrid cat-gut-rot stench in its wake. A large mass emerged from behind the toilet. Multiple furred filaments spidered out from its center. It was using its hold on my leg to pull itself toward me.

I turned to run, yanking at the trapped leg. There was a small amount of give, but not enough. I grabbed the door frame and tried to haul myself out. Disgust filled me as the moisture from the clinging appendage seeped through my jeans to my skin, a sick warmth added to the already cold dampness.

Another tendril snared my thigh. Now both legs were caught. I pulled with all my might, but couldn't breach the doorway. The protrusions continued to seek out my body and limbs, twining around my torso, legs, and arms. The granddaddy of all fur-tendrils reached my throat, and the strong smell of damp cat food and stagnant intestinal juices hit me. The cold, wet strand felt like a thick band of steel wool. I couldn't move my arms to pull at it or try to loosen it.

To my horror, the coils maneuvered my body, turning me against my will, stocking feet easily sliding around on the linoleum. My gaze fell on the mirror, my reflection revealing what looked like a steel wool-encased mummy. Only my face was free.

A loop shot around my forehead. Viscous fluids leaked down into my eyes, causing them to burn. I blinked frantically to clear my vision, but the world only blurred more. The tendril pulled my head forward so that I was forced to look down to the floor and the amorphous blob that awaited me—a matted mess of fur and smooshed-together chunks of cat food, plus what might have been a bit of intestine.

The creature squelched with every movement, a thick, wet sound that made me want to vomit. Only fear of my own puke becoming animated like this glorified hairball kept my gorge at bay.

As I tried to focus on the vomit monster, from the corner of my eye I made out another approaching tendril. This one came for me with slow, dreadful purpose.

It inched forward.

It touched my mouth.

The combination of vomit odor and the sensation of slime against my lips caused my gorge to rise again. I clamped down my jaw and squeezed my lips together with all my might.

Unfazed, the creature used the tip of the tendril to pry at my lips. I gagged and murbled out a close-mouthed yell that turned into a scream that vibrated up through my sinuses. It continued to wriggle against my lips, a sensation that defied explanation, like being tickled with a gelatin-coated hair sponge, but grosser. It smelled like cat breath magnified a thousand times. My nasal passages burned.

I fought to keep my mouth closed, but the creature pried its way in. Like a soggy, slimy invading army, its tendril staunchly marched across my tongue and down my throat, suffocating me even as the flavor of rotten cat food and the intense acidic taste of stomach acid coated my taste buds. Tears flooded from my eyes, clearing some of the glutinous muck from my vision.

Fully down my throat now, the appendage expanded inside my intestines. I felt like my guts would explode. By some miracle, I freed a hand from the matted cat fur and grabbed the clammy, mucus-coated tendril, pulling as hard as I could. But my hand kept slipping, lubricated by the abominable goo, and the tendril continued burrowing deeper into my body.

I strained against my binds, struggling to breathe past the thing blocking my airway. It abraded my mouth, lips, and chin. My panic ramped up, causing my heart to pound all the harder. I had no idea how this thing had come to be, but knowing its origin wouldn't matter if it killed me.

My other hand broke free, and I grasped the tendril with both fists now, squeezing as hard as I could to keep my grip. Smaller filaments wrapped around my wrists and yanked, but I resisted their efforts, determined to save my life and pull this putrid thing out of my body.

A *merowp* sounded from somewhere below.

Sasquatch rubbed against my leg, headbutting it. I tried to make a sound of warning, but couldn't. I felt several more rubs, then Sasquatch let out a questioning burr. *Yes, you dumb cat, your hairball is killing me.*

Then came the unmistakable sound of her eating.

Had a tendril not already been feeling around in my digestive system, I surely would have barfed.

Blocking out, to the best of my ability, the sounds of Sasquatch's gobbling—wanting but not wanting to know if she was, oh god, consuming the monster hairball—I made progress, slowly pulling the abomination out of my mouth. I could feel it scratching its way up inside my chest now, free of my stomach. My nose ran with my own mucus mingled with hairball ooze. It felt as if I were breathing through liquid, blowing bubbles through my nostrils. Any second now I would suffocate. All while my cat ate her own sentient vomit.

I fell to my knees, barely feeling the wet squish as I landed on some portion of the creature. I could feel myself weakening. The monstrosity took advantage of my slackening grip and renewed its journey into my intestines.

Closing my eyes, I gathered the last of my strength and pulled, working the tendril, hand over hand. No way in hell would I die this way.

It came all the way up, the tip tickling its way past my tonsils before gliding out of my mouth. I threw it down with a splat and flailed at the abhorrent entity, kicking it aside and writhing to get away. Sasquatch made a disgruntled chirp and scampered off. The cabinet below the sink was just within reach. I flung open the door and pulled out the bleach and enzyme cleaner. Tendrils grabbed for the smooth bottles, but failed to find purchase. I managed to pop the top off of each and douse the hairball with the two liquids.

The protuberances withdrew immediately. Still holding the bottles, I struggled to my feet and drenched every bit of the creature I could get to. It writhed and shook, arching away from me. Emptying first one bottle, then the other, I threw them down and scrambled into the hallway, slamming the door shut and leaving the thing to dissolve in silence on the other side.

Sliding down the wall, I swiped at my eyes, getting the last of the goo out of them. Sasquatch sat in the hallway, grooming herself, her giant eyes fixed on me in silent threat.

"Oh, no you don't." My voice came out in a rasp, throat aching at the effort. I stood up and grabbed her, running to the back door to toss her gently onto the porch. "Go eat some grass and throw up *outside*. Then maybe I'll let you back in."

I limped to the kitchen sink to wash my mouth out with soap, then swallowed down a bunch of vinegar. It stung, which gave me a certain sense of peace. I'd have swallowed bleach if it wouldn't kill me, but vinegar would have to do. Every trace of that thing must be eradicated.

Through the screen door, I heard Sasquatch.

Horka, horka, horka, blap.

When the Leaves Quiver

Sonora studied the coastline as their boat sped toward the dock. Tall, lush trees seemed to cover the entire island in a variety of greens and blacks that moved in ripples against the sea breeze. Their speed lent a coolness to the hot summer air, the mist blowing off the water a sweet relief against the burn of the sun.

"Land ahoy!" yelled Lou, one hand firmly on the throttle, the other steering the boat. His bald head gleamed bright red. Sweat soaked the back of his shirt in an elongated triangle.

"We all see the land, Lou. You don't have to announce it." Rusty swept soggy hair out of his face, tucking it beneath his wide-brimmed hat. Then he took his glasses off and cleaned them on his shirt.

"Just wanted to be sure you didn't miss it with those squinchy eyes a' yours."

Sonora laughed and shook her head. So far, they'd been on three planes, a bus, and now this boat together. The guys were somewhere at the intersection of amused by each other and ready to slit each other's throats. Sonora had mostly kept to herself, writing about the journey so far and postulating about what they'd find on the island. The local government had banned travel here. Whether that ban came before or after tales of a murderous demon inhabiting it, she wasn't sure.

Their interest lay in the fauna said to be on the island. Rare creatures were rumored to live here, kept safe by the demon. Most stories like this were based on a hint of truth, which meant there was probably something to discover, as well as some sort of predator that had scared away the people. Frequently, governments blew these things up to keep a safe place to conduct experiments or keep a private setup. That was something else they had to be aware of when moving around the island. Satellite photos showed nothing but dense foliage, however, causing Sonora to conjecture that it wouldn't be the case this time around.

In order for them to get here, bribery had been involved. Lou had greased some palms and arranged for them to travel across the water when no ships would be around. They had a narrow window with which to get to the island. The window to return to the mainland was even narrower, and they'd have to leave at precisely 6 AM in five days or risk arrest. Even worse, the locals policing the water tended to blow ships away and ask questions later. Knowing all this, the fear of a predator on the island wasn't one of their main concerns.

Aside from greasing palms, Lou was a bit of a bodyguard for hire. Ex-special forces, ex-SWAT, he was still beefy and a sharp shot. His forearms were the same size as Sonora's calf, and she was well-muscled herself from field work and workouts. Rusty, on the other hand, was tall and slim. He was here to study the flora and help solidify the paper Sonora intended to write about the island's non-human inhabitants. Irritable by nature, he was incredibly smart and could be sweet at times. When no one was looking, anyway.

Lou docked the boat. The pier was in poor shape, leaning to the side, the wood splintered and broken in spots. "Wait in the boat until I make sure we can safely get to shore this way." He took his job seriously. For the money Sonora was paying him, he'd better.

Jeans clad, Lou stepped onto the pier, rope in hand to tie them up once he'd made sure the whole thing wouldn't buckle under him. The pier wobbled slightly, but held. He jumped in place, which created more movement, but no breakage. He looped the rope over one of the posts and walked over the pier to land, where he bent over and studied the pier where it met soil. "It's reinforced with concrete. We should be fine."

Sonora released the breath she'd been holding. "Great. Why don't we hand off the supplies to you to get them on land first?"

Lou nodded. "Sounds good."

It took about ten minutes for them to get the boat fully unloaded and pack up their gear for the hike. The maps they'd gotten their hands on were old ones, but not much should have changed. The island had never been inhabited, at least not by the type of people who built permanent buildings. There had been paths, but those would certainly be overgrown by now, the island having been allowed to run rampant on its own. But the undergrowth on those old paths would be sparser than the rest of the jungle they now faced. Or so they figured.

Lou studied the map then tucked it into one of the pockets on his vest. Without a word, he turned and led them to the forest, pulling a long, angled blade out of a sheath at his waist.

Rusty stopped. "What the hell is that?"

"It's a kukri," Lou responded. He didn't turn around.

"That's really helpful, thanks."

"You're welcome."

Sonora didn't really know what a kukri was, but she figured it was sort of like a machete, only more aggressive, from the look of things. She passed Rusty where he still stood and caught up to about a foot behind Lou, leaving him plenty of swinging room. Footsteps rustled behind her as Rusty started moving again.

Lou studied the edge of the jungle, peering closely at the ground. He touched the vines and branches, nodded, grunted, then started hacking. They progressed slowly along the chopped-up path. The leaves and grasses on the ground were thick, a sweet scent of rot rising as they tramped through them. The trees grew close together. Sonora felt almost agoraphobic as she traveled behind Lou.

Rusty muttered and tripped his way through at the rear of the small cavalcade. "Can't you do something about the stuff on the ground?"

Neither Lou nor Sonora responded.

Sweat poured down Lou's head and neck, both bright red from the sun and exertion. He grunted and breathed heavily, but made no other sounds. His hits with the kukri were rhythmic, with bursts of increased hacking on particularly tough branches. The vines and branches fell to the ground, adding to the detritus there, causing them all to trip occasionally.

Sonora felt hot and clumsy, her own body covered in a thick sheen of sweat. "Do you need me to take over?"

"No."

Three hours in, they reached a surprise clearing. The trees abruptly stopped. Even the grass didn't grow in the circle, which measured about as big across as the speed boat they'd arrived on. The soil was dark and loamy, soft under their feet.

Lou heaved a deep breath and sat down. He pulled out his canteen and took a long pull of his water before lying back on the ground.

Sonora slumped down a couple feet away and drank her own water. It was warm and tasted metallic from the canteen, but it brought some relief from the deep thirst scratching at her throat. She watched Rusty sink to the ground, shed his backpack, and drink thirstily from his own canteen. "Seems like a good place to camp, doesn't it? I doubt we'll find somewhere else this clear."

Lou replied, "The soil might be a little soft, but we'll see if the tent spikes go in far enough and hit solid ground."

As she lay there, Sonora thought about the animals she would find. As far as she knew, the only mammals on the island were rodents, but there should be a wealth of insects, birds, and amphibians, if not reptiles. She'd never gotten to go into an area with no idea what to expect at all. She felt like a pioneer. Waves of excitement went through her at the prospect of getting started. The sun was lowering to the west, but if they got camp set up quickly she might have time to explore the jungle directly surrounding them.

With this thought in mind, she jumped up, already feeling the ache of her tired muscles from the hike in. "You guys ready to get started?"

Rusty groaned and thumped his head back against the ground. "Right now?"

"We need to be set up before it gets dark, and I'd really like to look around a bit tonight."

Lou stood, followed by Rusty, who sighed all the way up to his feet. They worked quickly to get the tents up and a basic fire pit created. All three finished with sweat-soaked clothing. Humidity dampened the air like rain suspended mid-air. No wonder it was so green on the island. The plants had so much moisture to thrive on.

Sonora pushed her sopping hair out of her face and pulled it back into a proper ponytail. It hung limply, the wet strands sticking to her neck. Frustrated, she wrapped it up into a bun and tucked her hair into a hair tie. Grabbing a small pack, she tucked her notebook, pen, canteen, and camera into it. She stepped into the trees, careful of her footing now that she was studying instead of cutting a swath through the jungle. Rusty would want to look at the plants when he started looking around.

The temperature instantly lessened now that she stood in the shade of the massive canopy above her. Leaning her head back, she looked up into the leaves. They were so dense, all she could see above about fifteen feet was darkness, deep and mysterious. What creatures hid up there among the highest branches? She ached to find out, but knew that likely wouldn't be this trip. She'd need to focus on the animals she could reach in the time she had. The paper might get them funding and even support from the local government to do more extensive studies in the future. That's what she should focus on.

A fallen log sat, partially sunken in and covered in a thick, blue moss. Sonora bent down, one knee in the dirt, to examine it. Rotted wood was often a great place to find all manner of creatures. It provided shelter for some, food for others. Picking up a nearby stick, she poked at the log where it appeared to be soft. She didn't want to collapse the whole thing, just open up one small area to see inside.

With the light fading, she could just make out movement inside. Some sort of insect activity. She took out her notebook and made a quick note about where she'd found the log so she could come back in the morning. She also made a note to pack a flashlight next time due to the limited light that could penetrate even here, steps from the clearing.

A shush of sound fell around her, the leaves in the trees quivering far up in the canopy. Down here, all was still. No wind, no movement of foliage. A deep groan sounded. A sound that made her feel as if the trees would crack under the pressure, though she still couldn't make out any visible movement. The shadows deepened, and Sonora realized it was time to go back out into the clearing. It was too dangerous to be in here with no visibility and no idea what might be moving around her. Pit-pats, plops, and various types of movement rustled around her. The beautiful sound of living organisms in their safe harbor of home.

Sonora walked back to the edge of the clearing and paused for a moment, letting the evening noises move around her. She loved the sounds of nature.

Sadly, the sounds of Rusty interrupted. "What do we have for dinner tonight? It's in your bag, Sonora."

"I'll check. Give me a minute." She allowed herself a moment to set everything down and stretch. She went to her supplies and grabbed a green ribbon, which she tied around a tree at the spot she'd entered the jungle. It would have been a good idea to mark on her way back from the log, but she'd forgotten to bring the ribbons. Before checking the food, she stuffed several of the ribbons into the bag she'd be taking out with her tomorrow.

Behind her, Rusty sighed.

Lou growled and said, "Shit's sake, Rusty, you can wait one damn minute."

"You know you're hungry, too, Lou. Don't act like you aren't."

"We're all hungry. We'll still be hungry in five minutes. Chill out."

Sonora's stomach growled now that food was being discussed. They hadn't eaten anything except trail mix in hours. She already missed being alone in the jungle. Just feet from where she now stood, there'd been peace for twenty minutes. Tomorrow there'd be plenty more. She could get lost in the jungle all day, exploring, seeking, discovering. Butterflies of excitement fluttered in her rumbling stomach, and she placed a hand there to calm the feelings roiling there.

Having pushed it as far as she could, she went to her supply bag and dug out a large can of chili. She tossed it over to Lou, who caught it easily. "You've got the pan, Rusty," she called.

Lou had already started the fire and rigged a stone to put the pot on. Sonora sat down away from the fire and the two hungry, squabbling men to take some notes. As she did so, she realized the utter absence of sound in the clearing. The men's voices, the crackling of the fire, the sound of her pen across the paper, these were the sounds she heard. No bugs flew around her. No birds chirped out here. Silence had fallen as soon as she'd stepped out of the jungle.

Curious, she stood up and walked over to the closest stand of trees. No sound. But the moment she stepped into the trees, a chorus of nature sang. Here there were bugs, night birds, tiny feet scurrying through the leaves on the ground. There were chirps, tweets, squeaks, and every sound imaginable. The temperature had dropped as soon as she stepped through, but that was to be expected. The sun hadn't reached this far during the day to heat it up.

Tiny glow bugs drifted around in the air. They resembled lightning bugs, but the lights were brighter and an array of colors. They stayed steady, illuminating the tree trunks around them. A lizard shot into the light, skittering around the trunk. It had six legs. It tilted its head and shot two tongues out, snaring two of the glow bugs and drawing them into its mouth. They continued to light up, tracing a path down its throat and into its stomach, where they slowly faded.

When the lizard took off running again, it circled around the trunk, climbing higher. To Sonora's surprise, the tree began to quiver. The whoosh she'd heard earlier occurred again, but this time the tree rose straight into the air, soil sprinkling to the ground in a patter.

The trunk came down a foot in front of her and slammed into the ground. It sent more dirt flying, striking her in the face. She screamed and backed away, hands up to shield herself.

Something moved behind her. She jerked her head around just in time for another tree to lift into the air. This time she tried to watch where it went so she could dodge, but it lifted too high, and she lost sight of it.

The entire jungle seemed to shift. Trees all around her rose and fell.

Sonora spun away from the trees as they fell. She couldn't tell where she'd entered the jungle. Dirt flew, trees slammed.

One of the trunks landed directly in front of her. It knocked her backward, and she fell out of the trees. She hit the ground, the air knocked out of her.

The chaos followed her into the clearing. The dim light of the setting sun disappeared, replaced by pure darkness. Sonora rolled over toward the fire, where the two men stood, stunned.

"What is it?" Lou yelled.

Sonora didn't have an answer for him. The only thing she could think to say was, "The trees." She managed to stand, just in time to feel something coming toward her, a movement of air pressing on her. She stooped down out of reflex and looked up.

The fire illuminated a smooth surface, covered in leaves. The center cracked then opened, revealing a gaping maw full of rows of sharp teeth that looked like carved wood. It lowered toward them, but jerked back with an echoing scream when the heat of the fire touched it.

"Run!" Sonora yelled. She turned toward the path they'd come in on, not waiting to see if anyone followed her. It was easier going than it had been coming in, but the ground remained uneven and littered with detritus that caused her to stumble. She kept her feet, barely, and ran blindly in the dark.

Footfalls approached her from behind, stumbling just as she was. A voice that sounded like Rusty's grunted. She refused to turn, to see if he'd fallen. All she could think to do was run, panic removing every other thought from her mind.

She had no idea how long she'd run, but it felt like forever. Her legs, already tired from the hike in, gave out and she fell. Frantic, she climbed back to her feet, but fell again, a wayward branch catching her ankles. Her breaths came out in short gasps, and she flopped the rest of the way to the ground, desperate for air.

It was in the stillness that she realized the thuds from the trees had stopped.

She lifted her head and strained to see into the darkness. Everything looked normal from here, but she could barely see a couple feet in any direction. Feet pounded toward her. Lou was the first to loom out of the darkness, Rusty close behind him.

Lou bent down and helped her to her feet. Then he bent over, hands on knees, panting for air. Rusty leaned against a tree.

"Don't touch it!" she screamed.

Rusty jerked away from it. "What?" he asked, hands held out

in a question.

"It's the trees. The trees are moving."

"This one's not."

Sonora didn't answer. He was right. It wasn't moving. Maybe they didn't all move like the ones they'd run from.

"We need to get to the boat," she said.

Lou nodded and straightened. "Let's go."

They picked their way back along the path, cautious now that things had calmed down. It took another hour, but they broke through to the coastline, the boat bobbing in the water a happy sight. The moon had risen, blessedly full, and it lit the dock and the rocking waves.

Sonora broke into a run, determined to get on the boat and away from the island. The men ran with her. Their footsteps pounded over the wood of the dock. It shook with their weight, swaying more the closer to the end they got. Sonora jumped from about a foot away from the end of the pier and landed in the boat. She moved to the front to get the motor started.

Lou was the next to jump onto the boat. He stepped next to Sonora and turned on the light bar in front of the windshield.

There was a crack, a splintering of wood, and Rusty screamed as the pier crashed down toward the water. He slipped beneath the surface, wood splashing around where he'd disappeared.

Sonora moved toward the side, but Lou grasped her arm. "Worry about the boat. I'll get him."

She nodded and turned the key. The boat started up after several sputters, loud against the crash of the waves. Cautiously, Sonora reversed the boat and maneuvered it closer to where Rusty had fallen. Both she and Lou jumped when Rusty popped out of the water, gasping for air. He splashed, trying to gain control. A wave slammed into his face, and he went under again briefly before bobbing back up on the other side of it.

Lou leaned over and grasped Rusty's outstretched hand. He started to pull him into the boat, but Rusty's hand slipped, and he crashed backward into the water.

In the jungle, the crashes came again. It was hard to see in the moonlight, but it looked as if half of the jungle had stood up.

It approached them on legs made of tree trunks. From this distance, it looked like a daddy longlegs: round, centered body, with long legs. Except there were hundreds of legs, all rising and falling in their own rhythm. The body swayed between them, the surface rippling.

"Get him in here!" Sonora called.

They once again clasped hands, and this time Lou got him onto the boat. Without waiting for him to gain his balance, Sonora gunned it, shooting straight ahead into the ocean. The boat rocketed over the buffeting waves, but sped forward.

Sonora looked back, only to discover the creature close behind. It entered the ocean waves, body hovering far above. The legs crashed down all around it, getting closer to the boat.

"Go, go, go!" Rusty yelled, looking back and forth between the creature and Sonora. Both he and Lou still stood in the boat, hands gripping the side.

Sonora looked forward, pushing the boat to its limit.

One of the legs hit the boat, and it rocked onto its side, nearly tipping, before straightening back out.

The legs surrounded them, crashing into the water, sending waves in counter patterns to the ones naturally occurring. The boat rocked severely. Nausea pumped through Sonora's body, but she fought it back.

Behind her, Rusty screamed.

Sonora turned, only to see Rusty shoot up into the air, one of the tree trunk legs sticking through his torso. She saw the shocked look on his face before he was whisked upward.

"No!" Lou leapt up and attempted to grab Rusty's leg. His hand brushed the other man's foot, but he wasn't able to grip it. He slammed back down into the boat, almost falling over the side before catching himself.

Sonora willed the boat forward, physically leaning toward the bow in her urgency.

They outran the legs. When Sonora turned to see why, she realized the creature's body was getting closer to the water. As the depth increased, it became harder for it to walk through the water. "Yes!" she cheered.

"Don't slow down," Lou called.

"Not a chance."

Another ten minutes, and the creature disappeared below the waves.

"I hope it drowns," Lou said.

Sonora nodded, the adrenaline abruptly leaving her body. Exhaustion filled her, and various aches and pains cried out from all over. She eased back on the throttle, but didn't stop.

Lou slumped into a seat. He put his head in his hands. "I couldn't get him in time."

Stars twinkled above them, winking against the velvety darkness of the sky. The boat evened out, less rocking, and they moved steadily forward in the direction of the mainland.

Just as Sonora began to relax, sirens sounded and a spotlight hit them. A second spotlight joined it, then a third. Two of the boats moved in front of them, cutting them off. She pulled the throttle all the way back and let the boat drift to a stop.

"Just raise your arms and don't say anything," Lou mumbled from her side. He stood beside her, his arms in the air.

Sonora raised her own arms and waited, wincing against the brightness of the lights.

A loud voice came over the water, amplified by a bullhorn. "Prepare to be boarded."

Four men jumped over from the third boat. One stepped forward and threw Lou against the control panel. Another grabbed Sonora and jerked her arms behind her, shooting sparks of pain through her shoulder. She gasped, but didn't speak.

"What are you doing here?" a man asked her.

"We're scientists. We were on the island."

"The island is forbidden. What were you doing there?"

"I was studying the animal life. We didn't mean any harm."

"You've brought more harm than you know." The man's face sunk, his eyes drooping. He looked tired.

"What do you mean?"

"You'll see. Soon enough. No more talking now."

The men hustled them from their boat onto one of the official ones. Two of the men stayed behind. When the officials started their boats in the direction of the mainland, the two men followed behind in the rental.

"Where are you taking us?" Sonora asked.

"You're being arrested."

"Aren't you supposed to read us our rights?"

"You have no rights."

Fear sunk into Sonora's stomach. She was being arrested in a foreign country. They could lock her up and never let her out. She wouldn't get a phone call. Somehow, even though she'd known this was a possibility, it hadn't seemed real to her before. Not something that could actually happen. Everything had gone so seamlessly until the island had turned on them.

"Don't say anymore," Lou whispered. One of the men near him shoved him with the butt of his rifle. He put his head down and stayed quiet.

Sonora studied the men around her. They all looked grave. Far more serious and unhappy than the situation warranted. One of them stared at her, lip curled, eyes narrowed. She looked away, afraid of the rage in his eyes.

When they reached the pier at the mainland, the men quickly unloaded the boat, pulling their prisoners off with little effort. They pushed Sonora and Lou ahead of them, occasionally shoving one of them in the back. A small building stood in the direction they were walking. Light poured out of its windows. A figure moved across one of them, casting a shadow onto the ground outside. It stopped, a face peering out at them. Then the figure moved, and a door opened, spilling a new rectangle of light that reached Sonora's feet.

The prisoners were shoved inside the building and forced into hard, metal seats. "Stay there," said the only one who had talked to them so far. He appeared to be in charge.

"Embassy," said Lou. "We need to speak to someone at the American Embassy."

No one responded or acknowledged he'd spoken.

"Did you hear him?" Sonora asked. "We're Americans."

Again, no response.

Sonora fell quiet. Obviously, these people didn't care who she and Lou were or where they were from. The men talked in hushed voices, urgency clear in the rapidity of their speech. Tension filled the room, fully palpable.

One of the men nodded and moved into a windowed room, closing the door behind him. He picked up a telephone and made a call, face grave. His movements became frantic, free arm waving in the air as he spoke. The hand clenching the phone whitened.

The phone call went on for a few minutes, but when he hung up, the man looked calmer. Apparently, he'd gotten what he wanted.

Finally, the man who'd spoken to them before approached where she and Lou sat. He stood before them, hands behind his back, legs spread. A militaristic rest pose. "We have called for evacuation. You'd better hope it arrives in time."

"In time for what?" Sonora asked. "That creature drowned. Is that what you're talking about? It sunk into the sea."

"The ghoul cannot drown. It does not breathe."

"Ghoul?"

"There's a reason that island is closed off. We've lived decades without trouble from the demon, but now you've brought it to us. Our truce no longer exists. You have destroyed us."

"That's a little dramatic," Lou said. "Surely you have weapons to use against it."

"We have weapons, though probably not up to American standards. They are untested against the demon. We don't know if it can be killed."

"Why are you bothering to arrest us then? Why not let us go so we have a fighting chance?"

The man turned away and left them again. No one else looked at them or talked to them. The men scattered, packing items. Two men came out of a back room with stacks of weapons, distributing them to the other soldiers. The energy was tense and frantic.

The percussion of helicopter blades approached. The soldiers moved faster.

The ground shook, a series of thuds feeling like miniature explosives going off. One of the windows cracked. Another shattered.

"Uncuff us!" Lou yelled.

One of the men looked toward their leader. He nodded. The

man uncuffed each of them. "Let's go."

Sonora followed him out the front door, soldiers pouring out in front of and behind them. In one direction, helicopter blades beat at the air. In the other direction, the creature lurched from the ocean, water pouring off its body. It shot one of its legs out and gored one of the soldiers, lifting him into the air and shoving him into the mouth on the bottom of its body. His screams cut off abruptly.

Sonora turned her back on the creature and ran toward where the helicopters approached. She didn't know where the landing pad was, if there even was one. All she knew was safety lay in this direction. Beside her, the building crumbled, multiple trunk legs slamming through it. A piece of brick hit her in the side, pain shooting through her torso. Something sliced into her cheek. Blood ran warm down her face.

She'd lost track of where Lou was in the disarray around her. Men yelled, gunshots exploded, some in staccato, some as random booms. There were screams and the sounds of the creature's legs hitting the ground.

More buildings stood ahead. Some had lights on, but most were dark. A pajama-clad couple ran out of one of the buildings. A leg shot through each of them, pulling them screaming up into the air. Sonora ducked as the woman's body flew over her, bound for the creature's mouth.

The legs crashed into more of the buildings. People emptied out of some of them like ants, flooding the street. One house to her left exploded inward under the force of three of the legs, just as a light turned on. A short yell burst out, only to be silenced.

An explosion sounded behind her, heat washing at her back. It pushed her forward, and she almost fell. The creature screamed, a sound that hurt her ears, and the night lit up with flames.

One of the helicopters landed ahead of her. Sonora ran harder, determined to make it to the chopper. Unsure how high the blades were, she ducked as she drew near, squat-walking her way toward the now open door. A man in uniform leaned out, reaching for her.

Her hand met his, and he gripped her firmly, pulling her toward him even as she lunged for him. He fell backward.

Sonora landed on him and promptly rolled off, looking back toward the horror occurring in the direction of the ocean.

The monster was massive. Flames lit it up as bright as day. Now she could see that it was covered in leaves, the jungle come to life. Its legs found targets everywhere, buildings crashing to the ground, bodies flying up toward its mouth. There were only two soldiers remaining, as far as she could see. And Lou. He limped toward the helicopter, one of his legs turned at an odd angle.

"Faster, Lou! Come on!" she called.

One of the legs, still sporting the green ribbon she'd tied on it, hit him directly. He crumpled under its weight. Sonora turned away, sickened and flooded with guilt. She moved away from the door, so the soldiers could pull others in with them. Several more choppers had landed and were pulling those who made it to them inside.

A leg hit the blades of one of the choppers and was rapidly whittled down. The creature screamed again. The blades broke into pieces, the shorter pieces still stuck to the rotor spinning faster.

People bailed out of the broken chopper and ran toward the one Sonora was on. She watched in horror as two of them were taken out, leaving only three still running. "We're at capacity!" yelled the man who'd pulled her in. "Take off."

"No, we have to help them," Sonora yelled, moving toward the doorway.

"If they get on this bird, we're going down." He slid the door shut and settled into the seat.

Sonora watched the people as they grew smaller below her on the ground. They diverted to another helicopter. The last sight Sonora had of them, two of them were skewered by the monster, the third pulled onto the helicopter, which took off immediately.

Another helicopter rose near Sonora's, but the monster knocked it out of the air. The damaged helicopter plummeted to the ground, exploding when it hit.

A different kind of helicopter flew past the one Sonora was on. She craned to look out the window. This one had weapons mounted on it, and a rocket of some sort burst forward, lighting the night sky. It slammed into several of the monster's legs, and the creature stumbled. Flames sped up toward the body, reaching it as a second rocket tore into its center mass.

The monster fell sideways toward the ground, its legs sounding like falling lumber. It slammed into one of the still standing buildings, flames sweeping toward the people fleeing.

Constant screams still penetrated the interior of the helicopter, louder than the rotating blades. The creature's remaining legs flailed in the air as it tried to stand. Another helicopter swooped in low, dropping bombs directly onto the jungle monster. It exploded, the legs falling still.

Sonora settled back in her seat, vowing never again to trespass. Not even for the chance of discovering a new species.

The Punishment Quadrant

Lenore resented being sent out to Quadrant 46.

Nothing happened there. It was nothingness, space within space. An echoing chasm of boredom.

In short, it was a punishment assignment.

She'd broken the rules, yes, but the infraction had been minor. It certainly didn't warrant being shunted off into deep space to monitor the abyss.

Okay, so she'd slept with the boss's son. Peter was a year older than her, and definitely old enough to not be under his mother's thumb. Of course, Lenore was paid to be under the wretched woman's thumb, but hormones had won out, and he'd looked so hot that she couldn't help herself.

If Cindy didn't want her employees having sex with her son, she shouldn't invite him to work engagements.

Lenore, steaming, approached the last checkpoint before entering the quadrant. One of the Gorillac boys was working it tonight, visible through the glass in the mini-station. The thick fur on his chest puffed out of the neck-hole in his spacesuit. She watched as he crammed his helmet on, the hair squashing down and getting trapped. There was no *way* the seal could be airtight. Then again, word was that the Gorillacs didn't need helmets, but liked to fit in. Plus, that's where the mic was.

He slid out a tray and said, "Identification, please." His voice was deep and gravelly, piped directly into her ship.

Having already pre-loaded it, Lenore pressed the button that sent the claw out from the side of her ship. It had a case on the underside, which it slid into the tray, ratcheting as the claw moved back to hover. The ship was a clunker, too, and not her usual assigned one, but they'd claimed hers was in for repairs. She knew better.

The Gorillac, whose nametag showed a name almost as wide

as his chest, and mostly illegible, studied the ID then pushed the tray back through. A smirk crossed his mostly hairless muzzle. "What'd you do to get this assignment?"

"I could ask the same of you," she retorted.

His laughter followed her past the square orbiting station, him obviously keeping the mic keyed so she could hear his amusement far longer than was necessary.

When the deep silence of space set back in, she realized she missed the sound. To fill the silence, she clicked her tongue twice to start her music via the mod in her ears. Her favorite Benathian instrumentals filled the small ship, the clang of metal and the shriek of moon rock scratches soothing to her soul. If the ship were bigger, she'd get up and dance.

She also slapped an illegal dome light at the peak of the dome shield over her head and set it to cycle through various light shows. Portable mods were the best new thing since the music implants, and Lenore always got the newest and best thing. Out here, who would tell on her? The Gorillac? Good luck to him getting anyone to believe him.

Setting the coordinate sphere, she let the ship follow the patrols on autopilot. Her lights blitzed out into the darkness, and she took pleasure in thinking that somewhere out there, someone was wondering where the strange, colorful lights were coming from.

It was while she watched an especially flamboyant burst of lights that she saw something unusual. Something that froze her so solid it felt like her heart stopped beating for a moment.

A tentacle.

Then her heart started beating again, she took a breath, and shook her head. There was no possible way she'd seen a tentacle. There were no tentacled aliens anywhere in the surrounding quadrants, and especially not in this one where life had never been reported.

She reached up and turned the dome mod off before turning on her spotlights. They penetrated the darkness for a significant distance, but she couldn't see anything. No, she had definitely imagined the tentacle.

To be safe, she did a full circuit of the quadrant before relaxing. There was, as expected, nothing out of the ordinary.

The patrol took up three hours of her twelve-hour shift, too, which was an added benefit. One-quarter of the way through her shift, and all was well.

Lenore turned on the light show again and settled in for the rest of her shift, pulling out a snack and the tipple of Zarconian liquor she'd snuck on board. Now it was a party.

This time, the tentacle left no doubt as to its authenticity when it swung out of nowhere and clocked the ship, scrambling the instruments briefly before equilibrium could be regained.

Lenore reached for the spotlights again, flipping the switch to turn them on.

The tentacle disappeared where the white lights hit it, but was visible in the rainbow array of colors coming from the mod.

Visible or not, it was still wrapped around the ship. From what she could tell, it had slowed her speed by a small amount, but was, in general, floating right along with her. What she couldn't figure out was what the tentacle was attached to. Other than her ship. The entire dome showed only the tentacle, growing larger as it stretched toward the back. She couldn't see the backside of the ship to know what body controlled said tentacle. Tentacles didn't just exist on their own, after all. Did they?

Finding it more comfortable to be able to see the tentacle, she turned off the floodlights and let the mod be the only light source. The colors danced over the tentacle, keeping it mostly visible, which at least meant she could track its movement. The appendage disappeared anywhere the color array wasn't hitting. The same was true when she went full dark.

Lenore was torn between terror and fascination.

An alarm sounded, the digital display giving a readout that stated the exhaust was blocked. She toggled the exhaust switch, hoping to reset it. This old tin bucket was probably just rebelling about the creature affixed to its carcass.

The alarm went off again, and now the ship shuddered. Other alarms joined the first.

The tentacle adjusted itself, pulling back partway along the dome. Another, smaller, one joined the first, crossing over it. Then three more, all smaller than the original.

The ship juddered again, this time dying completely.

With the power out, her mods went dead, no longer able to remotely feed off the ship's power. She now sat in silence and darkness. Cold seeped in rapidly and the oxygen seemed to thin. With the ship down, she couldn't send out messages. The Gorillac wouldn't expect her for ages, and by the time he noticed she was missing, she'd be dead.

The tentacles disappeared.

Rather, she could no longer *see* them. They were there, but she couldn't tell what they were doing.

A suctioning sound filled the ship, coming from the rear. Then, as the exhaust petered out along with the ship's power, a roar rang up the exhaust pipe and into the ship, reverberating throughout it and making her ears ring.

The ship lurched. The roar sounded again, followed by more frustrated sucking.

A metallic shriek sounded, followed by a bunch of creaking. Her windshield cracked. The ship was experiencing extreme pressure.

Lenore stood and pressed her hand to the crack, making sure she couldn't feel anything. The crack was only at the external level, or so it seemed. The windshield was specially built to withstand cracking, even in the case of a shutdown. It would take a lot to make it crack more deeply, but it seemed to her that the creature could do it. It was impossibly strong already.

The creaking intensified. Another small crack appeared at the top edge of the windshield.

Lenore would die immediately if a breach occurred.

She went to the power box to see if there was anything she could do. This ship was a piece of crap, but it ran well enough and had passed inspections. There was a chance she could jumpstart it if her stun gun had enough juice.

Racing to the control panel, she popped the personal storage drawer open and took out her purse, dumping everything on the floor. As another crack appeared in the windshield, she grasped the stun gun and returned to the panel.

"Please, please, please," she whispered, eyes closed.

The ship's metal shrieked again, and the roof visibly crumpled inward.

Lenore held the stun gun up and pressed the button.

Nothing happened.

She whimpered, but tried again. A single spark shot out.

Shaking the stun gun, she tried one more time.

This time, the full electrical arc shot out between the prongs, and she pressed it to the primary power circuit. The power roared to a start, but she wasted no time on relief. She made her way back to the control panel, removed the safety from the emergency shield switch, and flipped the switch, sending an electrical field around the entirety of the ship. The lights inside flickered, the ship trying to die since most of the power had been diverted to the exterior.

The tentacles were once more visible, stretched tightly over the windshield where it was cracking.

With another jerk and a series of small judders, the ship leveled out, bouncing in place once. It died, then restarted automatically, her mods following soon after. The lights now fell on empty space once more. The creature was gone. The music throbbed in her ears.

Lenore left as quickly as she could, speeding past the checkpoint without stopping. The Gorillac could report her. He was on his own.

One thing was certain: Lenore owed Cindy an apology. No more fun with the boss's son. It wasn't worth it. Not if it meant flirting with exhaust-sucking, tentacled creatures in deep space in the punishment quadrant.

Yellow Fever

The city of Savannah smelled of brackish water, rich soil, garlic, and seafood. Ship horns blared across the river in intermittent interruptions. Old buildings hid behind reaching, moss covered trees, and tourists walked the streets. Claire took it in, happy to be back. She hadn't been here since childhood, and now she got to introduce her husband to her favorite city.

"Hey, Jimmy, you hungry?"

Jimmy looked over from the passenger seat. "I could go for a burger."

"A burger? Absolutely not! Nobody comes to Savannah for a burger. I've got the perfect place to go."

"The stomach in me trusts the stomach in you."

Claire pulled into the driveway of the house they'd rented for their trip. The house was quaint, a pale blue with wooden shingle siding and white columns out front. Claire had carefully chosen a house within walking distance of the downtown area, so they could walk most of the trip. The grass was green, the yard sodden from recent rain. Water seeped into her shoe when she missed a step on the moss-covered stones leading to the stoop.

They stowed their things in the bedroom and hurried outside for their short walk to the novelty restaurant Claire remembered from her childhood. The front consisted of aged wood, brick, and windows. Inside, a wooden pirate stood in the corner next to the hostess stand. A twenty-something girl in black and white clothing greeted them and escorted them to a table.

"Your server will be Mandy. If you're interested in a tour, let her know and she'll make sure you get one after your meal."

"Ooo, a tour!" Claire said. "Let's do it."

They ordered off the menu and sipped real sweet tea while they waited for the food. A tour group walked by during the meal, and snippets of the female pirate's speech drifted to them. "They're not sure what these tunnels were for, but there are eight miles worth under the city. Unfortunately, due to disrepair and high risk, all the tunnels have been sealed off. Some say they were used to hide bodies during a yellow fever outbreak, others that they were shanghai tunnels, like you hear about on the west coast, and still others say they were simply to transport alcohol and other goods from ships on the Savannah River. We like to believe there's a bit of truth to all of it."

Jimmy reached out and touched Claire's hand. "We're definitely doing the tour."

Once they'd filled up on enough sweet tea to leave them floating for a week, they went on the tour, fascinated by the combination of old buildings that had been cobbled together to make what was now one large restaurant. They got to peer down into the entry of one of the sealed tunnels, where they saw money that had been dropped down as if it were a fountain, as well as glass bottles, gum, and other detritus.

Back outside, they walked past gorgeous oak trees dripping with Spanish moss. Sweat ran down the small of Claire's back. "If you liked that tour we should go do one of the night-time trolley tours. Maybe they'll say something else about the tunnels."

"What are we going to do until then?" Jimmy wiggled his eyebrows at her.

She laughed. "Very seductive, but a nap sounds better."

His shoulders slumping playfully, they wrapped their hands together and headed back to the house. Once inside, the air conditioning felt luscious, its icy fingers dancing along Claire's sweat-covered skin. She flopped onto the couch and patted the cushion next to her. Jimmy sat beside her, laying his head back on the cushioned couch back. Claire shifted so she was lying on her side and placed her feet in Jimmy's lap. They stayed this way for a while, skin growing damp where it met.

Claire had just started to drift off when an odd shifting sound occurred toward the back of the house. She jerked her head up. "What was that?"

"What?" Jimmy mumbled.

"That sound. Did you hear it?"

"It's probably the A/C."

Knowing he was probably right, Claire let her head fall back onto the armrest. Of course there'd be weird sounds in an unfamiliar house, especially an older one.

Jimmy's soft snores lulled her to sleep.

~~

Claire awoke to a dark room. She missed the warmth of Jimmy's body; he must have woken up before her. She sat up, reaching for her phone on the table.

It wasn't there.

She felt around in the dark. The glass surface of the table felt cold against her palm. In fact, cold permeated the room.

"Jimmy?" she called. "Can you turn a light on?"

He didn't answer.

Sliding onto the floor, she used both hands to seek the phone.

Somewhere in the darkness, something scuffed across the hardwood.

Claire froze. Her eyes, already wide in the darkness, now felt like they took up half her face. She strained to track the sound.

Another scuff sounded, followed by the creaking of a floorboard.

"Jimmy?" she whispered. Her heart pounded, mouth dry. She swallowed and tried again, a little louder. "Jimmy?"

He didn't reply. Jimmy wasn't one to play pranks. He wouldn't do this to her. Something was wrong.

The air to her left shifted.

She shied away and fell to the ground, scrambling until she came up hard against a wall. Dull pain throbbed through her skull. She held her hands out to ward off anything coming her way.

Nothing came.

It remained quiet. No sign of Jimmy. No sign of anybody approaching her. No sounds.

Claire quaked where she sat, fear-spiked adrenaline pumping through her system. She didn't want to move, yet she knew she had to. There was no sense in sitting here waiting for something to happen.

Sucking in a deep breath, Claire stood up, keeping her back against the wall.

The light switch would probably be near the front door. If not there, somewhere near it.

She took the first step and studied the shadowy lumps around her for movement.

Another step.

She had the urge to bolt for the door, but something within her told her whoever was here would come for her then, like a predator responding to a running animal.

Each measured step brought her closer to the front door.

Her foot hit an object on the floor. It tumbled away, clunking across the wood. She froze, looked around, then bent over to see what she'd kicked.

Her hand fell on something soft, but solid. A shoe.

Panic clawed at her throat, but she kept her hand on it, feeling around until she established it was just a shoe and not attached to anyone.

Clutching it to her chest, she continued her painstakingly slow journey to the front door. Her foot hit a creaky board, and she stopped, heart fluttering. Her body buzzed, nerve endings on fire with hyper awareness.

Damp cold wafted at her back, sending an icy chill up her spine. A dank smell that brought to mind sewers and moldy basements hit her. She broke into a run, one hand clutching the shoe, the other held out before her, stretching toward the front door.

It was only a few feet away.

Now one foot.

Inches from the door, a blow fell on her back.

She flew forward. Her hand hit the door, followed by her head, but she kept her feet, dizziness notwithstanding.

Her hand fell on the cool slickness of the doorknob and she turned it.

She pulled, but the door didn't budge.

A cold touch on her shoulder made her shriek, and she turned, placing her back against the door. All she could see was a void in front of her, pure darkness. She lashed out with the shoe and made impact. A grunt sounded, and Claire screamed and hit the figure again.

A cold, clammy hand locked like steel around her wrist, aborting her movement. It squeezed until she had to let the shoe go to clop on the floor.

Claire fought back, kicking, hitting with the free hand, screaming. She used her entire body, but her strength was nothing compared to theirs. The figure stepped into her, limiting her impact. Its entire body was cold, and Claire felt dampness everywhere it touched. Still, she squirmed and bucked, hoping to loosen part of its hold.

The light turned on, blinding her momentarily. In between blinks, what she saw made no sense. There were eyes. Yes. That was the first thing she saw. But no face. All she could see were eyes; wet, ropy hair; and what looked like vines or some sort of plant life. Up close, the amplified sewer odor choked her. Humidity came off its body in waves.

Another one moved up behind it, and she now faced two sets of dark eyes. She couldn't make out any other features on this one either. The one holding her spoke, and it sounded wet, as if water dripped down its throat. The words bubbled, and they made no sense. "It hungers?" The voice tilted up at the end like a question mark.

Claire shook her head, not sure if it was asking if she was hungry or telling her it was hungry. Or something else entirely. Surely the safest answer was no. No, she wasn't hungry. No, she wasn't food. "No."

The closest one picked her up with little effort and slung her over its shoulder. Moisture seeped through her clothes. Disgust squirmed in her belly. Together, the creatures walked down the hallway toward the back of the house. Turning left into the bedroom, they entered the closet. Straining to see where they were going, Claire twisted, but could only see empty hangers and a closet wall.

They moved backward now, and Claire had to draw herself back to avoid hitting the floor as it rose to meet her. The carpet had been rolled back, and a musty smell floated up from a square opening in the floor. They were going below the house.

A single burning torch lit the space, lending an amber glow

to the otherwise gray surroundings. The walls were earthen, with spots where the structure had crumbled, leaving gaps in the wall and holes in the ceiling. Runnels of moisture ran down the walls, creating a muddy walking surface. It sucked loudly at the creatures' feet as they walked.

She lost all concept of time as they trekked. The blood in her head had started throbbing from hanging upside down for so long. Every time she tried to change position, the creature's arms tightened painfully.

"Where are you taking me?" she asked.

They completely ignored her. Not that she thought they would answer, but she had to try. Every once in a while she threw out another question. "Who are you?" "What do you want with me?" "Where are we going?" They ignored them all.

Her terror seemed to have reached a plateau. Her heartbeat had calmed, but perhaps that was just because all the blood in her body appeared to now be in her head and extremities. Theories of what the creatures planned to do to her swirled through her head, but nothing made sense.

The sound of the rushing river filled the tunnel. The mud seemed deeper than it had before, and the water now poured down the walls and directly from the ceiling, dripping on her back and head. The odor of the creature amplified as it got wetter. She gagged. She tried breathing through her mouth, but that just made it so she could taste the creature, too. Her tongue felt coated with a layer of brackish mud.

At one point, so much water came down that she thought the tunnel was collapsing. Everything shook, and the roar of the river was so loud it thundered through her head. Here, the tunnel had been shored up with rock and brick, the ceiling a smooth archway of brick with many missing pieces. Several inches of standing water covered the ground, the creatures' steps now a swish rather than the slurp of mud.

Time passed. The rumble calmed, the roar diminished, and the tunnel returned to its previous level of damp versus sodden. Surely they hadn't gone *under* the river. The whole point of the tunnels was getting things to and from ships, wasn't it?

The space widened into a cavern of some sort, and the creature unceremoniously dumped her on the ground. The air in her lungs puffed out at once. It took her a minute to regain the ability to breathe. Once she could, she looked around. Stacked around the walls of this cavern were irregular burlap shapes, maybe about five feet long, though the lengths varied. Some were much longer, some significantly shorter. Some of the burlap lay open, bones and human skulls littering the floor. There were more creatures here, as well. One of them walked across the cavern, footsteps crunching as it walked over bone debris. A moan sounded from somewhere off to her right, and she squinted into the flickering torch light.

Jimmy lay on top of one of the burlap bundles, which she now assumed to be bodies. Blood had dried on his head, coating his face in a dark brown layer of gore. He opened his eyes, which rolled around in the sockets vacantly.

"Jimmy?" she ventured. When none of the creatures made a move in response to her voice, she tried again, louder. "Jimmy? Wake up."

He didn't respond.

Claire had no idea why they'd been brought down here, but what she knew was that they needed to escape. She had to get over there and help him.

All but one of the creatures moved to the far end of the cavern and grouped together into a huddle. Odd sounds emitted from them, more like grumbles than words. She couldn't make out what language they must be speaking. It wasn't familiar.

Eyeballing the creature that still stood over her, she got to her feet. Its eyes met hers, but it didn't move.

She took a step backward, watching the creature. It tensed.

She held her hands out in front of herself, palms out, a placating gesture. Pointing to herself, she then pointed toward Jimmy. When the creature just continued to stare at her, she took another step backward. It didn't relax, but it also made no move toward her.

Taking a deep breath, she turned her back to the creature. Her entire body stiff, she walked slowly, but steadily, toward Jimmy.

Footsteps crunched behind her.

Still, she moved forward, bracing herself. She could feel the dampness of the creature at her back, like a wall of humidity.

Claire reached Jimmy's side and squatted down next to him. The creature stepped over beside her, but didn't touch her. This, at least, was okay.

She placed a hand on Jimmy's cheek. He felt hot to the touch, clammy. Whatever they'd done to him, he was feverish, an infection of some sort already running rampant within him. His breaths came irregular and raspy. From all the blood on his face and matted in his hair, she had to assume he had a concussion. Moving him would be tricky, especially as they'd have to be running from these creatures. But it had to be done. There were other tunnels branching out from this cavern. As long as it had taken for them to get here, she figured going back the way they'd come might not make sense. Surely, another of these tunnels would get them to safety more quickly, but how was she to know which one?

Afraid to move his head any more than she had to, Claire shifted her hand down to his chest and shook him. Her hand sunk down with a squelch, his chest mushy and pliable. She'd placed her hand right where the breastplate should be. Gently, she felt around. There were hard, sharp objects amidst the mush.

Horrified, she withdrew her hand. They'd broken his ribs. Nothing protected his heart or other organs, as far she could tell. There was no way in hell he'd be able to get up and run. There was no telling what other damage had been done to him. Her heart stuttered. "Oh, my love, what did they do to you?"

His eyes had closed, but now they opened and seemed to focus on her for a moment. A slight smile lifted a corner of his lips. His lips cracked open, and Claire leaned closer. When he spoke, it sounded wet and garbled, but she understood. "I love you."

"I love you, too." Tears fell down her cheeks, pain filling her chest. "I'm so sorry."

"Get. Out." His eyes closed again.

She touched her head to his as gently as she could. "I can't leave you."

He groaned. Blood bubbled from his lips.

A sob escaped her throat, and the creature lurched toward her. She stared back at it, meeting those odd, dark eyes.

In one swift move, it grabbed her and threw her into a pile of burlap covered bodies several feet away. A sickening crunch sounded, pain leaping through every part of her body. A shattered bone beneath her dug into her side, slicing into the skin.

From her vantage point on the ground, she could see all the creatures, plus the broken form of her husband. The one that had thrown her now approached her again, and she attempted to scramble away from it.

It was faster than her. A solid, damp foot came down on her side, and something inside her gave with a blindingly painful snap. It felt like a rib. She shoved at the foot on top of her, but couldn't budge the creature. It removed its foot long enough to pick her up and slide her back to where she'd originally been thrown. The burlap felt scratchy against her skin, and it smelled like mildew and rotten meat. The shattered bone once again poked into her back. This time, her own rib poked back.

The creature put its foot back on her, sending a sharp pain through her torso. Nausea swamped her. She fought against the pain and the need to vomit, but wasn't able to hold in the whimper that escaped her lips.

The noise from the creatures amplified. She looked that way, distracted from her pain. As one, they moved toward her husband, feet crunching through the bone fragments. They circled him, blocking her view.

"Get away from him!" she screamed, but it came out weak and breathy, straining at the busted rib. "Leave him alone!"

They ignored her. Even the one still standing on her stomach watched them, paying her no mind. Her weak struggles accomplished nothing.

A tearing sound preceded her husband's screams, and the creatures leaned in.

She fought harder than before. It was like hitting a boulder.

Jimmy's screams became gurgles. Wet sounds emanated from that direction.

Straining, Claire dug her hand beneath her body, inching her fingers until they hit the sharp bone beneath her. She scrabbled the best she could, finally hooking a finger over it so she could drag it out.

Jimmy no longer gurgled. The wet sounds continued.

Claire's finger slipped off the bone, and she tried to shift her body. The creature looked down at her. She glared back.

As soon as it looked away, she thrust her hand as far as she could and hooked the bone again. It was large, maybe a femur. It shifted beneath her, running along much of her back.

The creatures slowed. Claire knew she was running out of time to get away. She refused to think about her husband, knew she would dissolve if she did. His screams played over and over in her head.

The sharp edge of the bone was free from her. Close.

The creature lifted its foot and bent toward her. Her turn to die.

Freed of the weight, Claire threw herself sideways enough to get the bone out, ignoring the insane level of pain that hit with her movements. She wrapped her hand fully around the shaft of the bone, lifted it, and stabbed it into the creature's foot with a primal scream. The bone squelched as it sunk into the foot, but it penetrated.

The creature let out a high-pitched scream, which caused the others to turn their way. A gap appeared between two of them, and she saw the pitiful remains of her husband. He'd been flattened, most of him gone. A couple ribs still arced up from where his chest should have been, but they were white as if they'd been sucked clean.

With a sob, Claire struggled to her feet and ran, bone still clasped in her hand. The creatures blocked the other entrances, so she returned to the tunnel she'd originally been brought through. Darkness waited ahead of her—the torches must have gone out. She held her left hand—the one not holding the bone—out to her side, trying to keep track of the wall so she didn't slam into the sides of the tunnel.

The ground was uneven. She stumbled, but kept running.

Squelches and grumbles echoed down the tunnel from behind her, and she ran faster, pushing herself as hard as she could. If they caught up, they would kill her.

She couldn't tell how close they were.

The rumble of the river grew ahead. Knowing she was close to that part of the tunnel gave her the energy to keep going. A mild glow far ahead told her at least one torch must still be burning.

The creatures now shrieked, echoing each other. They hunted her, calling to each other in the dark.

Ice filled her veins.

The ground became sodden, and soon she found herself knee deep in water. She remembered how easily they'd moved through the mud and water, and knew she would lose ground to them until she hit dry dirt again. She paused long enough to thrust the bone into the ceiling above her, where water already streamed. It felt like the water flow increased. It would have to be good enough.

She took long, springing steps, her body pushing against the strong resistance of the water. It felt like she was running through gelatin. The water now reached her waist.

Splashing behind her indicated they'd reached the deeper water.

The water became shallower.

A wave hit her back. She stumbled and fell face first into the muddy water. Choking on the fluid filling her throat and nose, she half crawled, half swam until she could regain her feet. The mildewed odor of the creatures reached her. They were gaining.

The mud still caused her to struggle and slip, but each bit of progress spurred her on. The creatures splashed along behind her. She listened hard for the moment she could no longer hear them splashing. Then she'd know they'd hit the dry ground.

A torch burned ahead. It illuminated dryer ground, as well as seriously degraded ceiling and walls. For the first time, she turned to get a visual on the creatures. They created a dark wall, mere yards behind her.

Fighting every urge within her, she stopped and chipped away at what looked like a particularly weak point in the ceiling. Chunks of dirt fell, getting larger. Something hard, a brick perhaps, painfully bounced off her shoulder. She dug harder, yelling now, throat straining. "Crumble, you bastard!"

Dirt slid down around her feet. The creatures were too close, maybe five feet away. With a final thrust, she brought down more of the tunnel and turned to run. The clack of brick and stone followed a rumble of earth, and she looked back to see half the tunnel filled with dirt, more coming down. The creatures attempted to scramble over it, spider-like in their movements.

Claire ran out of the light, forced to feel for the walls again. More light teased ahead of her. She had no idea how much longer until she hit the steps up to her rental house again. It had to be soon. Her energy waned as she ran, the adrenaline blocking some of her pain. Her lungs felt strained with her heavy breathing.

A victorious yip rang out, and she figured they'd gotten through the blockade.

Her hand hit something solid sticking out of the tunnel wall. She stopped and felt what seemed to be a wooden beam. It shifted when she pushed on it. She dropped the bone and shoved at the beam, working it back and forth until it loosened from the wall enough for her to pull it out. Dirt and stone fell on top of her, and she went down with the weight of it. Using the board for guidance, she worked her way along it toward what she hoped was an exit in the right direction. Dirt filled her mouth and nostrils, stinking of centuries.

Her hand broke through the dirt before her head. It felt like she'd been buried forever. No telling where the creatures were. Dirt in her ears muffled sounds. She dug until her entire body was clear, then broke into a run.

Her head jerked backward.

Something had her hair.

She reached back and felt the solid, wet hand of one of the creatures wrapped around it. Pulling as hard as she could, she freed her head, losing a handful of hair with a sharp, burning pain as it ripped out of her scalp.

Here was the torch she'd seen in the distance. Behind it, the stairs leading to safety.

She climbed the stairs on all fours, already smelling the clean air above her.

Her head rose above the floor. Shoulders now. She reached one hand forward and snagged carpeting to pull herself up.

What felt like moist steel encircled her ankle. She slipped backward, chin glancing off the top step. But she held tight to the carpet, arm straining. She pulled herself up and kicked backward with the free leg, making contact.

The hand on her ankle loosened.

With one final, guttural yell, she reclaimed her ankle and escaped through the hole in the floor. She slammed the door back down on top of it. Not finding a way to lock it, she shut the closet door and moved the bed against it.

Then she ran again. One final sprint to the front door. Every inch she gained was an inch toward freedom.

Her entire body slammed against the door, and she grappled with the lock.

The bed rasped across the flooring in the bedroom.

Grumbled yelps bounced down the hall.

The locks undone, Claire threw open the door and raced out into the humid heat of the night. She fell down the steps, scraping her knees and palms, but pressed on.

Screaming for help, she reached the road and stood in the middle of it, staring down the headlights of an oncoming car. She threw her hands out, palms open, willing them to see her, to stop.

The car screeched to a halt inches shy of her.

She ran to the passenger side and opened the door. A stunned man looked back at her from the driver's seat. "What are you...are you okay?"

"I need to get to the police." She climbed in.

When he only looked back at her, she screamed, "Now!"

Without a word, he took off. Claire slumped into the seat, her aches and pains swelling as the adrenaline flowed out of her system. She struggled to breathe against the poke of her rib and the ache in her chest. Her husband's battered body filled her mind, guilt overwhelming her. He'd only come here because of her. His absence already hurt her soul, filling her with an emptiness she couldn't process.

Something touched her arm. She jerked sideways, away from it, eyes opening. The man, concern on his face, pressed his cell phone against her arm. "To call the police," he said.

"Thank you," she whispered. No energy remained in her body. She was pain and emptiness.

"911, what's your emergency?"

She paused a moment to think through how best to get them

to listen to her. "There was a home invasion at our rental. My husband is dead."

The last thing she felt was the phone tumbling from her limp fingers. It thumped onto the floor of the car. Then all went black.

~~

Claire came to in the hospital, the bright white of the walls a glaring starkness in her sight. It still hurt to breathe, but she felt the mild relief of sleep and pain medication. An IV fed into her arm. Her chest felt tight, like they'd wrapped it.

A nurse came into the room, his face friendly. Wisps of fine hair teased at his cheeks and forehead. "You're awake."

Claire started to speak, coughed, tried again. "Police. I need to talk to the police."

"There's an officer outside. I just need to check your vitals, then I'll let her in."

The nurse was efficient, and after checking her blood pressure, O2, and pulse, he stepped out and called for the officer, who quickly came into the room. She approached the hospital bed, but stopped shy of it by about a foot, giving ample space to Claire. "Ma'am, we found the house you were staying in, thanks to the man who picked you up, but we couldn't find your husband. We found some sort of entrance in the bedroom closet, but when we went down, we found the tunnel filled in a little ways down, with no way to get through. Can you tell me what happened?"

Taking a deep breath and bracing herself to argue, Claire told the officer everything.

Inside Me

Her lips are sweetly spiced with cinnamon and sugar from churros shared amidst the jangling violence of a carnival. They're soft, yet hungry, against mine. I'd kiss her all night if she'd let me.

When she pulls away, it takes me a moment to open my eyes. My lips feel bruised and full from the rush of blood to them. She's smiling, lips and cheeks all curves, eyes half closed. I ache with the need for more.

"Good night," she says. Her fingers trail down my arm, leaving behind a warm reminder of their passage. Cold swirls around me in the absence of her body heat and sensual energy. A ghost of her presence lilts over my skin.

I watch her leave, the sway of her hips mesmeric. My breath catches when she turns to look back at me one more time, and I raise a hand in an awkward wave. Her long hair glides like silk over her shoulders when she turns away again

The short walk to my apartment passes in a blur of physical memory, my body a tyranny of pleasant sensations and yearnings that overwhelm my senses.

Then the tingling begins in my lips, gentle at first, but growing in urgency. They're warm as if I've eaten hot chilies. I run my fingers over them and find that they are hot to the touch, as well, pulsating. It takes me a minute to realize they're pulsing in time with my heartbeat.

At first, I smile. It reminds me of her, of where I was just an hour ago. As first dates go, this was the best I've ever been on. A chance meeting at the library, numbers exchanged, a date set up. I hadn't expected her to actually answer when I called, nor did I think she'd accept my invitation. But she had. My very own dream girl, and she liked me back.

Conflicted, I type out a series of texts telling her what a great time I had, erasing each one after a moment of thought. Maybe it's too soon to contact her. I don't want to come across as needy or psychotic. Finally, I suck it up and send a text that says *Thinking of you. I had fun tonight.* There's nothing creepy about that.

The warmth in my lips intensifies, a raging fire. It feels as if my skin will slough off. I lick them, the cinnamon-sugar lingering. Racing to the kitchen, I open the fridge and shift items on the top shelf until I find the milk. My hands shake as I pour the milk into a glass. Some of it spills onto the counter, the floor, my shirt. Heedlessly, I gulp the milk down. It pours down my chin, soaking my shirt even more.

The heat does not abate.

I open the freezer and pull an ice cube out of the bin, rubbing it over my lips. It melts rapidly without bringing any relief. I can barely feel the cold through the intensity of the heat. My lips throb with it.

Grabbing another ice cube, I make my way to the bathroom. Not sure what I expect, I study my mouth in the mirror. My lips are visibly swollen as if I've been stung by a bee. They're bright red, the redness expanding outward, creeping across my face, down my chin and up to my nose. Somehow, seeing that they look as bad as they feel makes the pain worse. Once more, I try to soothe them with the ice cube, now half melted in my hand. It turns to liquid within seconds, a mist rising from my lips.

With dawning horror, I realize I can see them moving, squirming. This isn't just the pulsating I felt earlier. Something is under the skin. Inside my lips.

My phone buzzes, indicating a text. I ignore it.

When I press a finger to my lips, they writhe beneath it. There are small, worm-like movements. I put my face close to the mirror and squint to see better. There are green things moving under my skin, dim against the pink of my lips. They seem to be multiplying and growing quickly. As I watch, my lips swell further, the surface undulating with the movement within.

My phone buzzes again. This time I take it out and press the text preview to bring it up. She's written me back: *The night's not over yet.*

I shove my phone into my back pocket once again and press my lips closed. Something has to make them feel better, to bring me some relief. It can't be what it looks like. There's absolutely no way this is happening.

The green things are roiling, pressing against my swollen flesh. They started out the thickness of thread, but they've now become the size of spaghetti. One breaks free of my lips, the green now vibrant against the paleness of the skin surrounding them. It wiggles and inches its way along, working itself down into my chin.

More worms break free, pressing into the flesh surrounding my lips. They look like veins. Only veins don't move like maggots.

Another buzz vibrates my phone. I don't want to see what she's said now.

Instead, I race back to the kitchen, digging through the drawers. I toss aside a wooden spoon, a slotted spoon, mixer blades. I'm not sure what I'm looking for until I see the zester lying in the bottom of the drawer, buried beneath the rest of my cooking utensils. I grab that and a pair of tongs and return to the bathroom mirror

The buzz comes again. I set the zester and tongs on the edge of the sink and pull it out to read the newest texts.

I'm inside you.

Can you feel me?

This time I toss my phone into the tub and turn my full attention back to my lips. It's not just them anymore. The worms have spread out, seeping like an infection into the rest of my face and down my neck. I can feel them working their way through my flesh. It's not entirely unpleasant. The burning discomfort has eased some, becoming more bearable. For the most part, their movement itches, even tickles. Mostly, it just feels foreign.

My phone vibrates against the porcelain of my old clawfoot tub, loud and echoing within the constraints of the space. It irritates me as the buzzing of a fly might.

The worms have grown more, multiplied. They are now the thickness of unstretched yarn. My face writhes with them now, one approaching my eye. I can't let this continue.

The itch has deepened, competing with the burning sensation. I find myself clawing at my skin without meaning to, leaving furrows that quickly fill with blood. It drips down my face, a crimson serpent. My skin looks like a disturbing road map of green and red lines. There's an intense pressure in my lips, which have become distended like burgeoning egg sacs, ready to burst. My teeth ache, and I realize I've been clenching my jaw.

The worm reaches the flesh of my lower eyelid and disappears, plunging out of sight as if it has gone deeper beneath the surface. Soon, I can't feel that one anymore.

Another one reaches my adam's apple, and the rough sensation causes me to cough. A crack appears in my top lip. It's not meant to stretch this much. The worms still in response, but start back up again almost right away.

They're now as big around as a phone charging cable. Pain has replaced the itching and burning, pure and sharp. I now know what a tree must feel as creatures burrow inside it, creating tunnels and laying eggs, slowly but surely overtaking its entrails. Every movement feels as if something is forcing its way through my face, digging away at my skin, rending the nerves. Another crack appears in my upper lip, followed by a first in my lower lip. My lips have ripened, preparing to give birth to the monstrous worms within.

Something presses at the back of my eye. There's an intense pressure, ceaseless, persistent.

Then it is through. It feels like an eyelash in my eye. It's a dull pain at first, but it sharpens and shifts. I can't stop blinking, tears forming only to spill from my eyes and run down my cheeks. The tears form clean swaths through the blood.

Leaning even closer to the mirror, I stare until the worm in my eye becomes visible. As the pain increases, I cannot keep my eyelids open. They shut against the pain. During the brief moments I'm able to open that eye, I realize I can see the shadow of the worm within. Not just in the mirror, but in my vision. It has grown once more, at least the thickness of a maggot, and it is tunneling through the viscous liquids of my eye.

Below, the worms have spread out, burrowing their ways

across my chest. I tear my shirt open, popping a button off. They're in my left breast, competing with the visible veins there. One works its way toward my areola. My skin feels like boiling water looks, a constant roiling beneath the surface. Sensations blur together, and I can no longer tell what burns, what hurts, and what itches. My lips are the worst of it, a confusion of agony and irritation.

My phone rings now, the music sounding canned as it arises from inside the tub. I ignore it, but it plays again and again until I can't take it anymore. I tear my eyes away from the mirror and cross to the tub, retrieving the still intact phone. Not even a crack from having been thrown. I turn off the ringer and take the phone with me, setting it on the sink.

As the worm reaches my nipple, a strange burst of pleasure hits me, quickly overtaken by pain as the worm violates the nerve it has just caressed.

The eye-worm is still in my vision, and it becomes hard to see with the shadow filling the space.

Picking up the zester, I steel myself for what's to come. The pressure in my lips has become unbearable. The first pass with the zester is tentative. My nerves scream with the pain of it and blood beads like crimson pearls on my lips before running down from them. Between the zester and the worms, the zester is the least of my pain. The second time is easier, sharp metal biting into my flesh, tearing at the nerves at the surface of my lips. A worm pokes from the mangled flesh left behind, and I grab the tongs, try to grab it. They're too unwieldy. Instead of the worm, I grab my lip, pinching it.

Dropping the tongs, I open the medicine cabinet and search for tweezers, tossing medicine bottles, toothpaste, a razor, my toothbrush, and more until my fingers find the comforting form of the tweezers. I close the medicine cabinet so I can use the mirror, and I zest my lips once more, this time also scraping across my chin. There's blood everywhere, my flesh maimed and looking vaguely of hamburger meat, but paler. More worms become visible, a much darker green than they'd appeared beneath the skin. With the tweezers, I grab one, pulling slowly, but firmly. It stretches, thins, and I fear it will break.

The worm writhes against my machinations, trying to free

itself.

I pull harder.

Finally, the worm pops free, and I drop it into the sink, looking for another one. Ignoring the pain, I plunge the tweezers in after a worm just below the surface. Once more I stretch it out, pulling harder this time. It thins and resists my attempts. It has reached almost a foot in length, my hand far from my face. I feel the tug from within.

This time it snaps, sending one half of the worm slingshotting back into my flesh, where it quickly disappears. Like earthworms, these ones seem able to continue moving even after being severed. The half still clasped within the tweezers jerks and writhes. The blood that leaks from the severed end is blue.

I drop it in the sink and go in for another. They seem to know to avoid the surface now. They're going deeper. My nipple screams with the pain of a worm eating its way through the sensitive nerves there, so I take up the zester once more and rake it across the raw nerves. The agony is exquisite. The worm there is the size of an earthworm, and I grasp it easily with my tweezers, pulling it slowly from my breast.

This time, I don't allow it to become too taut. It stretches, but I know not to pull to the breaking point this time. Even as I pull it on one side, the other part digs more deeply into my nipple, attempting to chew its way back inside me. I remember what I learned when fishing and both give and take, inching it out bit by bit, losing ground when necessary, only to regain it a moment later. The worm is plump and juicy, already well-fed from its time inside me. It glistens with my fluids.

When the worm finally breaks free, I am filled with a quick wash of relief and exhilaration, short lived as they may be. Somehow the worms are propagating even more rapidly now, with what looks to be thousands of smaller worms spreading out from the larger ones. The largest worm is the size of a wooden spoon handle. It's moving down my stomach. Every millimeter is misery, a shrieking chorus of nerves.

I try to use the zester over the large worm, but it isn't going deep enough. Each scrape fills with blood, blocking my view of the green creature inside me. I drop the zester and plunge the tips of the tweezers into my stomach above the center of the worm. It twitches inward, reacting to the stab. Then it quickly lengthens and keeps moving downward. I stab at it again, blind to the sensation of tiny stab wounds, so full of the feel of worms moving throughout my body now. The sense of movement within me is confusing, causing a sense of vertigo. Within and without, all is motion.

Wiggling the tweezers, I tear the skin further, allowing for easier egress. When blue blood mingles with the red of my own, I know I've reached the worm enough to grab it. I can feel it in the grasp of the tweezers, and I pull, careful not to sever its thick body with the intensity of my grasp.

I cough while struggling with the worm in my stomach, and tiny worms spray from my mouth. They splatter in the sink and against the mirror.

The worm pulls out in a long "U" shape, and I change my movements to try and pull one side out first. The tweezers are too sharp against the thicker worm, and they squeeze it, cutting through its body. I grasp the worm with my fingers, dropping the tweezers into the sink, desperate not to lose my grip. It feels thick and sinuous in my grasp, an ever-changing mass. It's so large that I wrap my entire hand around it and pull. It shouldn't be as strong as it is, but I'm losing against its ability to burrow with both sides of its body. No matter how much of it I get out, there's still more inside me.

The larger the worms get, the more the riotous sensations within me become pain, misery, agony.

A knock sounds at the door. It's late. No reason for anyone to be here. I'm too busy to check on it.

A strange, high whine is emitting from my throat. I'm scared, desperate, disgusted. I want these things out of me. I try to stop the sound, but it simply becomes more guttural. A scream waits at the back of my throat, a queue of terror.

The knock comes again. "It's me!" she calls through the absurdly thin door. "Let me in. I can help you."

I don't believe her. She did this to me. Why would she help?

One side of the worm breaks free from my skin, and I increase my grasp on it, pulling as hard as I can without breaking it. The side that's outside my body jerks crazily, thumping into my hand. It bites just below the knuckle of my index finger and starts trying to burrow into my hand.

I'm now fighting both ends of the worm in different places, but I'd rather have it in my hand than in my stomach. I ignore that end and continue yanking at the portion inside my stomach. There's a lot of bone in my hand for it to have to get around. That's what I tell myself.

She knocks again, and I walk toward the front door, still struggling with the worm. I grunt at the effort of fighting it, of the fine skill it takes not to tear it in half or let it go.

The worm in my eye has gotten so large that I can't see with that one at all and an incessant ache works its way backward into my skull. There's pressure like with my lips. It's going to burst at any moment.

My hand finds the lock, and I turn it before twisting the door handle. As the door opens, the worm pops from my stomach. I wrench its mouth from my hand and throw it on the ground, stepping on it and deriving a grim satisfaction at the sensation of it bursting beneath my shoe. Blue blood squelches from it, staining the floor. Still it squirms, but it doesn't concern me anymore.

Its brethren do.

I look up, my grin a rictus on my face. I must look feral.

My eye bursts, warm liquid running down my cheek. The worm inches across the bridge of my nose toward the other eye. I should be worried about it.

Yet there she is, as beautiful as she was earlier. She smiles at me and steps inside, shutting the door quietly behind her. I see now that beneath the lipstick her lips are blue. The fullness I'd so admired holds back a torrent of horror aching to spread. She touches my face and pulls me toward her, eyes intent on mine. I can't break free of her gaze or her grasp, and I lean in until her eyes blur enough that mine can close.

Despite the poison of her lips, I covet more.

Incident at Ben E's

Shrieks rent the air. A cacophony of violence permeated the surroundings—thuds, screams, garbled yells, body hitting body, and loud music. The scents of sweat and feces battled those of baking dough and cheap beer. Flashing lights blinded Isabel.

Isabel's migraine grew to epic proportions.

"Mommy!" yelled her youngest, Grady. He ran up to her, flushed and sweaty, his blond hair standing up where he'd shoved it away from his round face. At five years old, he was three years younger than his big brother, Jack.

"What's up, Grady?"

"Is the pizza ready yet?"

"Not yet. It should be here any minute. Do you need some more tokens?"

He held his plastic cup of tokens out to her and shook it to make it rattle. "Nope. I still have lots left." His mouth formed a pout. "I'm hungry."

"Soon, baby. Go play one more game, and I bet the pizza will be here when you're done."

His face lit up. "Okay!"

Isabel sighed and picked up her beer. Pre-kids, she'd scoffed at the idea that a place geared toward children would serve alcohol. Now that she had two of her own, that alcohol was sometimes the only thing that got her through their all-too-frequent visits to Ben E. Pepperoni's. There was always some kid having a birthday party.

Wasn't there somewhere else they could hold them?

No, there wasn't. She'd checked.

Another gulp of beer went down with a pleasant warmth.

Luckily, most of the moms were of the helicopter variety, and she'd been left alone to guard the table. Her boys were both in sight, so she kept an eye on them without hovering like a psycho.

Speak of the devil. The mom who always reminded her of Betty Boop was heading her way, eyes fixed on Isabel's face, overly warm smile spreading across her mouth. The woman's hand grasped that of a chubby five-year-old girl with brunette pigtails and an upturned nose. The little girl's face was bright red, her mouth wide open as she shrieked, "I don't wanna' sit down, Mommy!"

Isabel took a breath and prepared for the idiotic small talk currently bouncing its way toward her in the guise of a 34DD Kewpie doll with ruby red lips. She straightened and pasted a smile onto her own face.

"Suzanne, how are you?"

"Oh, great! Can you believe the weather we're having? So warm."

"I'm enjoying the heat. Then again, it *is* June."

Suzanne plopped herself down across from Isabel. She placed a manicured hand on Isabel's arm, while still maintaining a hold on her struggling daughter, who flopped around on the seat beside her. "So true. I miss the steady temperature in the Bay. Seventy degrees, year-round."

Suzanne never failed to work in how much better life had been in "the Bay." The husband had moved them out here for a job, and it had apparently been the end of the world to leave California for Colorado.

"That does sound lovely. Though I think I'd get tired of the same temperature all the time. There's something to be said for the changing of seasons. Sometimes I just want to snuggle up with a warm sweater in front of a fire, cup of hot tea in hand."

"I'd rather wear shorts all year. But I've got the legs for them." Suzanne giggled, lifting a shapely leg so Isabel could see just how made for shorts it was. Yep. Definitely shorts-worthy.

Isabel wore a pair of jeans and a t-shirt. The air conditioning was always set to arctic at these places. She thought about showing how t-shirt worthy her arms were, but decided against it. The size of her thighs would surely be turned on her, as usual, and she'd be forced into a snipe fight: veiled insults pushed through bared teeth meant to look like smiles.

She took a deep swig of beer instead, and said (quite graciously, she thought), "Your legs are toned! Do you work out?"

Isabel had asked this question in various forms before, and knew the answer before it came out of Suzanne's mouth.

"I should, girl, but I stay toned just from my day to day. Lucky, I guess."

Lucky, my ass. Isabel had sighted Suzanne exiting a gym, great big sunglasses hiding a portion of her face. Why she'd lie about something like going to the gym was beyond Isabel, but she liked to test Suzanne every once in a while to see if she'd cop to working out.

Either way, the woman had legs to envy.

Suzanne gave Isabel a visible once-over. "Do you go to the gym?" she asked in a tone that said she knew the answer. This was her standard gambit. If Isabel said yes, Suzanne would question the point in going to the gym, with thighs like Isabel's. Say no, and she'd recommend Isabel try it, or point out that maybe that's why her thighs were so full.

Hot, steaming, and smelling like canned spaghetti, the pizza arrived just in time. Two teenaged employees wearing red shirts slid the pans across the table. They slapped a pile of paper plates beside one of the pans and took the number placard with them. Instantly, the table filled up around Isabel, moms bringing their kids over to the surrounding tables and sliding into the adult table. A flurry of activity took off around her.

She waited until everyone had gotten their pizza, then served up a slice of cheese to each of her boys.

Mom conversations swirled around her. She attempted to make the right facial expressions and noises, but the pain in her head and increased excitement surrounding her made it hard to focus on any one person. If she put her head in her hands, like she so desperately wanted to do, it would only bring undue attention. She focused on her plate and the high-pitched voices, letting them run over her like water.

Excited yells ripped Isabel out of her brief meditation. She looked up to see what the newly enhanced roar was about.

The animatronic band had begun singing. The grinding, metallic creaks of their rusted mouths were almost as loud as the voices blaring from the speakers. Their wide, empty eyes stared into the audience. How kids found these things fun instead of terrifying, she had no idea. She didn't even like walking by them, especially when they were still.

It felt like the animatronics were going to reach out for her at any moment. Maybe pull her into their gaping, lightly-hinged jaws and crush her to death while they sang.

Ben E. Pepperoni was the most frightening of them all.

A squirrel with two giant teeth, its fingers more talons than anything else. The others held instruments, which would surely slow them, but Ben E. didn't. His hands were free.

The pizza had only worsened the migraine, and Isabel got up to refill her soda, hoping the caffeine would offer some relief. When she came back, her seat had been taken and she was forced to choose between standing or asking everyone to slide over in the booth.

Instead, she went to the kids' table and sat with her boys. Both were sweaty but cheerful. Hopefully they'd sleep well tonight.

She was fending off a chubby hand going for her drink when the lights dimmed. The animatronics slowed to a freakish speed, voices low and almost slurred. Children screamed. Parents yelped. A drunk father's voice carried from somewhere off to her left: "That shit's creepy."

One of the kids at the table knocked his drink over, sending a fizzy mess across the pizza and Isabel's shirt. She shot to her feet and grabbed napkins from the dispenser. The soaked paper shredded, making the mess worse.

The lights went all the way out.

Startled shrieks and gasps bounced off each other in the dim room.

A small amount of light filtered in the front windows, but it didn't reach far. Isabel could make out the people around her, but couldn't see the back end of the restaurant.

The animatronics had gone silent. Only the brightness of their eyes showed, a sinister beacon in the dark.

A voice from the back end of the restaurant sounded, lapping at the walls, vibrating within Isabel's head.

"Stay calm. Do not try to leave. You will be exterminated."

Of course, this statement did nothing to keep everyone calm. Now it was the adults screaming. Grown people stampeded toward the front doors, where a single hapless teen employee stood ready to check the stamps on children's hands against those of their parents. The tide of parents holding sobbing children knocked her over, trampling her. Isabel never heard a sound from the teenager, so sudden was the onslaught. Abandoned children screamed for their parents. When the doors wouldn't open, fistfights broke out.

Isabel took hold of her boys and brought them into the safety of her arms.

The lights came back up.

This time, when the voice came, Isabel watched the flapping jaw of Ben E. Pepperoni move with the words: "You were told not to leave. This is not calm. We can only take this as a threat."

Beside her, Grady and Jack froze. Their bodies went rigid, eyes wide.

She nudged Jack. He didn't respond.

"Jack? Grady?"

The other kids had frozen in place as well. Silence filled the place as everyone focused on their children. The air buzzed and filled with the scent of ozone.

Then all hell broke loose.

As one, children lunged at the closest adults. Grady went for Isabel's throat while Jack grabbed a plastic fork and jammed it into her arm. The teeth broke, barely penetrating the skin, but he kept grinding the broken plastic against the wounds.

She pushed Grady out to arm's length. He tried to bite her arm, her hand, anything within reach.

Jack gave up on the fork and raked a hand across her face. His nails bit into her skin with a hot slice of pain, but they missed her eyes. He swung again. She jerked her head out of the way just in time.

Suzanne screamed behind her. The sound diminished into a gurgle.

Fighting her own battle, Isabel couldn't turn to see what had happened.

She held Grady's arm, keeping him far away from her. For Jack, she grabbed a fistful of his hair and kept him at arm's length. They each struggled against her. Luckily, they were small—but both seemed stronger than usual. Wiry limbs swung at her, nails clawed, teeth gnashed. Her babies had become feral animals.

An infant in a car seat wiggled its way out of the blanket swaddling it, then rolled out onto the floor. It inched toward her, leaving a trail of drool on the matted carpeting.

Something jumped on her back. The munchkin voice of a toddler growled in her ear. Teeth sunk into her neck.

Isabel screamed and let go of Grady to rip the toddler off her neck and bring it over her shoulder. Blood dripped down the little girl's chin. Her tiny, sparkly pink sneakers kicked out, right into Isabel's stomach.

With an "oof," Isabel dropped the girl to the ground. Both the girl and Grady took off running, headed toward a group of adults who seemed to have bested their birthday party of two-year-olds.

The infant, meanwhile, had reached her. It lifted its head—something it shouldn't have been able to do at that age—and locked its gums onto her ankle.

This, at least, didn't hurt, and she turned her attention elsewhere, hand still locked around the struggling Jack's arm.

Suzanne rested in a puddle of blood, her throat ripped open, eyes glassy. Her daughter was nowhere to be seen. Other bodies lay strewn about the room. Kids ran all over the place, making leaps they shouldn't have been able to make, taking down adults at least three times their size. One little boy gleefully used a pizza cutter to scalp someone's grandma where she lay helpless on the floor, her walker several feet away.

Isabel shook the infant off her foot and marched behind the counter, past the cheap toys and ticket-counting scales. She straight-armed her way through the swinging door and into the kitchen. On the far side, a wooden door bore a placard stating, "MANAGEMENT ONLY." The lock grabbed her attention. If she could find the keys, she'd have a lockable room. Most of the other doors in this place were swinging doors that didn't even latch.

She crossed the kitchen to the door, yanking Jack with her, and cautiously nudged it open with her foot. Inside, a twenty-something male lay, twisted into an impossible set of angles. A look of shocked fear still stamped his face. Hiding in here with a dead body didn't appeal to her. She grasped his ankle and tried to pull him, but she couldn't move his body while still holding Jack. With a sigh, she released her son, knowing he would either attack or run.

He ran.

At least it gave her time to get the manager out of the room. He was still heavy, but, with both hands and a lot of putting her weight into it, she managed to pull him backward, ankles limp in her hands. His body grudgingly squeaked across the tiled floor. Inch by inch, she dragged him backward. Finally, his head cleared the door, and she dropped his feet. They landed on the tile with a thud and a smart tap from the hard soles of his shoes.

A ring of keys glistened in his hand; she grabbed it and tried her hand at locking the office door. The third key she tried worked.

Victory!

Chaos still sounded from outside the kitchen, though muffled. That meant there were still survivors. A quick look around the kitchen showed her plenty of deadly items, but she didn't want to kill any of these kids if she could help it. If the kids could just be locked up until a way out of this situation showed itself, everyone remaining might survive.

Defending herself, on the other hand, was completely doable.

Isabel took a roll of duct tape out of the office and proceeded to tape on as much armor as she could put together. A large metal strainer went over her head, pizza pans went on her torso and back, and plastic wrap covered her limbs. She went through several boxes of the wrap to make sure the sheeting was thick enough to resist teeth and unclipped fingernails.

As a final touch, she put on the thick oven mitts and picked up two giant ladles. These, at least, would be good for shoving children away or knocking them out cold. Whichever seemed best.

Armed and protected, she burst out from the kitchen to stoop down behind the prize counter.

She stared through the glass, past the paddleballs and

plastic spider rings. She'd created a significant clatter during her run, but no one was paying her any attention. A group of children held a dad down while a pre-teen used the hammer from a Whack-a-Mole to try to beat him senseless.

Isabel waded into the bodies of the children, shoving them away. The pre-teen, she knocked out with a ladle. Better a concussion than death. He slumped bonelessly to the floor, head hitting with a solid thwack.

Okay, so maybe a double concussion, but still better than death.

The dad, unaware he'd been saved for the moment, used his newly-freed hands to strike out at Isabel.

His fists rang off the metal strainer, echoing around in her head and amping up the migraine even further. She'd forgotten she even had that sucker. The reminder was not appreciated.

"Cut it out." She put her weight on him until he stopped trying to hit her. "I need you to help me. There's no time for you to panic."

"What *are* you?"

She realized how odd she must look, and that her face wouldn't be fully visible to him through the strainer. "It's not important. There's a room we can lock these kids into. We need to figure out what else we're dealing with here."

Much to her relief, he nodded. Okay, he understood well enough.

While she had been talking to the dad, children had come up behind her and started trying to gnaw through the plastic wrap. She shook them off and led the way to a mother being drowned beneath the soda fountain. Rescuing her was easy enough. With three adults now, they started gathering children. With her arms covered, Isabel could grab more than one at once, but the oven mitts made it hard to hold them well. She was forced to grab one at a time, which slowed things down.

They developed a rhythm where each grabbed a kid and met at the office door. Then Isabel would hold the kids already in the room back with the ladles, to allow the other parents to shove the kids in.

After twenty minutes, they had about thirty children in the room, with ten adults helping to gather them. The children slammed their bodies into the door and yelled incoherently.

Isabel went to find the infant that had gummed her earlier. She passed by a man whose head had been shoved through the screen of a video game. His body still twitched, random sparks shooting out from the damaged circuits inside the machine. The bodies she stepped over were a mix of adults and children. She pushed the horror from her mind as she continued her mission.

She'd found Grady and wrangled him into the room with the other kids, but Jack was missing somewhere in the mess.

Nothing moved, which meant...he had to be dead.

No. She wouldn't allow herself to think like that. Surely she just hadn't noticed when someone had found him and put him in the room. He had to be in there.

Or...he was out here, but unconscious.

Still, she choked up, thinking that somewhere among this litter of dead bodies, her baby boy lay, eyes empty and dead, body broken.

She wiped her eyes and continued searching for the baby.

It writhed only a few feet from where she'd originally left it. Somehow it hadn't been trampled. At least, not visibly. Isabel bent down to pick the baby up.

Underneath the table by the baby, Jack crouched, teeth bared in a feral snarl.

He opened his mouth wide. A voice—not Jack's—emitted from it, his lips not moving: "You have forced our further actions."

A screech sounded that was so high and sharp that it felt like ice picks were being shoved through Isabel's ears, into her brain. She fell backward, slamming her helmeted head on the table behind her with a clang that continued to ring through it for a few seconds. Something on the table fell with the sound of breaking glass, and the hoppy scent of beer dripped down onto her and the baby.

She wiped beer out of her eyes with her mitted hand and studied her son. His eyes had rolled to the back of his head, showing only the whites.

He seized under the table, limbs slamming into the ground.

The screech stopped. Now she could hear something moving in the vents overhead. It thundered throughout the ceiling, sounding like hundreds of temper tantrums.

Any second now, whatever it was would break through.

In her arms, the baby stopped writhing. It stilled, sucked in a breath, and began to cry, the normal cry of a normal baby. It hadn't made a sound other than grunts since it had worked its way out of the car seat. Now it cried like any hungry, beer-soaked, confused baby would.

Isabel drew her eyes from her son and looked down at the baby. It no longer tried to bite her, and its head was settled firmly into her arm, no longer straining upward.

From what she could tell, the baby no longer suffered under the control of whatever had possessed all these children.

Jack's body stilled.

Isabel crawled to him, arm still snuggly wrapped around the baby. Holding it close to her chest, she wrapped her other arm around Jack and football-carried him toward the kitchen, where the others still gathered.

Her son was limp in her arms, but she could feel him breathing. She had to believe he'd be okay so she could press on. *Both* of her sons depended upon her to find a way out of this situation.

Just as she reached the counter, the noise in the vents stopped. She froze, looking up.

The metal duct directly above her swelled, pulsating. She dove over the counter with a clatter of her armor, Jack and the baby tucked as close as possible to protect them.

An explosion rang out above her.

She hit the tile. All the breath rushed from her lungs, and she gaped, trying to pull oxygen in. Something pelted her from above.

Rolling to her back, she saw small, furry creatures raining down around her, coming from the duct. They were slightly bigger than rats, but striped in purple and white. Each of the creatures tucked and rolled, coming up to their feet and turning on Isabel.

Finally able to gasp in a breath, she clambered to her feet and pushed through the door into the kitchen.

"Block the door!" she yelled.

She set Jack's limp but still breathing body against a wall, then settled the baby into a large metal pan filled with hand towels.

Several of the parents had scurried to the door, pressing their bodies against it to hold it closed. Isabel raced over with a broom and slid it through the handle so the door couldn't be pulled outward.

Isabel looked through the galley window set into the door. The furry creatures had round, black eyes and six fingers per hand, of which they had five. They cartwheeled faster than they ran. Frankly, she found them adorable. Were these really the creatures they'd been fearing? Surely they could overcome them with little effort, now that there were no children to sic on their parents.

The creatures cartwheeled into a large pile, which quaked and melted.

From the puddle of fur formed from this gathering, a single large creature emerged. It let out a mighty roar.

From the locked room, the children's voices rang out in a sweet, yet eerie, chorus:

"Now you die."

Their banging against the door and walls ceased. The ensuing silence struck Isabel as particularly terrifying. As a mother, she knew silence meant something was afoot.

"What do we do?" one particularly frantic father asked, pacing back and forth.

Isabel suddenly thought of what had happened earlier with the beer and how it had seemed to settle the baby almost immediately.

She used the ring of keys on a large door across from the office, where the alcohol was stored. Inside were multiple kegs of beer and jugs of cheap wine. She didn't know if the wine would work. She didn't know if she was right about the beer having worked.

At this point, there was only one way to find out.

"Help me move this keg to the office," she called.

Two of the parents not holding the door came to help her. They rolled the keg across the tile floor to the office doorway.

Isabel had never had to tap a keg. She looked at the others. "Does anyone know how to open this thing?"

One father stepped forward. "I do."

It didn't take long for him to prepare the keg. He and the others looked to her for what to do next.

Before she could say anything, two events occurred simultaneously:

The doorway leading to the office where the kids were locked up sucked inward.

And the door between the front and the kitchen disintegrated as the large purple-and-white body of the furred creature slammed into it, bowling over the shocked parents that had been holding the door.

The kids poured forth out of the office. The parents were now under siege from both sides.

"Spray them all with beer!" Isabel yelled.

No one listened. The large creature swept two adults off their feet and slammed their heads together, dropping the limp bodies to the floor. The children surged over the nearest adults, overpowering them with sheer numbers. Isabel got knocked over while trying to get to the keg.

She crawled, feet thundering around her on all sides, bodies slamming to the ground beside her. One particularly large man dropped directly on top of her, knocking the air out of her lungs. She clawed at the ground in a panic until her lungs opened up enough to get a breath in.

The body was hard to push off her, but she managed it with a lot of profanity and effort. His bulk slumped to her side, and she crawled the rest of the way out from under it. The adults were all under attack, leaving only her to finish the trek to the keg.

Isabel arrived at the keg and pulled herself up to a standing position. The metal armor she'd decorated herself with earlier clattered against the keg, drawing the attention of both the creature and the children.

She tried to spray the beer using the hose the father had attached.

Nothing happened.

Heart in her throat, she tried again. Still nothing.

She kicked it, breaking her toes with an audible set of crunches.

"Pump it," a man called, voice weak.

Isabel remembered seeing movies with kegs. She grasped the handle and pumped as rapidly as she could. But the movies hadn't told her how many times she had to pump it. She was afraid to stop too soon and blow her chances.

Several children attached themselves to her body, trying to chew through the plastic wrap. It held true, though the ends had started to unstick. The pressure of their bites through the plastic still hurt like hell, but at least they weren't breaking the skin.

Meanwhile, the creature lunged into a rapid cartwheel, fur ruffling as it flew through the air. One of its hand-feet crushed the head of a man struggling on the ground, causing an explosion of bone shards and brain matter.

The creature reached her seconds later, knocking her away from the pump.

She slammed into the wall, children flying like pins in a bowling strike, dizziness hitting her as she slid to the ground.

The creature roared one more time, then approached her, lifting a viscera-covered foot-hand.

Isabel cowered.

The baby let out an angry howl from its place in the pot, catching the creature by surprise. It turned to look at it.

Isabel threw herself forward into the creature.

Its body was soft and the fur silky. Her hand sank into its gut.

With one foot-hand in the air, and only one currently on the ground, the surprise attack threw it backward.

Isabel grabbed the beer nozzle and sprayed the children nearest her.

They dropped to the floor, unconscious.

She pumped more, eyes on the creature.

Its black gaze felt like a physical attack, energy crackling between them.

Bringing the spigot up, Isabel aimed at the creature and depressed the handle. Frothy, yeasty beer shot in an arc toward the adorable, yet terrifying, creature before her.

Beer soaked into its fur, causing it to ripple. Its body moved like the ground in earthquake footage she'd seen, almost liquid in appearance. It tried to roll into a cartwheel, but its limbs melted into a jiggling puddle, the rest of the body rapidly melting down to join it. Tiny forms crawled out from the puddle, stretching grotesquely, as if the individual creatures were trying to reform.

But none could reach a solid state. Instead, they liquefied, leaving thick puddles of sludge in their stead.

Around the room, children came to, crying in fear and confusion. Grady's voice pitched above the others. "Mama!"

"In a minute, baby." Isabel pumped more, spraying everything that moved. With her final set of pumps, she soaked the still-undulating puddle one more time, making sure to get every inch of it.

White foam fizzed atop the now pink puddle. All motion within it ceased.

Outside, sirens sounded.

Isabel dropped the hose from the keg. Beer splashed across her shoes, soaking into the fabric. She limped her way over to Grady, who huddled against Jack's side. Jack had woken up. His bloodshot eyes locked onto her face. "Mom?"

She bent down and brought both boys in, careful of the metal shields she still had strapped to her body with plastic wrap.

She kissed the tops of their heads. "I need you to both be big boys right now. Mommy has to go check something outside. Can you keep the other kids in here?"

Jack nodded, eyes large and solemn. He stood up, Grady still pressed to him, and called out to the kids. It took a few shouts, but the other children stopped to listen to him.

Isabel nodded, a small smile on her lips. She went through the shattered remnants of the doorway to the front of the building.

The doors opened easily—inward, toward her.

She wondered if they'd ever been locked, or if it had simply been the stupidity of a terrified stampede of people keeping them from opening. She'd probably never know.

A large shadow loomed outside the front doors. When she pushed through, she looked up, expecting to see a storm cloud blocking the sun. Instead, what looked to be a spaceship hovered overhead. It was smaller than she would have imaged. Then again, the creatures had been tiny. About the size of an old Cadillac, it stayed in place, a single ring in motion along the base. It was shaped like a cigar, long and thin, rounded at the tips. A plank of sorts led down to the roof.

In the parking lot, motorists stood outside their cars, gaping at the space ship. One determined woman approached it, using her cell phone to take pictures. She turned her back to the ship and held her phone at an angle to take a selfie with the ship.

A police cruiser slid into park not fifteen feet from Isabel. A man and a woman in uniform climbed out, staring open mouthed at the spaceship above them.

"You're going to need some beer," Isabel called to them.

Thank goodness Ben E. Pepperoni's had beer.

It was a lifesaver.

Story Notes

Dust Bunnies – This one has a pretty simple origin: getting a face full of dust. But also the imagery of a picky woman running a finger along a surface to test for dust. I don't remember what it was in, but we've seen it a billion times, that look of disgust and judgment when the finger comes away covered with filth. Plus, the act of trying to stay ahead of dust collecting in one's house is a horror story all its own.

A Few of His Favorites – This started with an image, really, of someone sitting in a lovely picnic setting and talking about the good times. I rarely know how my stories are going to end until I write the ending, but I knew I wanted a body under that picnic blanket.

Sweet Nothings – Did you know that some dentists (in Georgia, at least) were disposing of their teeth in the walls of their practices. There were a series of such discoveries during various renovations. I'd also been wondering how many psychologists/psychiatrists are a mess themselves, and the two came together. (Don't think I also haven't heard of the slots in people's homes in the old days where razors were discarded – fodder for a different story, perhaps).

Shelter From the Storm – I wanted to write a story in a Mad Max sort of setting. I hadn't really written anything post-apocalyptic, and I'd written a piece about post-apocalyptic stories being the new westerns, so I wanted to try out the theory.

Following the Rules – There was a skit on a comedy show (I can't remember which one, but considering the time period, most likely SNL) about two sets of parents switching out, and I thought it would be creepy to play with a child whose experience was to have a set of day parents and a set of night parents. It was fun writing from a child's point-of-view to try to tell the story with fewer details than an adult who understood what was going on might recount.

Root of All Evil – Not long after the COVID shutdowns first started. I belonged to the Horror Writers Association, and a few of us locals were writing stories together to put out an anthology. We were encouraged to each write something involving some kind of plant, and this was my contribution. That project went all kinds of haywire and never happened.

Tailgating – This was a call for a monster road trip. But it may be the oldest inspiration in this book. Back when I was a pre-teen, my family was on a road trip up Highway 101 from California to Oregon. There was a vast expanse where it was pitch black, no homes or buildings, and the road was pretty narrow. Someone came up behind us, pacing us perfectly, and I started spinning a tale about who might be in that car and their intentions toward us (my siblings were asleep, but I was an insomniac, so I was never going to be able to sleep). The longer I did this, the more I freaked out my parents. Even my calm, measured dad who loved horror novels inadvertently found himself pressing down more firmly on the gas and speeding up.

Darkness of the Concrete Soul – I have multiple siblings who are or have been cops, and the brother who first became a cop had a freaky experience near the beginning of his career. (This was probably a couple decades ago, so the details are a bit blurry, but the important part is the one I used.) A dead body had been reported in a home, and he was sent to look into it. It was night time, but cops always have a flashlight on them. Just as he was approaching the body, the power went out. When he turned on his flashlight, it flickered then went out, and there he was, in a strange building with a dead body and no light. That *had* to make it into a story.

The Killing Tree – I love to switch things up a bit, and as someone who grew up watching westerns, I'd never written one before. So I decided to try my hand at it. I also wanted to do a teeny bit of an homage to xenomorphs, so the creatures are lightly based on them.

Sweepers – This was a specific call for cyberpunk stories involving mods. I don't really write science fiction, but I grew up on a lot of sci-fi, too, so I decided to give it a try. It wasn't accepted for the anthology, and who knows if it was even representative of the genre. Still, it was kind of fun to branch out and write some science fiction since that's not a place I live a lot.

Psychosis – This was another call that I did not make it into, though I was a little relieved. Denver Horror Collective is another horror group I belong to, and they had put out a call for stories about Wendigo. The thing is, I was putting out a whole book about Wendigo and this was a non-indigenous call, so I was a bit uncomfortable, but because I'd missed opportunities to write anything for their other calls due to life circumstances, I figured I'd try it, but I wasn't writing about an actual Wendigo. Instead, I focused on something called Wendigo Psychosis, a very real condition reported long ago (though not so long ago that people should feel relieved) in areas of Canada where people thought they were becoming Wendigo, which to them meant they were possessed and needed to eat human flesh. This was also adjacent to COVID when we were all home bound, yet sales people still occasionally came to our door.

A Darkness That Evades the Eye – Oh look, another call where my story wasn't accepted. Though that was because they didn't feel it completely fit with where the rest of the stories had gone. The publisher did connect me with a friend of theirs who was doing another anthology, because they felt my story was good and right up the other publisher's alley. The new publisher accepted it...and then promptly went under. Womp, womp. The original call was for a travel guide of sorts. I'd like to write more stories set in this world with this group, so there may be more in the future.

Watched – This story was about exploring how someone could spy and harass someone digitally. Plus, I've shown a clear history of not trusting neighbors with some of my other stories...you really never know who you're co-existing with until they show you.

Coffin Birth – This was another "fun fact" inspiration. Coffin birth is when a dead woman's body expels her deceased fetus due to the buildup of gases that occur after death. It doesn't really happen in modern times because of embalming, modern science and medicine, and all that good stuff. But it has been found in rare cases archaeologically. I was intrigued and wanted to write something about it. It was also inspired by the MMIWG2 movement (Missing and Murdered Indigenous Women, Girls, and Two-Spirits), which is now more of MMIP (Persons) to include indigenous men. *Typehouse Literary* was nice enough to let me include a write-up about MMIWG2 in that issue, which I'll put after the story notes for those interested. It's also probably important to state here that I am Indigenous, as I've used some harsh words in the story.

Coulro-Psycho – This was an invitation to a magazine with a theme of twisted tropes in speculative fiction. I figured not many would be twisting horror, and I love a clown. Tucker and Dale vs Evil was an inspiration. I wanted to take a scary trope and make it the good guy, but have people dying as they tried to escape it anyway.

Hork – This came about from a discussion with my brother during a time where we were helping take care of my dad. I feel like it speaks for itself for cat owners. In reality, I swear to you I *heard* the sounds of my cat throwing up a hairball in the other room, but I never, ever found any sign of it. It was recounting this to my brother, also a cat owner, and my parents, who have had cats in the past, and joking about it having hidden so it could take me out later that inspired this story. I told them I'd write it, and I did. And it ended up in a "Best of" anthology!

When the Leaves Quiver – This was for a call for stories that I saw too late, but decided I wanted to play with anyway. They were looking for kaiju stories. I'd never written one, but I wanted to make mine a bit different.

The Punishment Quadrant – This was just me wanting to have a little fun with a science fiction story.

Yellow Fever – I'd wanted to go to Savannah, Georgia for ages. So long that I named my daughter Savannah, because I loved the sound of it. So when I finally got to go, I wanted to do all the things. One of the things I did was do a tour at The Pirate House, a restaurant cobbled together from multiple buildings that has the preserved entry to one of the tunnels leading to the coast. In many coastal cities there are various types of tunnels, such as the shanghai tunnels in Portland, that were supposedly used to transport goods to and from ships at harbor, but also to sneak drunk people out to ships, where they'd come to from their drunken stupor only to find themselves as staff on those ships far out to sea. But in Savannah, they felt they may have also been used to store the dead bodies of those who had died during a yellow fever outbreak. I'd also stayed in an AirBnB (though not in Savannah – this one was in Estes Park, CO), where there was a creepy trapdoor in the floor in a room adjacent to mine. I figure it was just a crawlspace, but this was a writing retreat and every single other person was in rooms on the other side of the house, so it was just me and the creepy trapdoor. It had to make its way into a story.

Inside Me – This was for a call for stories inspired by Alice Cooper songs. It sounded fun and I love a prompt, so I went online and watched a bunch of Alice cooper concerts until I found a song that inspired a story. That song was "Poison," and the line that inspired me was "I wanna' taste you, but your lips are venomous poison." Proceeds from the anthology go to Alice Cooper's nonprofit Solid Rock Teen Centers.

Incident at Ben E's – This was a call for alien stories. Have you ever been to Chuck E. Cheese? Then surely you get this story. It's crazy, chaotic, and loud, and some children lose their minds. I love horror comedies, and you'll find several in this book. I enjoy playing with the absurdity of horror sometimes.

MMIWG2 Information

In 2016, the NCIC reported 5,712 missing Indigenous women, girls, and two-spirits in the United States, with the DOJ only recording 116 of those cases, due to racial misclassification and misgendering. Other disturbing statistics include:

- 1 in 3 Indigenous women will be raped in her lifetime (USDOJ)
- 4 out of 5 Indigenous women will be impacted by violence (CSVANW)
- Homicide is the 3rd leading cause of death for Indigenous women ages 10-24, 5th for ages 25-34 (CDCHP)
- 95% of cases involving Indigenous women aren't reported by the media, and if they are, they get a single mention (UIHI)
- Indigenous women experience violence at a rate 10x higher than the national rate (CDCHP)
- Indigenous women are twice as likely to experience sexual assault than non-Indigenous women, with 96% of those being perpetrated by non-Indigenous men (USDOJ)

90% of violent crimes against Indigenous women are committed by non-Indigenous men, as per the DOJ. These are not tribal issues, but national ones that, without spreading the word, will continue to grow exponentially in this national epidemic.

Here's how you can help:

- Boost the signal—share missing persons reports and articles about the murders of Indigenous women
- Donate to projects that support the MMIWG2 (Missing and Murdered Indigenous Women, Girls, & Two-Spirits) movement, such as Native Women's Wilderness, Native Hope, National Indigenous Women's Resource Center, and Coalition to Stop Violence Against Native Women (csvanw.org), and MMIWUSA.org
- Advocate and vote for legislation that protects and supports Indigenous women

- Continue to learn more about the movement and the epidemic behind it, and help keep others apprised. A good starting place is the Urban Indian Health Institute (UIHI.org) in addition to the organizations mentioned above

Thank you for taking the time to read this information. That, in itself, is the first step to helping save and improve the lives of our Indigenous women, girls, and two-spirits, and to end this human rights crisis.

Dedication

This time, the dedication goes out to just one person. To my husband, Jeff, who stands with me no matter what. You are my person, the one I trust with all I have and all I am. I love you.

Acknowledgments

"Dust Bunnies" © 2020 Shannon Lawrence (*Novel Noctule, Issue 7*)

"A Few of His Favorites" © 2022 Shannon Lawrence *(Indecent Magazine)*

"Sweet Nothings" © 2025 Shannon Lawrence

"Shelter From the Storm" © 2019 Shannon Lawrence *(Vagabond, Issue 002: Apocalypse Edition)*

"Following the Rules" © 2020 Shannon Lawrence (*XVIII: Stories of Mischief and Mayhem, Underland Tarot Anthology Series,* ed. Mark Teppo, Underland Press*)*

"Root of All Evil" © 2025 Shannon Lawrence

"Tailgating" © 2019 Shannon Lawrence (*Amazing Monster Tales #2: Monster Road Trip,* ed. DeAnna Knippling and Jamie Ferguson, Borogrove Press)

"Darkness of the Concrete Soul" © 2025 Shannon Lawrence

"The Killing Tree" © 2022 Shannon Lawrence (*Particular Passages 2: East Wing,* ed. Sam Knight, Knight Writing Press)

"Sweepers" © 2025 Shannon Lawrence

"Psychosis" © 2022 Shannon Lawrence (*Madame Gray's Vault of Gore,* ed. Gerri R Gray, Hellbound Books Publishing)

"A Darkness That Evades the Eye" © 2025 Shannon Lawrence

"Watched" © 2021 Shannon Lawrence (*I is for Internet,* Red Cape Publishing)

"Coffin Birth" © 2022 Shannon Lawrence (*Typehouse Literary, Issue #24)*

"Coulro-Psycho" © 2024 Shannon Lawrence (*Twisted Tropes, Issue #1,* ed. Chuck Anderson)

"Hork" © 2024 Shannon Lawrence (*Carnage House, Issue #4)* (*Best of Carnage House, Year 1,* ed. Josh Darling and Jacque Day, Carnage House LLC)

"When the Leaves Quiver" © 2025 Shannon Lawrence

"The Punishment Quadrant" © 2025 Shannon Lawrence

"Yellow Fever" © 2025 Shannon Lawrence

"Inside Me" © 2023 Shannon Lawrence (*Dismember the Coop,* ed. Bert Edens)

"Incident at Ben E's" © 2019 Shannon Lawrence (*Amazing Monster Tales #3: It Came From Outer Space!,* ed. DeAnna Knippling and Jamie Ferguson, Borogove Press)

Other Books by Shannon Lawrence

Short Story Collections

Blue Sludge Blues & Other Abominations

Bruised Souls & Other Torments

Happy Ghoulidays

Happy Ghoulidays II

Novels

Myth Stalker: Wendigo Nights

Nonfiction

The Business of Short Stories: Writing, Submitting, Publishing, and Marketing

About the Author

A fan of all things fantastical and frightening, Shannon Lawrence writes primarily horror and fantasy. *The Killing Tree & Other Afflictions is the newest of her seven books.* You can also find her as a co-host of the podcast *Mysteries, Monsters, & Mayhem* and a columnist for *Rocky Mountain Reader.* When she's not writing, she's hiking through the wilds of Colorado and photographing her magnificent surroundings, where, coincidentally, there's always a place to hide a body or birth a monster. Find her at www.thewarriormuse.com.

Website: www.thewarriormuse.com
(For appearances, publications, and online store for signed copies)

Facebook: www.facebook.com/thewarriormuse

Instagram: www.instagram.com/thewarriormuse

Rocky Mountain Reader:
www.rockymountainreader.org/author/shannon